Sven Davisson
The Starry Dynamo

Sven Davisson is the founding editor of *Ashé! Journal of Experimental Spirituality*. A rebel-publishing pioneer, Davisson edited the small, yet groundbreaking, zine *mektoub* from 1989-1995. During that time, he also received a degree in Queer Theory from Hampshire College and studied photography with Jerome Liebling of New York's famed Photo League. In addition to *Ashé*, his work has appeared in *Abrasax: Journal of Magick & Decadence*, *sneerzine*, *The New Aeon*, *mektoub*, *Lambda Book Report* and *Velvet Mafia* as well as the collection *I Do/I Don't: Queers On Marriage*.

Books by SVEN DAVISSON

When Foley Craddock Tore Off My Grandfather's Thumb:
The Collected Stories of Ruth Moore & Eleanor Mayo
(Blackberry Books)

Ashe! Selections from The Journal of Experimental Spirituality
(Mandrake of Oxford)

THE STARRY DYNAMO

.

THE STARRY DYNAMO

THE MACHINERY OF NIGHT REMIXED

★

SVEN DAVISSON

REBEL SATORI

ACADIA

Rebel Satori Press
P.O. Box 363
Hulls Cove, ME 04644
Fax: (207) 669-4200
Online: www.rebelsatori.com

Author information: www.svendavisson.com

ISBN: 978-0-9790838-0-8

Contents

Acknowledgements

"Rant" appeared previously in *sneerzine*; "Winter-style Candies" and "Crux Ansata" appeared in *mektoub*; "Love Always, Jojo" and "The Snake of Time" were privately issued by Ananael Books; "Asceticism of Being," "The Rise & Fall of Rajneeshpuam," "Over the Hills & Far Away," "Spirit Guide" "Burroughsian Gnosticism," "No God Where I Am," "One Made for Exceptions," "The Plastic Ideal" and "If Not Now, When?" appeared in *Ashé Journal*; "Keep Your Rights" appeared in the Suspect Thoughts anthology *I Do/I Don't*; and "Et In Acadia Ego" appeared in *Velvet Mafia*.

Special thanks to all those who been inspiration beyond measure or attribution: Nathaniel Bamford, Chris Bold and Bill Malay; my satyr muses Trebor and Emanuel; Chris DeVere, Cookie Willems, Louise Lopez, Sal Sapienza, Jason McDonald, Jim McDonough and Scott Wilson; and the beloved *enfants terribles* Greg and Ian.

To
My Mother and Father

๕๑

I lost consciousness of everything but a universal space in which were innumerable bright points, and I realized this as a physical representation of the universe, in what I may call its essential structure. I exclaimed: "Nothingness, with twinkles!"...

"But what Twinkles!"

Aleister Crowley

The Night Machinery
Preface to 2006 Edition

This work is driven by a critical analysis of love, control and control structures. Speed, tight curves and resting hours reflect the core of spare nights. My own William Burroughs white knuckles at the crowded writing of the *Naked Lunch* wheel. The channeled voice pulls down the centripetal force—threatening me with the cut-up experiments, dragging Allen from him to me through time and television snow. Wandering thoughts fiercely intersect the course. Associates turned eighteen, graduated, overflowed. Control. (Capitalize this!) High school fucks spill out from locker-lined halls. Like a wolf, my best friends are imprinted upon me in the process. Only small unsuspecting objectives, from the first, hands guide me into the general population.

Burroughs' life slowly dissipates through a winter-morning's air. He artfully illustrated the ways of a growing rumbling cacophony. A shot straight up into the vein of culture announced his entrance. His cheat, a falling cascade of media and group utilization, stains the frosty ground. His work produced a crisis gang slowly surveying current conditions. A small smile reinforces his position and raises the corners of youthful buttocks. Knocking safety, Burroughs perceived that we are living a series of shuffled objectives and underlying near misses. He fought Control's plan and exposed the dangerous role of glamorizing the careenings of the body through the stages of death and living. He fought Control by reinforcing the concept of immortality.

Suddenly I was of the One God. Angry—choked by the gush of the Universe, depressed and caught up in a reality of contradiction. Blitzed-out on the frozen ground I even attempted to negate the dreaming subject. Despite this, I am bound to that bond of the first poem. Ginsberg walks on. Once again the One God and the Universe, secular Control is captured tightly by modern assassins.

People continue their attempts to eradicate free thought.

The mortal world is nonmagical lacking both dreams and any interest in multiple gods. Burroughs' experience, rising in the young, theorizes a universe done well forcefully predicated on myth and embracing death.

Homosexuality is the pursuit of multiple gods. From puberty looking forward, this is necessary for one to have hope—like the quality that was first love and finding the dream. What of this bulk of friends, so familiar? Buddies jacking at Control's voice frozen in playboy centerfolds? Each, possessed by an urgency, they move in a static One God Universe focused on His brilliance.

Burroughs' words are the painful period of a monopoly—forward projects set on Space, preparing for an artistic awakening of closeted teens. Immortality. Burroughs asserts life. They are exalted as if the One can truly find love again. Humanity moves, almost overcome, but looks back toward its own annihilation. Both support themselves in an avalanche of childhood memories, dreams and fears. Who is here to implement the work, chalking up the next word? Who will run these negative critiques to ground, lasering the problems inherent in humanity.

I continue my attempts at maintaining being a writer.

The proximity of everything says that life itself is a species. The end of all poems is always familiar at this stage. Can anyone be so contrite about the human subject? The complaint that this is a biologic dead end is completely false. This reflects an underlying uncertainty regarding the skeleton of our own nature. The only choice for humans is the connection between Poetry,

Time and a single Moment. This is our opening to the pleasure of mutating into our future. Is it really the first human impulse to become extinct?

Like a modern Nero, Burroughs argued as Control's delusions crumbled. Their set ended with the Now. You can't deny it masks itself behind experienced paroxysms. With an unexpected reading of the pleasurable, the One God Universe fades out in a Howl of post-pubescent lust.

All control systems claim the artistic outlet. They were the laws of the Universe. For an instant, the universe has opened into a great void. Don't be afraid when absolute control ceases at a new intersection line of ancient custom and new rationalism. The living have created an opposition poetry.

Have you ever felt that a magical universe, consisting of many gods, had managed to gain an upper hand? I ask.

We have the dream space. The road of realization is stained with dark sexual smudges. The magical universe, through his reach, has caused the covers to rend back from the form, the destruction of the human majority. While the still cloth bleeds conviction, the dreaming subject is again a virgin. He refused to be trapped in the dark, excited into his very depths. The One God is now controlled by unease.

The business of the One God Universe is a world pulled semi-clean from excrement. Excitement is its absolutes, where no darkness can be entirely normal. The deep breaths of receding power through these destructive minutes search for what is still familiar. It attempts to shrug through constructed contradiction and determined compulsive organization. A jerking dissonance overflows spilling out into the streets. Age and archetype in my dreams free critical thought.

I bet my ass on the arising of savage tribes. They stabilize in the daily ritual of "Me too!" They fight the impulse to become their own Control systems. Once they fall, catch your eyes on your own Eden.

God, backed now by secular powers, begins to look stupid. What was he getting from his power? Forced downtown, unable to find words, he wonders why the masses have stopped. His name was once Islam and Christianity, now in this new kitchen of realization he has lost even the protection of the glittering state. Long beyond the grab of childhood, secular leaders want his mother's money too.

What about that One God lost in a feedback loop?

Our sexual functions eradicate our intelligence—a bass rif off the page.

"I cannot without the One God," they scream from apartment 1.

But there is this sometimes when the magic downstairs creeps up and becomes a component in the human story.

Burroughs' work moved past the derelict rose of spirit and toward an eruption of immortality and evolution. The world may yet become a manifestation of life. Burroughs' work presents a narrow passage. The seas crash with myth, magic and the dream experience. Petals thread through the tide of a subversive magical universe. Two letters remain in the world— the music of the primal body: AH. The first will never miss you.

The One God. At one time his name an ineffable mantra. The universe. I think. You do. The sexual moan knocked loudly at the pen, only to tell me "Not tonight."

My magical universe. A door. Eyes begin to follow a white universe of many gods where the mark is pulled often into conflict. Fiercely the all-powerful, all-seeing God is knocked down again. Unlocked. The page resurrects archaic forms guiding me through human religion-myths. Cosmology forms where mutation of the living is a necessary corollary. The door opens with the winter-morning's air.

The image, tilting, careens over the body. Contradictions cloak the One God. Someone gives the heads up. He disappears back in despair. Suddenly, I am cosmology. Magic moves into the living choking it with another gush of the universe. AH.

Warning: the strength of inherent contradictions can be a meager space.

Once again a world of diverse gods, each grabbing the tape and assaulting the opposite page. Word Assassins.

People have their own objectives—their own painfully flaccid agendas. The mortal perceives safety as the familiar printed representation. Fags and the young know it as an artificial construction of Control.

Homosexuality is pursuit, from puberty a search for the promised land.

The outcome of Control's moving deployments. His fiction. A young man's epigram. This is a painful period an attempt to stand in a doorframe of symbols. Searching out the conspiracy, he finds love again. Agents surround him.

Can there be anything else but one's own nature? Even for those so deeply committed to remembering? Who stands behind a person at these moments? When the magical universe is pleasurable and spontaneous, is the intruder in actuality nothing more than a human feeling? Now you can't deny the impending engagement with the unpredictable, alive.

My existence. Free thought shakes the body. One cannot exist without Captain Kirk.

"You, there," Control attempts to get a last signal out. "Yes, I destroy the dreaming. It's a right cold break."

Don't be afraid when dreams work down toward the mystical experience.

Being becomes spontaneous and unpredictable, a final time. Whatever the form, it cannot be absolute.

The Machinery of Night

Chad drove that summer at full speed and hanging tight to the curves. Knuckles white on the wheel, at every moment the centripetal force threatened to drag him from the course. It was the summer he turned eighteen, graduated from high school and fucked his best friend. It was the first time in his life that he could say that he belonged to a group—that he had a gang with which to hang. They all lived fast doing nothing, while simultaneously maximizing every second. The lucky were living a series of near misses on a dangerous rode glamorizing death and living out their immortality.

Some among them were angry, some were depressed and the rest were too blitzed-out to care. All were bored. That was the bond that bound them tightly to one another.

By the beginning of that summer Chad was heading for the culmination of his high school experience. He had done well, but not as well as those who watched him had hoped. Like the bulk of his friends, he thought he was a writer. Each focused on his brilliance preparing for an artistic life. They exalted in themselves and provided support for each other's work, while chalking up negative critiques behind each other's backs.

The proximity of the end of his senior year had brought Chad to a point of uncertainty regarding the connection between his poetry and his future. As his delusions crumbled, he experienced renewed paroxysms of post-pubescent lust. It seemed that as his artistic outlet began to yellow and fade, his hunger for something else increased to fill the void.

Chad was no more confidant in the medium of sex than he was in that of poetry. That spring he was about to turn eighteen and still had managed to gain no progress down the road of realized sexual desire. Every day he moved closer to accepting that he was about to reach his majority still a virgin. He refused to discuss the root of his unease with even his closest friend Jamie.

After he showered, Chad pulled a semi-clean pair of black jeans from the family laundry and went off in search of a clean T-shirt. Following a few minutes search through his bureau, yet again the victim of his mother's compulsive organization, he found his favorite Circle Jerks shirt. He put in *The World Up My Ass* and began the daily ritual of polishing his 14 hole Docs. Once they were shining and laced, he began the trek down town to find Jamie. He stopped in the kitchen just long enough to grab his mother's money off the counter.

He heard the music before he rounded the corner and saw the building. He couldn't make out the group—all he could distinguish from the feedback was the bass rif. The smell of Mexican food assaulted his nostrils from the restaurant adjacent to Jamie's apartment building. Apartment 1 was downstairs, so number 2 must be the second story. Logical, but it took Chad a couple of minutes to find the entrance—a staircase tacked onto the side of the building and accessed from the end the alley. Chad moved past a derelict car partly blocking the narrow passage. He tested the first step, not immediately trusting the staircase that seemed to be a hap-hazardly added appendage to what once must have been a one family house.

As he moved up the stairs the music became louder. By the time he reached the apartment door, he could distinguish Henry Rollins' voice. He knocked loudly. When he didn't get an answer after a couple of minutes, he knocked again. Still no response. He tried the knob. Unlocked. He cautiously let himself in. He surveyed the cramped apartment. The door opened into a small entry-room beyond which was a combined kitchen, dining and living room. A long hallway led off the opposite side of the living room.

Chad could just make out the sound of a shower running down the hall. Someone was here at any rate. He moved into the living room area, maneuvering around the three over-stuffed thriftstore chairs that vied for the meager space. He sat down and grabbed the empty tape case from beside the small stereo. He now recognized the familiar Black Flag song that was just winding down. He scanned the song listing on the back of the *Repo Man* OST.

"Great song." A voice from the hallway surprised Chad. He sat up quickly. A young man stood in the doorframe a towel wrapped loosely around his waist. He had wet, spiky, black hair, a slightly pot-marked face, a bare-chest, tribal tat descending from his shoulder to encircle one nipple and a second smaller tat on his inside right wrist.

Chad quickly remembered that he was an intruder in the apartment. "I'm Chad—a friend of Jamie's."

The young man waved, "I'm Tiberius, but everyone calls me Kirk, as in Captain Kirk. I'm just going to get dressed. Be right back. Help yourself to a beer; they're in the fridge." Kirk turned and started to move down the hall. Chad watched him remove the towel from around his waist and dry his hair a final time. Chad felt his crotch twitch as he stared at the muscular ass walk away. All too quickly, Kirk disappeared into one of the doors leading off the short hallway.

Chad went to the kitchen and grabbed himself a Fosters. He grabbed a second for Kirk and then went back to the chair. He took a long drink off his can and set both before him. Kirk soon returned. He had put on a pair of worn, black jeans, a Never Mind the Bollocks T-shirt and gray-stained white tube socks. He immediately noticed the second beer. "Thanks man."

"So you must be Jamie and Sven's other roommate?" Chad said, taking another long drink from his lager.

"Guilty. I know Sven from Orono. We went to high school together. You still in school?"

"Graduating with Jamie this year."

"So it's almost over. What's next? Got into a college?"

"Reed. In Oregon. You?"

"Naw. I didn't bother to apply. I plan to take some time off. Learn by living a little. At the end of the summer I'm taking my bike across country for a year or so."

"Motorcycle?"

"Ninja ZX-10 that my dad gave me for graduation." He quickly finished off his first beer. "Another?"

Chad nodded. "Got a butt?"

"Sure. There should be some beside that other chair." Kirk headed off toward the refrigerator.

Chad stood and rummaged through the loose trash littering the small end table to the left of the other chair. He found a pack of Camels. He returned to his seat just as Kirk reentered the room two more cans clutched in his hands.

Chad smelled the butane even before he heard the grind of the Zippo's flint. A large flame came around the side of his head and up beneath the end the cigarette he had just placed between his lips. He noted that Kirk had strong hands and surprisingly clean finger nails. As the cherry glowed to life the Zippo snapped shut. Kirk set Chad's new beer beside him.

"Thanks. You're a real Emily Post," Chad said.

"Don't mention it. It's not often I entertain," Kirk responded sarcastically.

The sound of two people laughing and tumbling up the stairs announced Jamie and Sven's arrival. "Okay the party can start," Jamie said with a mischievous smile.

Chad laughed. "Looks like it already has."

"We've not even begun. We just dropped two tabs each during the walk over here." Jamie laughed in return.

Kirk crumpled his empty second can and winged it at Sven's head. "You fucker. I hope you don't plan on me baby-sittin' your asses tonight, 'cause frankly I have better things to do."

"Like what?" Sven replied. "What could be more exciting than hanging out with a couple of ball tripping freaks?"

"Getting' shitty. Me and my new bud were planning on cracking a case together. You're welcome to do your Timothy Leary impression all you want, just do it quietly."

Sven tossed the disfigured can back into Kirk's lap. "I'll just dig out the toy chest and be off."

Kirk dropped the remains of the empty can onto the floor. "Hey would one of you shitheads mind getting us another round of beers before you two settle down for your long winter's trip?"

"Sure thing," Jamie swung around and pulled two cans from the refrigerator. "Here you go."

Jamie and Sven settled into a sprawl on the floor in front of the chairs and couch. From the size of Sven's pupils, Kirk could tell he was well on his way to oblivion. Kirk would figure out some excuse to jet really soon. He found being around tripping people a bore. He would finish his beer though. The apartment was unusually hot, for early June, and even the metallic taste of cheep beer was cool and refreshing. He'd skipped dinner and was starting to feel the first edge of his buzz coming on.

Kirk leaned forward. With his right hand he rummaged through the jumble of tapes scattered around the portable stereo. He picked up and discarded several, before selecting a tape and inserting it into the player. He pressed play and the first track of *Let Them Eat Jellybeans*; Flipper's "Ha Ha Ha" began mid-song.

A cold swig of beer washed over the back of Chad's tongue and he watched Kirk slouch back into his chair. He took another swallow. Kirk was definitely cute—his type. His spikey, black hair reminded Chad of early Sid Vicious. His body was fuller and more muscular—a decided improvement over the gaunt ravages of heroin. He felt his cock begin to tug at his underwear. He was surprised that he hadn't noticed that Kirk's irises were so brown—almost black—giving his eyes an obsidian quality.

Chad began to wonder. He took another cold drink in an attempt to douse the first murmurs of hope that were beginning to bring their entangling stems up along his spine. Who knew? At 18, everyone seemed to be still in hiding. Chad reminded himself that he was one of them. He finished his beer.

"Can I get you another?" Kirk reached for Chad's empty can.

"Shit. I don't want to drink you out of house and home," Chad replied shaking the last drops out of his can before relinquishing his hold on it.

"Don't worry about it. My brew is your brew. Be right back; don't go anywhere." Kirk disappeared behind Chad's chair.

Chad leaned back sinking into the soft padding of the chair and his quickly engulfing beer buzz. Resting his head on the chair's back he closed his eyes briefly. Kirk was cute. Absolutely his type: punk, short hair, slightly muscular, cocky and 99.9% sure of himself. He couldn't resist the way Kirk carried himself. His ease within his environment exhibited an aura of control that seemed to animate his punk accouterments, his boots, jeans and T-shirt as if they were all parts of a fluid animation drawn with a single continuous line. That was also the problem; Kirk was too much his type, which meant that he was STRAIGHT.

Chad opened his eyes, drawn out of his reverie by the approaching sound of Kirk's Air Cushion souls. A cold sensation shocked his cheek as a beer can snaked in from behind to meet Chad's quickly outstretched hand.

"How you feeling?" Kirk sprawled into the opposite seat. The music had stopped while he was in the kitchen and Kirk scrounged for another tape. Chad immediately recognized the familiar goose-stepping intro *I don't want a holiday in the sun-a I want to go to the new Belsan I want to see some history Now I got a reason of an economy.*

"I didn't ask for sunshine and I got world war three," Kirk echoed along with the music.

A noise from the floor caught both their attentions. In his fuzzy beer brain, Chad had completely forgotten that there were actually four people in the room, not two. Sven and Jamie had been quietly playing amongst themselves. The noise that had attracted Chad's attention turned out to be a moan from Jamie. She was reclining on her elbows, her short skirt pushed even higher along her black fishnet thighs. Sven's hand disappeared up to its wrist beneath the small stretch of black spandex. The green glint of a Rolling Rock bottle was just visible against the tendons of his forearm. He appeared to be slowly moving the bottle in and out with a methodical twisting motion.

She was a bloody disgrace, the music drove unrelentingly on.

Chad moved his gaze to Jamie's face. Two white teeth emerged from her unnaturally red lips resting two indentations into the lower. Her eyes were closed—the rest of her face placid and serene.

Dragged out on a table in a factory

He shifted his eyes tracing back along Kirk's corresponding line of sight. He followed the conic field as it narrowed from Jamie's crotch, along Sven's arm, across Kirk's own outstretched booted leg to its terminus in his dark eyes. The pupils shifted left in recognition of Chad's attention. Kirk smiled.

"I think that's our cue to jet."

The smile was a warm hand clutching Chad's guts twisting them into a fearful mash of anticipation. It was a feeling Chad wished he could prolong. He feared the disappointment always edging just the other side of tension's dissolution. Kirk rose to his feet. His smile retreated to a shadow ghosting the edges of his mouth. He extended his empty hand to Chad who grabbed it and rose to his feet. He was surprised to find that he actually needed the hand to steady himself. He grabbed Kirk's arm for a second moment as he got his lateral bearings again. He looked up and again found himself in the expanse of Kirk's smile.

"I think we can both use a little fresh air." The smile continued. "I'll grab a couple for the road."

"I got to piss before we go anywhere," Chad said feeling suddenly foolish for some reason.

"Just down the hall to the left."

"Thanks. Be right back."

Kirk shot a glance at the two on the floor. Sven now had his head buried beneath the retreating folds of Jamie's skirt. A beer-bottle green long neck lay discarded to one side. "I think I'll meet you outside," Kirk snorted.

"Kewl."

Chad's mind raced with embarrassment as he peed forever. His head lolled back on his shoulders as his mind raced through the evening's events. Kirk was too good, he told himself. His paranoia crept back. He'd blow it. He'd dream and than it would blow up and, if he were lucky, he would end up with another friend to frustrate him. If he was unlucky... Well, it wouldn't be the first time. He shook his cock, momentarily distracted by the clear urine in the bowl. He flushed, zipped and double-checked that he hadn't accidentally pissed on himself. Everything fine, he turned and made his way to where Kirk waited.

On his way through the living room, Chad glanced at Jamie and Sven. Sven's bare ass met him. He was now fully on top of Jamie's limp prostrate body. At first Chad thought she had passed out, but he quickly saw that her eyes were focused and intently moving along the blank ceiling. He couldn't begin to imagine what she was seeing on the superb *tabula rasa*. "Shit Shit Shit," Sven interrupted his diversion, "Shit. I could come a million times. Fuck. I am going forever."

Chad continued the few steps to the stairway door. "You go right ahead, but it will be without me," he said trying to erase the image of Sven's pale bony ass.

"Is the creature with the two backs still at it?" Kirk asked as he descended the last step.

"Oh yes. Full glory. Claimed to be going for a record."

Kirk laughed, "He'll be spent and shagged by the time we get back, don't worry." He paused and seemed to check out their options. "Shall we take a walk along the shore? There aren't likely to be any rent-a-cops out that way."

They walked down the side street exiting left onto Main Street. As they crested the hill and began down the second block, Chad's heart squeezed painfully as he recognized the figure approaching him.

They cut down another small side street to a volunteer path that meandered along the shore an intruder across the expensive lawns. They walked in silence for several minutes until the last of the large homes disappeared behind them. Large black outcroppings of rock pushed into the night, silhouetted against the moonlit ocean. Kirk chose a flat rock and sat down motioning to the bench like surface beside him. Chad needed no second invitation to join him. As soon as he settled his butt against the hard surface, Kirk pressed an unopened beer into his hand.

"Hey, thanks."

"I always like to come prepared."

They spent another hour talking music and bands. They had similar tastes in music, not surprising in a circle based so heavily on a musical revolutionary impulse held over from the 70's backlash. The Sex Pistols, Clash, Dead Kennedies, Black Flag, Gang Green, Crass and Flipper. During their conversation, Chad decided Kirk had little respect for Sven, though he referred to him as his 'best friend.' As Kirk bitched about his roommate's stupidity, complaining about his use of drugs and emphasis on self-mutilation, Chad began to question his own dependence on his friendship with Jamie. He loved her, enjoyed being with her, but she could demonstrate a shocking amount of stupidity at times. Like tonight, tripping out on blotter and getting banged with no concern for anyone who might be around. But at least she was getting some. What was he facing? The end of the evening and a date with his right hand...

"Shit," Kirk abruptly interrupted his venting. "I got to crash. I have to work in the morning and it's almost three. Mind if we head back."

Chad stood up. "Not at all."

They walked back in silence. He had a little hope, but each time it crept too high, his hard-earned pessimism beat it back to its corner.

When they reached Kirk and Sven's apartment, the lights were still on but Jamie and Sven were nowhere around. The green beer bottle was the only reminder of their show.

"Do you need a place tonight?" Kirk asked as he began to unlace his boots.

"No," Chad paused. *How fucking tempting.* "Thanks anyway, but I think I can make it home."

"Okay. Be careful; it's a dark and dangerous world out there."

They laughed.

Chad turned to the door. "Night."

"Stop by anytime, all right?" There was that smile again.

"No problem. See you later." Chad flew down the stairs as he left Kirk's building. Christ it was like one of those moments in the crappy gay romances he used to read as a kid. A fucking Gordon Merrick novel. The voice inside him said loudly, *It's bullshit. Good things don't happen.* It is a dark world.

When Chad left Roasters with his afternoon caffeine fix, Kirk was waiting for him outside. He was leaning against the building, leg cocked, a stubby Lucky Strike hanging from his lip. A sleek motorcycle tilted on its stand at the curb, all shiny, meticulously cared for black and chrome. Kirk flicked his butt into the gutter in a small fire burst of red sparks and a hiss as it came to rest in a small puddle. He mounted the bike, righted it and kicked the stand up. "Get on." He motioned behind him.

Chad threw his coffee into the nearest trashcan and nervously climbed on, gingerly wrapping his arms around Kirk. Kirk drew his arms tightly around him. "You gotta hold on. All right?"

They took off. Kirk steered up the side street, turned down Main Street and out of town. The wind and the freedom quickly dulled the raw nerve of Chad's fear. He tilted his head down, using Kirk's to shelter his face from the wind. If I die, I die, he thought to himself. They sped past the small trailer parks that ringed town and the wharves at the head of the harbor—the smell of rotting fish mixing with the fresher salt air. The engine, wind, made them feel like he and Kirk were one unit—the shear strength of their speed melting them together. Chad let himself melt into the moment, wandering his mind over the land quickly passing on each side.

Though he hadn't had a reason at the time, Chad was glad he'd decided to shave his balls that morning. He loved the smooth feeling of them pressing against the clean softness of his

CK boxer briefs—an erotic layer between him and the hard impression of his zipper pressed against Kirk's ass.

Kirk was bent forward leaning into the bike. This forced Chad to lie almost on top of him. The speed, the cool wind and the undeniable heat along the surface of their pressed bodies gave him a painful hard-on all too quickly. It ran a hard wedge between their bodies. One that he feared was fully recognizable for its animalistic truth. Part of him hoped, nee prayed, Kirk would blame it on the exhilaration of being on the bike and pass it off without mention. Another segment of his mind harbored a more electric fantasy, but one that the fear of loss prevented him from allowing to fully form. His desire was so palpable he could feel it zing current through his nervous system. At the same time, he tried to force it back into its dark closed box.

They rode for over an hour. They circled the island. When they finally pulled up in front of Kirk's apartment, Chad's cock still remained rock solid. They reached Kirk's apartment just as Jamie and Sven were leaving. She had a backpack slung over her shoulder and he carried a six-pack in a crumpled paper bag.

"Hey Boys." She waved as she stumbled toward them. "We're going on a roadtrip," she screamed.

Chad glanced at Kirk.

Kirk looked at the two of them and paused. He shot a second glance at Chad, met his eyes and smiled. He turned back to Sven and Jamie. "Kewl."

Jamie paused a few paces from Kirk and Chad. "Sven's uncle loaned him his Caddie for the weekend."

Sven grabbed Jamie's arm and encouraged her to resume moving. "We'll be back sometime tomorrow." His speech was perceptibly slow and methodically drunk. "I want to make it to New Hampshire before the liquor stores close." He hefted the bag higher into the air.

Kirk checked his watch. "Well, you're goin' to have to break some speed records to do that."

Sven smiled. "I intend to." He turned and hurried after Jamie who was already half way to the car.

Kirk and Chad stood and watched until the car had started and pulled away from sight behind the corner building. Chad looked at Kirk hoping he wasn't showing his expectation and awkward feelings.

If Kirk did notice Chad's unease, he didn't evidence it. "You want to come up? If we're lucky they may have left us some beer." He walked toward the apartment motioning with his free hand.

"Sure." Chad followed.

Kirk went for their beers and Chad took his now normal seat in the living room. He leaned back his foot knocking a paperback off the cluttered coffee table. He looked behind him. Kirk still had his head stuck in the fridge looking for something that wasn't too rotten to eat. Chad reached forward and retrieved the book from the floor. Andre Gide's *The Counterfeiters*. He quickly put the book back on the table as Kirk approached. Chad looked up. Kirk smiled and handed him his beer. The smile was completely inscrutable. Chad translated it a million different ways in a millisecond and then just as quickly dismissed it.

Kirk hit PLAY on the CD-deck. *Never Mind the Bollocks*, again. They sat back and drank. Silence engulfed them both in the five minutes it took them to each finish their respective beers.

Kirk rose. "Want another?"

"Twist my arm."

The refrigerator door opened and closed. A slight touch of cold air grazed Chad's arm.

Kirk reached around from behind Chad and handed him a cold Red, White and Blue already open. "I got to take a leak; I'll be right back." A minute later, the toilet flushed and he heard Kirk's Docs return along the hallway.

As he waited for Kirk to emerge into view around the side of the chair, a hand touched his shoulder. At first it was normal, just resting, steadying oneself touch. It lingered, though. Chad caught his breath. Held his breath. Rather than disappearing, the hand got a little stronger. He continued to hold his breath. His chest began to hurt. The hand tightened and than was gone. Kirk came into view and dropped himself into the opposite chair. Chad realized he was still holding his breath and exhaled.

Chad's attention was again drawn to the book on the table. He raised his sight in a direct line from its worn cover to Kirk's face. He found Kirk's eyes looking directly at him. Unblinking. Kirk forcefully, aggressively, held his eyes. Then, just as unexpectedly, he smiled. Chad felt like he was having an acid flashback. He ran his fingers along the grooves of his chairs corduroy covering, focused himself and remembered to blink. Kirk closed his eyes and took a swig of his beer. Everything seemed to return to normal.

Chad checked himself again. His mind shot back and forth from hope to the inescapable thought that he was imagining everything.

Two more swigs and Kirk finished his second beer. He got up and went for a third. When he returned, he dropped a can into Chad's crotch.

"I thought you could use a little help."

Until the can landed, Chad had not realized how painfully hard he was. He looked up at Kirk standing a little behind his chair and to his left. Again, the hand landed on his shoulder. This time, however, it was definitely exploring his shoulder and the sharp ridge of his collarbone.

Kirk swung around to the front of Chad's chair and lowered into a kneeling position. He moved his face close to Chad's and a hand landed softly on Chad's erection.

Hot breath, ringed with the tang of fresh beer, warmed Chad's mouth and nose. He inhaled as much as his lungs could hold savoring the aggressive tartness. Kirk's hand tightened on Chad's bulge. Chad closed his eyes.

Chad's face was suddenly warmer. He kept his eyes closed. Kirk was closer. The warmth became wet as Kirk's lips met his. Chad moved his hands out to Kirk's sides just below his armpits. Kirk was on top of him, plunging into the chair almost knocking it over backwards with his weight. Kirk began kissing him aggressively. Acclimatizing, he returned the moist movement of Kirk's lips. A tongue was inserted between Chad's lips and teeth. It explored his mouth, running along his teeth, reaching toward his throat. Hands were everywhere Kirk's on Chad's body and just as quickly Chad's on Kirk's.

Chad slipped his hands beneath Kirk's T-shirt running his fingers against the soft, hairless flesh of his abdomen. He moved upwards to his ribs, and then followed the sternum fanning his fingers outwards seeking Kirk's nipples. He found one, ringed with its little halo of short hairs. He teased at it until it blossomed into a little sharp point between his fingers. Kirk was still kissing him—violently kissing him as if he couldn't allow even a second's pause. Meanwhile Kirk's fingers were ripping at the front of Chad's jeans, fighting with the top button. He grabbed at it until he had it open and the fly came down easily.

Chad felt air on his cock as Kirk brought it out into the narrow space between them. He encircled it and squeezed. His tongue slid farther down Chad's throat.

Somehow, sometime, they made it into Kirk's bedroom. Little more than a mattress amidst a clutter of empty beer cans and squashed cigarette packs. Chad was on his back diagonal across the mattress. Kirk was over him, kissing him his hands running a random grid across his flesh. Chad was doing his best to keep up with Kirk's pace, but the other's ferocity was more than Chad expected. His hands moved along Kirk's body.

Kirk grabbed Chad's wrists. He leaned forward pinning Chad's arms against the mattress. Kirk held them in position leaning heavily forward. He moved his other hand off the edge of the bed and blindly out along the floor. Chad tried to turn his head, but couldn't enough to see what Kirk was reaching for. Kirk kept his eyes fixed into Chad's while his hand scanned the floor.

Having found what it was looking for, Kirk's hand returned. It moved across the bed in a blur and shoved something deep into Chad's mouth. Chad strained to see what it was but couldn't—his eyes going cross-eyed. He began to taste it to feel it with his tongue and lips. Soft material. Cloth. Cotton. Then he realized, as his nostrils picked up the aroma of stale sweat. Kirk had gagged him with a pair of used underwear. Chad closed his eyes and absorbed Kirk's aroma. He could taste it as much as he could smell it. He opened his eyes after a second, when he felt Kirk moving again.

One of Kirk's hands continued to pin Chad's arms above his head. He used the other to pull Chad's legs up onto his shoulders. Chad rolled slightly backwards, his ass rising off the mattress. With his arms pinned and his legs on either side of Kirk's neck braced by his shoulders, Chad was wound tight and unable to move—or resist. His neck began to hurt, so he gave up lifting his head off the mattress to watch what was happening. He alternated between closing his eyes and studying the ceiling. Anything to keep his mind back on earth, so that he could savor what was being done to him.

It was first a cold hint of sticky moisture at his ass—more a cool breeze followed by an uncompromising push. Kirk's lubed cock was inside him faster than he would have ever expected possible. He felt the bristle of Kirk's black pubic hair crumple against his ass. Kirk moved all the way in on the first thrust. On the second, he lingered his stomach and chest pressed against the backs of Chad's thighs.

They awoke simultaneously, a single sprawled tangled mass on Kirk's mattress. They shared a cigarette in silence, both studying the far wall and ceiling.

Kirk was the first one to breech the near palpable wall of morning-after emotion that stood between them. "That was good." He took another drag. "Last night, I mean." He passed Chad what remained of the butt.

Chad finished it off and dropped it into one of the many empty beer cans littering the floor around the bed. "Yes it was." He felt stupid, but he had to say something. He didn't want to give too much away and have the night before disclose itself as the dream it must have been. He scanned the sensations from his body. Their legs were still woven together and, at first, Chad had trouble distinguishing what was his warm flesh and what was Kirk's. They were both naked and his body ached in a million different zones of leftover pleasure. Maybe last night did happen, he thought. He looked at Kirk.

Kirk was looking at him. A hard and determined look. "Want to go again?"

Before he could answer his face was grasped in Kirk's hands and his mouth was engulfing large portions of Chad's face.

After they had each come two more times, they stopped. Kirk passed Chad a freshly lit cigarette and lit a second for himself.

"I suppose we should shower and get dressed, before Sven gets back," Kirk said taking the butt from his mouth.

Chad took a deep drag to re-center himself trying hard not to look at Kirk's naked body so that he would be able to think with some coherency. "Yeah, I 'spose." He took another drag slowly edging away from ground zero.

"Don't get me wrong, but..." Kirk took a drag. "You know, I really enjoyed last night..."

"But..." Chad felt his stomach sink.

"Sven's my mate and..."

"Look," Chad tried to recover. "I understand if you two are... whatever..."

"No. No. He's my best friend, but he would never understand... this. He's an asshole about just about everything."

"Oh," Chad said relieved.

"He's a bigot, but we have been friends since junior high. This just wouldn't make sense to him. This will be just between us. I really liked it, but I just don't want to deal with any shit this summer."

Chad took the last drag on his cigarette and put it out. He held the last bit of smoke in until it was so painful he couldn't any longer. It made sense.

"This fall," Kirk continued, "I am going to ride my bike across country. Then, I don't give a shit what Sven thinks, or anyone else for that matter. Fuck 'em all! But, until then I just don't want to deal." He paused finishing off his own cigarette. "All right with you?"

"Sure. Whatever. Just as long as I get a little more of this." Chad lowered himself along Kirk's smooth body until his excruciatingly sore lips met Kirk's soft cock. Once inside Chad's mouth, it quickly grew again. Kirk leaned his head back against the wall, eyes closed, mouth slightly open.

It took Kirk only seconds to realize where he was and what was happening. He was on his side the weight of his bike pinning his right leg to the ground. He'd been riding. That was the last thing he remembered. He knew he was taking that turn too quickly. He moved his head slightly. Shit, his bike was crumpled. He attempted to roll onto his side, but found that he could not free his leg. He set his head back down on the asphalt. It was wet. Out of the corner of his eye he could see a small pool of darkness slinking across the ground, expanding away from his head. He reached a hand up to his hair. Wet. He pulled his hand into his line of sight. Shit: Blood. He must have really cracked his head, he thought. Then, suddenly, he noticed another pool of darkness growing on the pavement. This one shiny, metallic-looking, reflecting black light and abalone rainbows. A spark and then there was light followed by black.

"I don't see why you're so upset; you barely knew him. It wasn't like you were friends or anything," Jamie screamed into the phone minutes after telling Chad. "Christ, you are such the fucking drama queen sometimes."

pass i on

grind-into-me passion healthy passion cock-and-balls passion clothes-on-the-floor passion short-spiky-hair passion water-bed passion crumpled-sheet passion moaning-groaning passion leg-cramp passion dead-kennedies-background-music passion KY-middle-america passion thick-leg-slamming passion high-on-pot passion dazed passion crude-sexual passion no-question-of-god-watching passion angelic-dirty-street passion grateful-dead-skeleton-earring passion sex-pistols-t-shirt-thrown-over-chairback passion half-drunk-slurring passion black-14-hole-doc-marten passion huge-cock passion sacrilegious passion hell-brimstone-and-damnation passion satan-here-we-come passion junk-culture passion capitalism passion advertiser-pushed-trojan passion powerful-adult passion angry-childlike passion thelemic passion "I-am-the-god-of-hellfire" passion Da-Vinci-nude-David passion fast-jock-dominant passion long-hair-submissive passion uneducated-animalistic-pure-lust passion poetic passion passion passion

Somewhere On the Moon

I

Though Jamie and Chad arrived with easily an hour to spare, the small auditorium was already crowded. By the time that Allen Ginsberg entered through a small side door, people overflowed into the hall. A small shuffle and a slow dissipation of the rumbling cacophony announced his entrance. His bright eyes slowly surveyed the room and a small smile raised the corners of his mouth. He shuffled the ten feet to the low stage and its single, metal folding chair. He cleared his throat and introduced himself in his soft cigarette-spun voice.

With the first poem, Ginsberg captured Chad. Though rougher with age, he could detect the voice he had heard so often rising off scratchy vinyl. Its sound had a particular quality that was so familiar. Ginsberg's voice still possessed an urgency. His words tumbled over themselves as if the speaker was overcome by the avalanche of word racing to ground. Many of the poems were familiar: "In Society," "My Guru," "Complaint of the Skeleton of Time," and "Hum Bom!" The first set ended with an unexpected reading of "Howl."

During the intermission, a dozen people queued to get books signed. At Jamie's prompting, Chad reluctantly stood at the end of the line—his copy of *Collected Poems* in hand. As he shifted the book nervously from hand to hand, he noticed dark stains smudging the pads of his fingertips. His sweat had caused the cover's cloth to bleed a dark navy blue into his skin.

It was his turn and Chad took the seat offered. Ginsberg lifted the book, as if examining, for the first time, something that should be familiar.

"Where did you get this?" Ginsberg asked, surprised at the dissonance between Chad's age and the book's price.

"My father. I was working on a term paper about you last fall." Chad suddenly felt stupid. Before the words were all out, he realized how childish they must sound.

Ginsberg turned the book to the title page. "Really? And what was your theme?" He drew a small circle on the page opposite.

Chad groped for something to respond. It had been a high school paper and, as such, lacked any real depth. "The vision of Blake's rose within your early work."

A series of half-oblongs took shape around the first circle slowly forming the petals of a flower. *Rose of spirit, rose of light, Flower whereof all will tell,* he quoted as he continued to draw his childish flower. Within the center of the petals, he placed the two letters of the primal syllable "AH"—the first mantra, the universal sound of pleasure, the sexual moan. His pen then began to mark out the stem—a thin line curving below the lower petals. Before reaching the bottom edge of the page, the line swung up again crossing itself to approach the center forming a top-heavy figure eight. Ginsberg finished the line forming a serpent with two eyes and protruding forked tongue. The snake swung outwards to the left of the image tilting its head up and back as if appraising the "AH." Within the lower loop of the eight, Ginsberg added a small Star of David.

On the opposite page he signed his name below its printed representation. Below this, he placed the actual date between "1947-1980" and the Buddha's footprint, wrote "Orono" beneath the publisher's cities and added a second "AH" beneath the page's epigram. Things are symbols of themselves. He looked over his work and then handed the book back to Chad.

Chad rose from his chair. "Thank you."

"Thank you," Ginsberg said smiling.

Before Chad could say anything else a person behind him stepped in to engage Ginsberg in conversation. He had been waiting anxiously just to the side for the slightest signal that he could break in and embark upon an obviously rehearsed question. "How would you describe the mystical experience?"

"Trungpa, out at Naropa Institute, described it as stepping on the step that isn't there," Ginsberg replied, lighting a cigarette. Chad watched the smoke curl up past the hall's large NO SMOKING sign. "You know the feeling: the total loss of all reference points; being set suddenly and completely adrift."

The second segment of the reading proceeded much like the first. As before, the poems' beat held Chad. Jamie and he exchanged only the periodic smile of acknowledgment but no words. He was particularly amused by an unfamiliar poem "Ode to My Sphincter."

II

Scott shook his head trying to force the web of fog to dissipate. He knew he shouldn't have dosed at a party that would include so many jocks from his school. He now regretted not tagging along with Chad and Jamie. He didn't have much of an interest in poetry, but he had even less in jocks. Of course, the girl he had come with hadn't told him what the party was going to be like.

By the time they arrived, he was beyond the point where he could pull back to any level of control. They had each placed two tabs of blotter on their tongues before heading over. He had pressed another as they turned down the drive to the camp. He wasn't gone yet, but he knew that he was too far along. The only option was stay out of the way. He chose to move inside away from the front lawn and area surrounding the keg.

It had worked for a while. Everyone had left him alone. No one even bothered to come in and use the bathroom. Scott was busy studying a photography book—either a photo-essay on the builders of the bomb or a Max Ernst portfolio, he wasn't sure. A noise from behind startled him. He turned—trails flashing melting freeze-frame ghost images of the book's pages as he shifted focus. Tim had entered the cabin and was making his drunken way to one of the antique chairs near Scott.

He looked at Scott and smiled. "Christ, I'm fucked up."

Scott tried to sharpen the focus of Tim's face—mentally pushing away the lines of vibrant color that shifted and ran elegant patterns off his high cheekbones. "You're not the only one," he replied.

Tim leaned forward as he passed studying Scott's pupils. "I guess I'm not. Fuck man what are you on?"

"I dropped a couple of tabs... Make that three."

"Fuck. Are you all right?"

"I'm fine." Scott couldn't control an accompanying laugh.

"I guess you are, dude. No doubt," Tim laughed leaning back in a chair.

They both stared at the ceiling for a while. Scott kept shooting glances at Tim's languid body— a rag doll with the booze running through it. He kept blinking in order to better his appraisal of Tim's athletic build, running his eyes along his bare leg to the opening of his loose fitting shoots, up along his baggy pullover to his subtly developed arms. Scott could feel infrared waves of heat rise vertically in pulsating swirls from his crotch. A great over powering roller coaster of red light was driving higher across his abdomen careening up into his chest toward his throat grabbing at his breath.

Tim was tall—set with toned, lean muscles developed through high school years focused on athletics. He was star of the varsity basketball team, but somehow had escaped the ego generally associated with high school sports celebrity. Unlike many of his teammates, he was nice to just about everyone. He refrained from joining in with the other jocks as they harassed

Scott day in and day out. Scott's eyes continued to run their route upwards along Tim's body. He rested on his face and perfectly sculpted flattop. He started to hallucinate Tim's head closer to him, between his hands. His fingers jerked slightly. Each caress of the phantom hair sent a new wave spiraling outwards from Scott's cock. Over the short distance across the room, his eyes traced each hair while his fingers simultaneously sculpted its hallucinatory double.

Scott couldn't even tell if he was hard. It didn't matter. Everything was exploding into a multi-colored maelstrom and then dissolving to white. He blinked his eyes rapidly in an attempt to regain his sight. Without initially realizing it, he found that he had moved across the space separating their chairs. He now crouched in front of Tim. Close. Too close. His hand rested on the Tim's bare leg, just above the knee. He stared down. His breath caught again in his throat, as he realized how dangerously close his hand was to the loose leg opening of Tim's shorts.

Tim's eyes struggled sluggishly open. He blinked and looked down at Scott.

"I have always thought you were really cool," Scott said. He knew he sounded foolish and he knew he was not in control.

"Thanks," Tim replied nonchalantly adjusting his leg to move away from Scott's hand.

"I'd love to give you a blow job." Scott had always thought that Tim's easy-going nature might indicate latent tendencies.

Tim's eyes opened and his expression immediately shifted. "Thanks man, but I am really not interested. I got this girl out there that I have been waiting to jump." He sat up straighter in the chair pulling his leg farther away from Scott.

"Close your eyes and pretend. I don't care." Scott moved again towards the Tim's fly.

Tim stopped the hand just before it made contact. "Man, I'm really not into that. Okay?" He shot a look toward the door. "I'm going to get another beer. Thanks for the offer though."

Tim got out of the chair and maneuvered around Scott's hand. Scott dropped backward onto the floor kicking himself for being so stupid. He replayed the previous moments in a jagged concatenation; each memory cut into the next before completing, moved back and spliced again.

III

After the reading ended, Chad and Jamie lingered talking outside the auditorium. As she had just started to show her impatience, Ginsberg and his student handler emerged from the lecture hall. When he saw Chad, the old man's face lit in recognition and he began to make his slightly waddling way toward them. Jamie knowing well her part drifted into the background.

"It looks like my ride hasn't shown up. Do you have any other questions for me?" the poet asked.

"Well," terrified, Chad scanned his mind. "My father and I always wondered which came first Kerouac's *On the Road* or Holmes' *Go!*?"

"*Go!*. It was really the first Beat work. We were all hanging out together and Robert and Jack were being exposed to the same things. Both books center on the same people. Holmes just wrote it as a traditional novel, while Kerouac was working at creating something new and experimental. The anecdotes are all Kerouac's, however. Have you read much Kerouac?"

"Just *On the Road* and *The Dharma Bums*."

"Good. You should read *Mexico City Blues*. Of all of us, Kerouac was really the genius. What he did transformed writing. He was the greatest writer of the twentieth century and one of the greatest of all time.

"Early on we were both influenced by Blythe's *Encyclopedia of Haiku*. We wanted to expand beyond the language of the American novel as codified in Hemingway, Fitzgerald, Faulkner, etc. Like Joyce and Stein, we wanted to expand and rework the ways of crafting language and sound. Kerouac attempted, in his work, to transform the Jazz-African music beat into words, since he recognized it had the rhythm of speech. What he didn't know was that the music had begun in word, originally, and he was just taking it back to its source."

From the far end of the hallway, a forced cough and an audible clearing of the throat announced the arrival of Ginsberg's ride.

Ginsberg glanced over his shoulder down the hall and turned back to Chad. "There's my ride." He paused. "You're coming to my lecture tomorrow on Romanticism, I hope."

Chad was shocked and for a split second he couldn't respond—caught in the realization that Ginsberg may not have been simply killing time. "I'd been thinking about it."

"Well, maybe I will see you there. Good night." Ginsberg moved forward and, despite his diminutive stature, engulfed Chad in an expansive hug. He felt a whiskery kiss on his cheek and then the brush of hot breath against his ear. "Drive safely."

Ginsberg pivoted and shuffled down the hallway waving to the young bearded student who shifted his feet waiting at the hall's end.

Jamie slept the entire ride home closing her eyes before they even made it out of the parking lot. Chad, for his part, was exhilarated. He felt high—the car's tires flying on a black ribbon of excitement. They reached home quickly; it seemed nothing like the normal hour plus. He woke Jamie and dropped her at her house. It was a little after midnight when he pulled into his own driveway.

IV

Scott couldn't remember how long he had been lying there before he realized that the lower half of his body again needed his mind's attention.   Except this time, the urgent request was coming from his bladder.   His mind knew he had to pee more than his body could feel it.   He truly hated the intrusion of his bodily functions when he was fucked up. They always turned his trip around.   If he was with company, he would grow fearful that he would miss a control point and piss himself.   A pernicious paranoia would take over and cloud everything.   He felt his jeans. No, not yet anyway.   He moved past the bathroom and out the cabin toward the backyard.

As he descended the back steps, he found himself entering almost total darkness.   He was barely able to distinguish outlines of leaves reflecting moonlight.

He began to relieve himself.   His urine streamed noisily off the bushes in front of him.

"Oh isn't this fucking nice."   Scott heard a voice to his right. "I come back here to take a leak and a fucking faggot shows up." Scott could hear who ever it was move closer.   "Did you come back here to try to get a look?   Huh faggot?"   The voice was now very close, low and hard.

"I just came out here to pee," Scott replied trying not to sound panicked.   He turned, but could not make out the identity of the form now standing not more than a foot away.

"I heard what you tried to do to Tim.   You're disgusting.   A fucking pervert."

Scott felt a hand grip his arm.   Fingers tightened and it began to hurt.   He couldn't prevent being turned around to face his accuser.   The dark form moved even closer.   Now, their faces were six inches apart.   Scott could feel hot breath breaking against his face in even, controlled waves.   He regretted having

37

already emptied his bladder. "Look, I don't..." was all he managed before freezing completely. His mind was making up features to fill in the gaps that the low light could not. Red stripes flared off the silhouette like war paint. Neon green lines swirled and carved their way into the moonlit brow and buzzed hair.

"I hate you," the words formed evenly through clenched teeth.

It really was that simple, Scott understood in a coherent flash.

His assailant reinforced his statement with a single powerful right to the gut.

Scott felt all the air forcibly expelled from his lungs in one unstoppable exhalation. Pain seared up from his abdomen in streams of fire snaking explosions around his nipples. Arcing trails of crimson shot out from around his attacker in a demonic aura. Two hands met and shoved Scott to the ground. No quicker had he hit the hard earth than a body was hard on top of him a knee jabbing painfully into his groin.

A low growl: "I wish I could kill you. You know that?"

Scott didn't or couldn't reply. A fist connected with his jaw sending his head left into the packed soil. A stick jabbed his cheek dangerously close to his eye. The attacker stood. A heavy tan work boot ground into the dirt inches of his face. In his peripheral vision, Scott saw its mate arc back, level and descend. He braced himself for the impact. In a burst of white, he convulsed inwards toward his abdomen. His hands shot to his stomach in an attempt to keep the pain and light from ripping him in half. It began as broad slices of electricity pulsating outwards along a highway of nerves. They slowed and swirled with the acid. He could see it with the sight behind his eyes more than he was able to feel it. The white shattered into its multicolor components—spreading out in beaded riffs from his center. They cascaded like liquefying strands of glass beads along his skin. Scott grabbed one, feeling its heat, and began to climb it.

Others had joined the first attacker. Their kicks were now no more than punctuations. Each a new burst of white that quickly broke apart into its spectrum of sensation and myriad light. To Scott, the figures in the dark were air whipping around him. A cold wind cut into him magnifying the centers of pain—each an originating point of white. He grabbed at the swirling air. The figures' movements were fragmented by the jagged electric thread of his trip. Stilted like dancers in a strobe light. He attempted to analyze it. The mass of shadows and moonlight moved on their own. It broke down into cinematic frames until Scott thought he could discern its underlying elemental structure. It was voice, song—an animalistic chant of his attackers' manhood.

"How do you like it now, faggot? This will teach you. You're going to learn a lesson tonight."

V

Once he finally made it home, Chad could not fall asleep. His mind was still frenetic with his second night spent listening to the old poet. He gave up, turned on his reading lamp and pulled out his journal. He began to compose a letter:

Namesté Allen:

From a young unknown poet to a known old poet. After your reading at U Maine Orono, we talked in the foyer of Little 130 of Kerouac (Mexico City Blues) and his relationship to Holmes and Go! how he transformed the African beat (which was once word) to words (again) like Hulsenbeck at #8 Spiegelgasse, Cabaret Voltaire and Blythe's four seasons of Haiku. Tonight after your lecture on romanticism—reading Shelley, Keats, Blake—walking up the stairs to the Faculty Club we talked of Crowley and his resemblance to Shelley's breath machine. Just before I left, as you were getting your coat, you touched my arm and asked me how I was doing. It was all important but I bypassed what I meant to say.

Thank you THANK YOU It was not until meeting you that I realized how much the word image Allen Ginsberg (As Ever, Howl, et. al.) is tied into who I am. At the nadir of my self-worth, when the solution seemed to be Robert Penn Warren's Great Sleep, but eternally (or the myth we perceive to be such), it was your work that saved me. It was not acceptance; I've always known that I go "a little bit sweet for a poor freckled sun faced lad." Your writing was my first introduction to how homo-eroticism permeates art. It gave me a sense of pride and allowed me to carry my head high through adolescence, knowing that I was right.

You (actually the Allen Ginsberg young & beardless from a 1944 snapshot Riverside Dr., NY w/ Hal Chase, Kerouac and Burroughs) were my first lover and in some ways my father.

P.S. You know, I would have... maybe next time.

The next day he carefully typed the letter into his Macintosh and printed it for mailing. He addressed it c/o the University and knew that it was very unlikely that it would reach its intended recipient.

That afternoon as he walked home from school, he dropped the letter into a mailbox. As he turned to walk back toward his house, a single word broke the isolating silence of the side street.

"FAGGOT"

Chad's pulse quickened. At the word, his body tensed instantly. He turned his head quickly to look over his shoulder. At first he did not see anyone, then a shadow shifted beneath one of the large trees about fifteen feet down the road. A tall young man walked slowly into the open. Chad recognized him as a classmate, but did not know his name. He knew the kid's group and knew well their opinion of him. The boy walked toward him—his gait an expression of teenage self-confidence.

Chad knew he had little chance of outrunning him, so he stood where he was calculating potential escape routes. He gauged the distance between himself and the nearest house and compared it to that between himself and the boy. Too far. He decided not to run.

"Hey, faggot. I'm talking to you." Another shout broke the charged silence.

Chad turned fighting to appear calm. "Can I help you?"

The youth held up his wrist and than tilted it limply. "Can I help you," he mimicked in an exaggerated lisp. He stopped a few feet in front of Chad shifting his feet in the gravel as he stood. His eyes remained leveled at Chad unblinking, malicious. "Maybe you *could* help with something." He made an unmistakable motion toward his crotch.

Chad could not arrest the first sarcastic response that came to mind: "I don't do charity work."

The boy's smile tightened, his eyes narrowed. Chad could see the anger beginning to burn into his face. "Fuck you. You little cocksucker." He lunged at Chad with a hard shove to the chest. Chad stumbled backward and struggled to maintain his balance. The boy pushed him again punching him sharply with both fists. This time Chad fell to the ground. A sharp rock jabbed into his right hip.

The boy stood over him—hands set confidently atop each hip. He seemed to study Chad for a split second and then his hands slowly came forward to the front of his belt. He methodically undid the buckle unlooping the thick leather. "Let's see what you can do you, pussy."

Chad looked up at his assailant. "What does this make you?"

"A fag's mouth is the same as a bitch's when it's eating my cock," the young man stated flatly.

Suddenly their attentions were caught by the grinding sound of a car turning onto the gravel lane. The boy looked back at Chad and cleared his throat. The wad of warm spit struck Chad directly in the face. The boy turned and disappeared out of sight into the wooded shadows.

The car slowed as it approached. He heard the sound of a power window lowering as the vehicle drew along side of him. A middle-aged man leaned over from the driver's seat. "Are you okay?" he inquired.

"I'm fine," Chad replied—the cooling spit slowly dripping down the side of his face.

"Are you sure?" the man persisted.

"Yes, I'm sure."

The window rose and the car moved on down the road.

EPILOGUE

Nashville? Who did he know in Nashville, Chad wondered. He flipped the postcard over, probably one of his summer friends stopping in the midst of a cross-country road trip. He noticed a return address rubber-stamped into the upper left corner, obscuring the card's caption: ALLEN GINSBERG, NEW YORK, NY.

Beneath, familiar handwriting:

Thank you for your letter. I wished you had talked to me longer. I spent quite a few bored hours alone in my hotel room. Remind me when we meet again whether it be at Orono, Naropa or somewhere on the moon and we will pick up where we left off. Love, Allen.

Ode to the great poet
of the west

To Trebor Healey

In the west one stands
a minute high point
amidst the vast and open,
the wide Pacific stretched
tranquil and smooth.
So in contrast to
the bottle-green Atlantic
sharp with whitecaps
driven before the nor'easter.

Along the downeast coast
the land is close in
shoulders hunched
as if man and land
huddled down together
against the weather
and salt brine air.
Our hills we call mountains
and name them after
great explorers
and benefactors.

Even two centuries on
one knows this land
cannot be held by man.
No matter how many deeds

let all men know
by these presents,
this land is no more
ours than it was
the Indians' before.

We pass through and on
leaving our traces
shells and plastic
but never holding long.
No vast acreages
with fence posts
to hold them down,
only a few hardscrabble
clutching to the scar of rock
at water's edge.

Winter-Style Candies

The human syndrome needs only flesh to show what it can do.
—Ruth Moore

"I think you do not love me, but be kind and do not tell me tonight."

My eyes followed the white gloves as he pulled me onto the bed of snow. Fiercely but with marvelous panting he pushed my head down on his young breast. Like a wolf perhaps, he held me in both hands guiding me through the winter-morning's air. He shot straight up his chest, some falling to the frosty ground. I sucked his nipples, down his hard stomach onto his cock. Like knocking an opponent off, he guided it into my mouth. He fought my careenings over his body. He thought he would disappear. Suddenly I was choked by another gush of warm sperm. The frozen ground was made slippery. His strength kept me upright as we walked on. Once again assassins.

The people on the floor danced painfully—the fat, aging lesbians, the mortal fags and the young. I was only interested in the young, for they had most forcefully embraced death.

Homosexuality is pursuit. From puberty looking for first love and finding it in buddies jacking off to playboy centerfolds. From there, moving to the painful period of awakening as closeted teens. One finds love again, but looks back to childhood and thinks, who's next? "Be good and you will be happy." Everything says that life is a stage, but can anyone be so completely false to his own nature? even for one moment? When pleasure is a human feeling? Now you can't deny sex is pleasurable and, of course, it could be gay sex. My body is shaken by a strange grief.

"You were his great friend?"

"Yes, I was. For an instant—a toothy blowjob and a disemboweling."

"Don't be afraid when ancient custom cradles you to bed," the living advice of the Old Ones.

"Have you ever felt, before this moment, like you were a genuine human?" I asked.

We had been discussing the precise moment that possession takes hold. I felt a dread go through me. Whatever the form, the convict must feel similar when, excited to the very depths, he enters "come out with your hands up. No funny business, now; we've got you surrounded." Excitement is entirely normal. "Why are you asking me of other men?" His mind quivers but could manage excitement. The deep breaths in. "I'll explain in a minute." His eyes shine. I shrug, trying to seem safe and he overflows with the archetype in my dreams that arise several times, like savage tribes. Even "Me too" becomes a chant of exultation. I catch his eyes, they're attacked by a sadness. What was he getting at, why had he brought up women? He glittered with some reason that would have surfaces, while engulfed in the memory of a going. No jumping to conclusions. Some change memory of the "What about when you are not of your upbringing/conditioning? What about right now?"

Our sexual functions are pleas. "Sure I'd like to be... But you're too busy already to become my friend, aren't you."

"I cannot without you."

"But there's this sometimes... I feel the deep, being close to you. I like it and find it necessary to utter such. I like it when you sleep."

Under that rush of the primitive, we're making love— already the joy of a savage is reborn. I think about actually breaking the manifestation of life. I kissed him and the seas crashed and the stallions pawed the air. The bells and the doves and flowers all did their thing.

After his fevered ejaculation, a savage thread tide of exhilaration remains in the body. "The rocks will never miss you."

People Change

It was not until the second knock that Chad realized someone was at the door. He got up from the couch and groggily made his way to answer it. He'd fallen asleep. He turned back toward the television—Suburbia now three quarters finished. The last thing he remembered was "Jimmy Hung Himself."

As he rounded the corner into the front hallway, he could see T.J.'s short, curly red hair just at the edge of the door's small window. He heard him knock a third time.

"Well, hey there."

"I thought you'd never wake up." T.J. pushed his way into the house, before Chad could open the door and get out of the way.

He clasped Chad's hand and gave him a zealous hug before taking off his light jacket and throwing it onto one of the series of hooks that lined the left wall.

"That must have been an exciting movie," T.J. said walking into the living room.

"Suburbia. It's really good, actually."

T.J. watched the TV for a couple of beats, tilting his head with exaggerated inquisitiveness. "Looks like more of your punk shit to me."

Chad lunged at T.J. and caught his unsuspecting friend in a strangle hold. "It's not shit."

"Uncle. Uncle! All right. It's not shit. Whatever you're into..."

Chad let him go. "My parents are out of town this weekend."

"I know. What do you think brought me over?"

"Want a beer?"

"Does the Pope wear a dress?"

"I'll take that as a yes. Just a minute." Chad disappeared into the kitchen. T.J. heard the refrigerator door open.

T.J. clicked the VCR's STOP button and then EJECT. He rummaged through the tapes in the case beside it, thought about a couple and chose his selection. He slipped the tape into the opening and prepared to relax on the couch. The opening scenes of *Terminator* began to play on the TV screen.

"Here's your beer. Don't hesitate to make yourself at home."

"Don't worry I won't. So, Chad, my man, what have you been up to. I haven't seen much of you this semester?" He motioned for Chad to sit beside him.

Chad swallowed the first cold swig of his PBR and took the place T.J. indicated. T.J. was his best friend—best male friend might have been a more apt description. They had been close since junior high. Once they were nerds together and now they were growing into coolness simultaneously, but along distinctly separate paths. While Chad was inventing his individuality through the leather jacket ripped jeans and combat boots of punk, T.J. was moving into the carefully prepared garments of his very preppy family. This past year they had not had much to talk about. Chad continued to hope that they still remained close and he was very glad T.J. would still stop by on his own. Chad had long ago given up on his obsession to get together with T.J. in anything beyond friendship. They had jerked off together when they were going through puberty, but he doubted that T.J. would acknowledge it as anything other than adolescent need.

Chad quickly checked his reverie to respond to T.J.'s query. "Getting my school work together. You heard I got into Reed, didn't you? You got into Yale, right?"

"Of course I knew about Reed. My mother's the town gossip you know."

"How could I forget?"

T.J. smiled. Chad had long ago decided that this expression was his best feature. T.J. opened up when he smiled—his whole personality threatening to spill out around the edges.

T.J. placed his empty bottle on the coffee table. "Got another?"

"Sure I got a couple of six. Jamie's new boyfriend bought them for me when he visited her last."

Chad ignored T.J.'s grimace, but reminded himself not to mention Jamie again. She and T.J. had fucked on a pretty regular basis the previous summer. He now made no bones about his negative opinion regarding the direction her appearance had taken since.

Chad quickly returned with more beer.

After a third round, they ordered a pizza and put in another SciFi movie. The sun fading outside, the room sank into darkness.

"Did you understand your geometry homework?" T.J. turned to Chad as the credits rolled. Several more empty beers littered the surfaces about them.

"I think so. You want me to help you with yours?"

"Maybe later. I'm too drunk right now to care." T.J. glanced over at Chad and smiled his smile again.

"You still got that movie? You know the one we stole from the video store that time?"

"That porn thing? You want to watch that?"

"It's good for a laugh."

"I think it's down in my room. We can put it in down there, if you want."

"Sure I'll meet you there. I got to take a leak first."

"Grab a couple of beers on your way through."

"No problem."

They made their separate exits and within a few minutes converged in Chad's basement room. He already had the tape in and a naked threesome was earning their money on his small TV screen. Chad's section of the basement was small, having been halved by the addition of a garage several years ago. The cramped quarters meant that the bed provided the only clear space for anyone to sit. Chad sat cross-legged on his small twin bed, leaving just enough room beside him for T.J.

T.J. handed him his beer and bounced his way onto the mattress. "God, look at her tits." He watched the TV and smiled.

Chad grunted a response that he hoped resembled agreement. He had trouble removing his eyes from that smile to the screen.

"Do you think they're real?"

"Huh?"

"Her breasts. Do you think they're real or fake?"

"I don't know. They do look a little large to me."

"What would you know?" T.J. laughed.

Chad hoped that it was nothing more than a friendly jibe. But, then, they'd been friends long enough that T.J. had to know more than he let on.

T.J. removed his eyes from the screen to look at Chad. "Have you fucked her yet?"

"Who?" Chad had no clue where this had come from.

"Jamie?"

"Jamie?" he asked, surprised. "We're just friends."

T.J. didn't seem to acknowledge the second half of Chad's response. "Don't bother. She's not worth it."

Chad was about to defend his other friend, but when he looked over it seemed like T.J. was back into analyzing the porn. He decided the safer choice was to let it drop.

"Christ. It's been so long that even something this corny gets me up."

Now Chad was surprised. "You don't have to go there."

"Why not? We've been there before."

Chad looked over at T.J. who was in the process of unbuttoning his jeans.

"I've got to do something about this. Pass me the KY you keep in that drawer, will you."

"I don't..."

"*Bullshit.* Now give it up."

Chad chuckled to mask his unease and opened the small top drawer of his end table. He extracted the small, half-used tube. He turned to hand it to T.J. who was now standing pulling his shirt off over his head.

"What are you doing?"

"It's nothing you haven't seen before. I got something that I have to take care of."

"You're drunk."

"Your point? Now come on. Race you."

Chad decided he had nothing to lose. He was drunk too, after all, and this was an opportunity he was not about to pass up. He bounced off the bed and ripped his T-shirt over his head. By the time he had dropped his pants and boxers to the floor, T.J. was already back reclining on the bed stroking his erection.

He had seen T.J.'s body before. He had a small treasured collection of photographs they had taken after a drunken party when they were sixteen. He had studied them often for the next couple years as he nursed his obsession. T.J.'s body was hairless, except for a shock of reddish brown at the immediate vicinity of his cock. His balls smooth and Chad wondered if he shaved them. His skin was milky white, coated with a copper spread of freckles across his shoulder blades and down both arms. He was slender and his ribs still ghosted through as Chad remembered they had in those old photographs. His small pink nipples rested on a subtle bed of pectoral muscle. His erect cock was longer than Chad remembered and veered to the left.

Chad raised his eyes along T.J.'s torso to his face. He met two blue eyes looking back. T.J. was smiling. It lit up his freckled face, shifting his crooked nose, broken in a JV basketball game. Chad smiled back.

T.J. gripped his cock tightly in one fist and brandished it toward Chad. "They say there's nothing to it."

"To what?"

"To giving a blowjob. I'll probably give someone one, someday. It's not like sex or anything. Just helping another guy out."

"Whatever," Chad replied looking down at his own growing cock. He sat now on the bed beside T.J. squeezing a small amount of the lube onto his palm.

T.J. reached over and grabbed Chad's hand moving it away from Chad's erection toward his own. "It feels better if we help each other."

Chad swallowed as he felt the warm, smooth taughtness of T.J.'s flesh pulse in his hand. He squeezed and absorbed the novelty of feeling someone else's skin slide along his palm. T.J.'s hand squeezed in recognition along Chad's shaft and slowly glided up and down its length. They leaned back in opposite directions along the bed.

Chad watched his hand move in its rhythmic motion up and down T.J.'s prick. He was caught with an impulse and thought: What the fuck?

T.J. looked up in surprise as he felt Chad's mouth envelop his dick. He smiled. Chad closed his eyes. T.J. bent his head and like wise took Chad into his mouth.

They shifted positions. T.J. swiveled on top of Chad—pistoning into his receptive mouth. Chad ignored the periodic scrape of T.J.'s teeth for as long as he could.

"Less teeth."

T.J. looked back over his shoulder. "Sorry."

Chad felt himself drawing close to orgasm. "Stop. Stop, I'm getting too close."

T.J. stopped again glancing back at Chad. "Why?"

"I don't want to come yet."

"Why not?"

Chad guided T.J. off him and into a reclining position along the mattress. He moved up and brought his face close to T.J. Chad shut his eyes, tilted his head and moved forward. He briefly felt his lips graze against T.J.'s.

A hand shot up against his chest and held him back. "I don't kiss."

Chad was a little taken a back, but relaxed again as he felt T.J.'s hand renew its ministrations on his dick. "Whatever."

"There are other things..." T.J. said.

Chad looked at him and was instantly cognizant of what he meant. T.J. placed one hand on Chad's shoulder, the other on his cock pulling it down and forward. Chad bit his lip and sank into a deep intake of breath as T.J. guided his cock toward his ass.

"Wait." Chad reached into the still open drawer beside the bed and pulled out a Trojan, which he handed T.J. He heard the rip of plastic and within a few seconds felt hands rolling latex over his head and shaft. Chad bit his lip and tried to relax.

Chad winced at the first pull of rubber making contact with T.J.'s tight sphincter muscle. He could sense T.J. tense and then visibly will himself to relax. Chad pressed forward with his head with more insistence. Suddenly he was inside T.J. He felt a rush as he realized that the head had passed through the ring of muscle and was now gliding into T.J.

T.J. reached down into the space between them and began working his own cock.

"Oh God, I'm going to come," T.J. groaned throatily. "*Oh shit.*"

Chad quickened his thrusts as he felt T.J. tighten with his impending orgasm. He felt himself cross that point as T.J. shot come out across his chest.

After several quiet moments, T.J. rolled over and sat up. He swung his legs off onto the floor. Looking down, Chad slipped the condom off his softening cock and tossed it basketball-style into the trash.

"I'm going to go shower off. Want another beer?"

"I think I'll pass for now." Chad lifted his head and looked down at the Pollock drops of white fluid dripping off T.J.'s chest and stomach. "I've got to shower off too."

"Suit yourself. Don't mind if I grab one on my way, do you?"

"No, not at all."

Chad glanced at his clock's oversized red numerals, rubbed sleep from his eyes and looked again. 6:38. He looked over toward T.J., who was trying to quietly pull on his tangled jeans. He caught the line of Chad's sight a quick smile passing across his face and all too hastily fading.

"I've got to get to work. My father's expecting me to help him get some stuff done."

"On a Saturday?"

"He says that if I want to take over the company one day, I have to give up the concept of weekends."

"Sounds like fun," Chad said sarcastically.

"Fun." T.J. pulled his shirt over his head—the last glimpse of white flesh hidden from Chad's view as T.J. smoothed the cloth down over his stomach. "I'll see you around, I guess." He slipped his feet into his sneakers, but neglected to tie them.

"Don't be as much of a stranger."

"Don't worry. Later man." T.J. turned and bounded up the stairs.

Chad heard feet tread across the entry hall immediately above. "T.J...." he called after him already knowing it was too late. The echoing click of the door meeting its jam told him that he was right.

He fell back asleep thinking of T.J. and wondering what would come of the night before. When he re-awoke and looked at his alarm clock, he was surprised to find it already afternoon. "Shit." He rolled onto his back and looked at the ceiling.

He heard someone moving around upstairs. Shit, he thought again. One of his parents was home and would have found the evidence of his drinking. He slowly rose from his bed and, grabbing his robe and towel, proceeded upstairs.

His mother was in the kitchen. She was wearing her jacket and was in the process of organizing her purse. "Slept in, I see."

"Yes." He looked hard at the linoleum flooring. "I have exams next week and I need all the rest I can get."

"Well, that's good. Just make sure that you are ready for them. Your acceptance to Reed is still contingent on you continuing to do well. You know your grades haven't been that great this quarter."

"I know, mom. Don't worry." He turned and began to walk to the shower.

"It's a mother's job to worry," she answered softly. "Your father and I are going to your Aunt Alice's. I am meeting him at the golf course and we're going from there. Alice's husband has taken another bad turn and she needs us at the house to look after the kids while she is at the hospital. We'll be back either late tomorrow or early Monday morning."

Chad resumed his walk to the bathroom. "No problem, mom. I didn't have anything special planned."

Chad's mother closed up her purse and turned toward the door. "I left some money on the counter for you. Just in case you wanted to order take out or something." After getting no response from her son's receding form, she continued, "Make sure you eat while I'm gone."

"No problem. Alice is waiting."

She heard the bathroom door close and the scratch of metal as the hook and eye connected.

Chad hesitated for the hundredth time that evening. He was frozen, his hand poised over the last digit in T.J.'s number. Shit, why couldn't he make the call? They had been friends for years; he had called him a thousand times. He looked at the handset studying a small smudge of paint for what felt to be hours. He turned back to the tiled pattern of digits. He dialed, but again his hand froze, poised inches away from the final number. Fuck. He plunged his finger home blindly striking the button eight. He felt as if he had dove off a cliff. He held his breath waiting for the first ring hoping that it would be busy.

The phone rang. His heart clenched within his chest and he was forced to intake a breath. After the phone's second assaulting ring, a pleasant female voice came on the line.

"Hello."

"Hello Mrs. Hughes, is T.J. there?"

"Sure, just a minute." He could hear her voice muffle as she put her hand over the mouthpiece. "Thomas John, the phone is for you."

"Chad?" she asked returning to the phone. "How have you been? Your last weeks of school going well?"

"Everything's going great. I'm going to Reed in the fall."

"Your mother mentioned that. Congratulations. Oh, here comes my son. Say hello to your mother for me and don't be such a stranger around here."

"I'll try not to."

"Hello?" T.J.'s voice took over the receiver.

"Hey T.J. How's everything?" Chad tried his best to sound natural and calm.

"Fine. Look, Chad, I'm right in the middle of something. Can I call you back?"

"Sure." Chad's whole chest seemed to cave in.

"Bye."

Before Chad could reply, he was left with the dial tone cutting into the first harsh bite of numbness.

He waited throughout the evening absent-mindedly trying to do homework intermixed with bouts of pacing the confines of his small basement room. He jumped when the phone rang three hours later, but it was only Jamie asking if he wanted to go out for coffee. He felt like a complete loser as he declined. The realization had already taken hold in his conscious mind: T.J. was not going to call him back.

Maybe he had become caught up in what he was doing, Chad rationalized with himself. A knowledge that hit him like an elbow in the gut told him otherwise.

For the remainder of the school day, Chad felt sick to his stomach. He could not get the image of Scott's bruised face out of his mind. His only diversion the continuous and persistent intrusion of his anxiety regarding T.J. He had not managed to run into him at all that morning and, as was his usual, T.J. had left campus for lunch. Chad had caught a glimpse across the field, but the distance was too great to catch his eye.

His two preoccupations kept him from concentrating on his calculus class that immediately followed lunch. Images of the shock horror of Scott's appearance and T.J.'s naked body intercut themselves like a demented gore/porn combination. He could not keep the two grotesquely contrasting intrusions out of his mind. Twice his calc teacher had to make her presence physically known to him in order to elicit responses to her questions. His next period was physics lab and T.J. would be in that with him. They did not sit near each other, but there was usually an opportunity to talk during their forty-five minute practical.

As his physics instructor finished his preliminary notes on the board and the last of the students settled in their seats, Chad grew increasingly apprehensive. T.J. had not come in yet; his desk remained conspicuously vacant at the front of the second row. A quick look shot out the window to check the parking lot informed him that T.J.'s car was gone. His Jeep, PICASSO, no longer occupied its usual space near the football bleachers.

His physics class dragged. He could not keep his mind off T.J.'s absence. The weeks of no communication was closing him into a painful claustrophobic cell. When the final buzzer sounded, he didn't even bother to sort out his homework—just grabbed his jacket and headed for his Scirocco. Not wanting to go home and face the boring tightness of his room, he drove directionless through town. He had no particular destination, maybe he would stop in and grab a slice of pizza.

He didn't bother slowing down when he reached the pizzeria, however. PICASSO stood out prominently among the small row of vehicles parked along the curb in front of the building. After verifying the familiar license plate and driving past several times, he could not bring himself to pull over and go in. Two factors drove his reluctance: he couldn't get up the nerve to face him and he feared being disappointed. He had known T.J. since they were twelve, but suddenly everything was different. He was attempting to navigate an entirely new course and he was increasingly unsure as to the extent that their paths aligned. Chad was slowly reaching the conclusion that T.J. was going through his own ordeal processing the exchange, that, ironically, he himself had orchestrated. He was beginning to accept his suspicions that T.J.'s agenda was not Chad's. No matter what T.J.'s desires might be, Chad knew that he was the victim of other powerful, crippling imperatives.

After three passes by the pizza joint, T.J.'s Jeep unmoved, he turned home.

He waited by T.J.'s locker long enough to be getting nervous. Really fucking nervous. People were staring. People didn't care. He was just being stupid. He cared. But no one else gave a shit about him or where he loitered. As ever, he was nothing. His pulse increased, simply beating faster with the catch of breath in his throat. Nothing cliché... just abject fear as he spied T.J. approaching.

Seeing Chad, T.J. broke away from his group of friends and, without eye contact, approached his locker with steeled determination.

"Hey what's been up with you," Chad shot through the edge of silence.

"Nothing."

"Do you want to get together tonight... to talk or whatever?"

"What's there to talk about? Look... I am really not interested in hanging out with you anymore."

"But... before, you said you thought..."

"People change." T.J. walked away.

all day I kept that
  note in my pocket
dreading the opportunity
  I would have to
  turn it over to you
making excuses
  you'll never know

Crux Ansata

Everyone says that life is acting without conscious initiative. To become obsessed with darkness, a darkness heard of only in furtive timorous whispers is unhealthy.

For an outside it must have been a complex construction of ghostly gossamer fibers—Imps melting through the forest stone steps which rose into the rock I leaned my head upon. He groped carefully with his hands alive in a half-dream of wine. A door opened overhead. A little fumbling opened the shirt which blended and glowed inward...and beyond it the forest. Dank. Primeval... below it into a worm-eaten subterranean grotto. We rapidly began exploring with our feet. The amoebas melting, locked, so that he freely offered another bowl. He seemed indifferent, naïve. The ground and the rock became dust over box pews.

Acting almost without consciousness—no more than an infantile dream—he raised the window and let himself down into the green tangible dark. His foot found a barrel sitting on the rubble-strewn floor. The vaulted roof seemed to rest on his shoulders. He was one of the many partitions segregating the sections of the basement. In a far corner sat a pot. He wore his green track shirt now covered with shadows. He saw a black archway alive with vibrant strobes. I felt a peculiar sense of oppression, as we descended down the face of the great spectral building... the green strobes and the rock at the bottom. He slowly scouted about with his eyes—finding a broken ladder which he rose to get. He moved it under the window. The green sank to the escape route. Bracing himself he needed cold.

His chin rested on a magnificent sounding board and his titanic gold ropes were slicked back and pushed away toward the pointed arches of the gallery. There was a scar on one cheek. Power columned over all this over his hushed strong pecs that billowed out leaden light as he reclined in the fading light. His denim—gray with the moonlight coming through the strange half-blackened panes of thick, big and swollen, strained creatures. His lips were slightly parted.

Hour-glass pulpit chest... dirty yellow hair a cobweb stretching over his face which was itself square and strong... is lowered to cluster around gothic arms folded across desolation that played a hideous tone crowned by a thick nipple. The moon sent its borrowed rays through muscular thighs and something strange came through the great windows that ran a stain across his crotch. Black could have scarcely foreseen the mystical painting created. But from the little I could, my back touched the wall. He... the design was largely in my head, so I could see drops of obscure symbolism enfold him. He spit his gum out and bent among the patterns of ancient saints depicting his big hand turning my face. I was open to question while he closed my eyes, hardly daring to show more than dark space with me coldly. His voice scattered about in it. "Turned into a fucking fairy." I noticed that the cobwebs could cut. "You sonnabitch, the only straight kid, but I was never one of your sluts—you asshole."

He moved still closer until the windows were so obscured by soot... He put a hand on the wall above the cipher, what this script represented... of sweat glistening on his arm. I could make out that he did not like them. His face came closer to mine, while his mind moved closer to his knowledge. Instinctively, I hushed concerning some of the ancient... I opened my eyes and he distinctly bore a startled expression. "Just as I thought..." one of the windows seems to hit his chest with spirals of curious luminosity.

"That's the thing, you are capable of kissing away form."

A shadowy *crux ansata* flew softly out of ancient Egypt. He slapped me hard across the face. In a rear vestry room, "I'll show you what a fucking..." With the back of his hand he made a cross above the altar. He slammed himself in closer to the primordial ankh of I Am. I was suddenly... arms went around me. Desk and ceiling-high shelves broke away as I was engulfed in hard hot muscles. Here for the first time, he ground against me. At his side, I found a rotting, brutal, determined hurt driven by mildewed, disintegrating memories. I was possessed by object horror, for I kicked and tried to get away. His were the black forbidding arms that drew me closer. I had never even heard of or pulled at his nipples in encouragement. His crotch whispered—the banned and dreaded against his stomach. He pulled with an immemorial formulae. He grabbed his time from the days of man's youth. His wet, deep kiss became tender, a positive shock ran my fingers over his chest. Those books had taught him much. He felt like a mound of molten things which most sane people never experience. He pulled away and looked down at me. His blond head only a furtive and timorous shake... he bolted from the room.

He descended the steps of the aging stone cathedral, not looking back as the heavy doors shut. "For all have sinned..." He turned the corner of the church and began down the path that ran between it and the stone monuments in the churchyard. From behind a crumbing black headstone, a small boy leapt into his path. He looked at the older boy with ancient eyes. "Pennies for the Queen. Pennies for the King."

When he did not respond immediately, the youth kicked him sharply in the shin. Brushing past the boy, he continued his walk. He kept his hands carefully in his pockets. Softly, with eyes cast down—as if to avoid looking up at the old rectory as he passed—"...and fall short of the glory of god."

Love Always, Jojo

Needing you. Please Please write back. This is where we always used to tell secrets as kids. Being a Scorpio, born on Halloween, I am an extremely horny person. I'm always walking around with my cock ready to burst out of my pants. Shaking himself, almost paralyzed with fear, Bran thrashed in closer, his sleeping friend under him. Feeling their bodies against each other, a whimper of yellow smoke appeared at his groin. I find the very motion of you a gentle breeze caressing. His throat ached as he felt the tranquil fierceness in his friend tonight. There's a guy here named Sean, and he reminds me of you. He has a brown mohawk. He's tall and really good-looking. Every time I see him smile I think of you and get really horny, I wish you were here. I've been doing pretty well, though I have been feeling a little bit lonely lately. I wish so very much that we could be together.

By the spring of 1939, the Gestapo had begun the routine placement of homosexuals in protective custody, under paragraph 175 of the German penal code. *It is such a drag to have to hide your sexuality.* As he stirred, he noticed a hand dangling illuminated by the moonlight. Cautiously he reached up and took the hand. *If my friends found out about me being a homosexual some of them would flip. I'm so tired of hiding it and lying about it.* Bran reached across for the lubricant. *If I could kiss anyone right now it would be you. I'm so tired of being afraid of people finding out about me being gay.* Straight fucking is nothing more than ritualized polarization. *Some of my friends are really prejudiced about gays and I wouldn't want to lose any friendships over it.* Results confirm the existence of the phobic type of heart rate acceleratory pattern among high homonegative males.

I went to Jamaica for a week. In Kingston we stayed with a rasta couple named Sister P. and Brother John for 4 days. Their house is on top of this huge hill overlooking this beautiful bay. Everything around was green and jungled. At every meal there were new kinds of food we had never tried before. In the day we would always walk 3 miles down a road to a river where we would relax in tropical pools of clear water. We slept in a bamboo hut elevated on stilts. Of the 57% of gay men who had served in the armed forces, eighty percent had had sex while on active duty. *Last week I was in the Infirmary sharing a room with this guy named Jeff. When he was lying in bed I got in with him and we laid together for awhile. When we kind of started to connect, these two guys from the room next door came in.* At night a member of the lagerpolitzei would sneak into the barracks in an attempt to catch someone engaged in their filthy queer behavior. *I had to leave so they wouldn't suspect anything. With you I don't feel ashamed or afraid to talk about anything.* Heterosexuality means remaining the victim.

I told you about him. His name is Sean. He came to school at the end of the year. We never really had the chance to become very close friends. Every time we looked at each other this feeling came over me, it was so intense. Sometimes we would sit in class and just stare and smile at each other. Wishing one of us would make the first move, knowing that the recognition was unavoidable. I never had the same feeling with anyone else before in my life. He was a senior so he won't be back next year. A Ouija board told me that we were lovers back in ancient Egypt.

He remembered when younger, initiation with the Vaseline jar and wet sweat—he and his brother cornholing in their basement. Once when the pants came off and his brother eased himself beside him, they felt each other through their BVD's. The contact of their naked bodies, hands massaging lats and deltoids, their lips meeting again viciously. Then the white cotton came off. He bent his head, his brother's cock bouncing in his face. There was an understanding of the nature of challenge. He met the cock ruthlessly. His brother freed his hands and seized his hair, a burst of soft laughter. Brothers always love each other.

I went to San Francisco this summer to visit some friends. I had a great time driving around, eating good food, going to coffee shops, smoking a little herb. I met a nice guy named Tom. We kind of fell in love with each other the first time we met. I went into a coffee shop late one night and he worked there. He offered me free coffee and we just started talking. After it closed I waited for him to finish closing up and I talked to him again. We were so into each other. He has the most intense blue eyes—I was lost in them. We both had friends standing around waiting for us to finish talking and who would have been really disgusted if we were to exchange addresses and phone numbers in front of them. A factor of 43% expressed a moral condemnation of homosexuals and homosexual behavior. *It sucks to be so closed about your sexuality. We had to part, but Tom said we'd meet again.*

Here it's a gray morning. I'm sitting in bed with that morning hardon busting the seams in my underwear forming a tent in my blankets. He held him on his back and lifted his legs over his shoulder. He pulled his hips into him. *Writing a friend who I have never seen in person. The hornyness of young teenagers.* Masturbation is a virtue. *I used to give pony rides to kids before our pony was stolen.* The other felt the nudge of entry, sweaty, locked legs, the cock growing into him. *I'm glad your friend helped you out. You must be very lonely working by yourself. If you ever get lonely let me know and I'll write you a letter everyday.*

I freaked out in my last class, geometry. The teacher kept putting me on the spot, making me go to the board when I didn't understand what to do. I'm so frustrated with school that I almost broke out crying in class. After class I ran up to the top of my favorite hill and screamed. He could never have expected any strength of character in a queer. *My cock burns I mean burns to be touched by someone. I look at your picture and your great letter and all I can do is fantasize about how it could be. It just hurts. I just want you to know that I love you and that if I ever stop writing for a long period of time I have not forgotten my wonderful friend across the country. I never will.*

Groups marked by a desire for traditional sex roles display a greater degree of homophobic behavior. *Since then Brian and I have been going out secretly. If it were to get loose Brian would lose his job. So we decided tonight that we should at least stop having sex because it's too risky.* The nuclear family is the schooling ground of the sexually repressive society. *I get mad sometimes when my mom asks me if I'm on to any girls. When my dad asks me about my girl friend I just tell him I'm not involved right now and I get real nervous like he can see right through my cover and GAY is written allover my face. I don't know why.* The strength drained as he felt himself being ripped, "No..." *I guess I'm paranoid he'll find out.* The answer that they teach our young people is simple: the growing number of homosexuals indicates a decline in American values. *I hate when I'm around friends and they talk about girls. And to show you're not a wimp or a fag you have to say how much you would like to sleep with her and really dumb shit. I can't do it anymore. Lying to them and myself.* Continued heterosexuality represents a compulsive annihilation of the human spirit. *I don't think I could ever come out to all my friends like some people do. I'd rather they found out on their own.* An exclusive commitment to one sexual formation means that one is just another good soldier. Only seven percent of the heterosexual males in the military had ever had sex while on duty. Without breaking the rhythm, "I fuck you good, Maricone." Smashing together bodies clamped with arms and legs, arms entwined, all muscles alert.

Anyways, I've been lonely as usual. Knowing that whether I have friends or no friends you're always there for me is the best feeling in the world. "That feels great." It had never occurred to him that sex between two males could feel good for both. *At the moment I am working for the person I am living with in exchange for board. I'm getting food stamps from the state but it's hardly enough to live on. My counselor (outside of school) has arranged a meeting between me and my mother tomorrow. Hopefully we can work something out so that I can get some support from her. I haven't talked to her for about 2 months since I ran away. I need help right now, bad. I have no money for soap, school supplies, etc. So far I've managed to stay in school keeping a 3.5, feed myself, board myself.* By January 1940 the complement for the camp was complete and they were taken to hard labor. *If I don't get some help from someone I'll have to drop out of school and get a job.*

I think that saying you're gay to anyone else that's not gay can limit your possibilities, paranoia and all. No one but you and myself know that I'm homosexual. I know that if I told everyone I met that I was gay my life would be miserable. It is also miserable hiding it, especially when I have to talk with other guys about how I like this girl and that kind of shit to keep them from suspecting me of being gay.

Love always,
jojo

75

The Snake of Time

Their eyes make contact.
"Plot evil against me."
"That goes with saying."
"Being a cop is a blue collar fantasy
and, therefore, I used to think it
utterly loathsome."
As he remembers a concentrated and
constant despair, his eyes narrow
"It would be so great."
"Thought I could, huh faggot."
"Yes, I really..."
A one eye black, tommy-gun black,
fuck standing up to being... eyes
crackling fateful love near erect with
the rebuff, as he quickly makes for
Tim. He unbuttons his fly, strains to
reach. Tim drops, crouching between
the outstretched legs, giving in. What
fragrance of heavy lifting, a musty
smell of sex, bleak perfume—it's
moving down over the bulge...
"Choke on... you want it don't you..."
Their talk is all lies... "Cocksucker,
watch out Yah now... strangle
yourself." Their high god creates
their crime—sex sessions with live
sync-sound with its own jagged
frequency. Mouth fucked in a blur
of heat desperate and crushing.

Total cock and ball boot in the face
passion... his mouth becomes a
fist... a slap across the face, still
broad and firm, warm and blunt
against his skin... smooth and warm
bruise. A vulture hovers over and
descends upon the two lovers of
God, the snake of time, sheathed in
the fear deep in the crotch.
Jimmy sighs. "As thought I had never
left, I am the one. I am the only
one... doing observing remembering
their work." His cock bounces, with
something like contempt, thick and
sturdy. He pulls the faded t-shirt
tossing it to the floor, and pulls the
tight waistband of his white boxer
shorts over his crotch. Tim's cock
springs up still warm and thick...
dirty Hüsker Du t-shirt crumpled to
the floor passion. The lovers and
their princes rebelled against the
sanctuary. The divine souls shall fall
by the word use of sex rays. Jimmy
runs his hands over his chest... and
raises his mouth above him. One god
embraceth the other taking their
souls in his mouth. Their breath
moves to the center—to his lungs, the
soul of Ra. The instant is filled; their
blue lips spring into being. To help
with everything familiar and
weakened, a crimson myth of dust

comes over the people. Jimmy fucks
hard with muscle. He is like any
other, a job—whisky mouthed
horizons to his heart. He relapses
onto the hungry part, the obscenities,
all at the same time, like tongues.

TASMAI SHRI GURUVE NAMAH
He goeth into Tattu, over his head,
a gradual expanding of the dragon of
pain. The universe smashed, the
cosmos goes dream consciousness—
the sight and sound's own excitement.
Something inaudible and obscene
radiates hate and death. They have
broken the covenant. The pendulum
stops I AM... apollonic radiance,
busted wires, broken ropes five feet
tall... He findeth there a pool of
semen and a dry old rose on an altar
heaped with hops. The Twin Gods,
the hands that guide the myriad,
look down to him for help.
Instruction they cry. "Put the trumpet
to the worship of your lips. I have
given you strength, all young men, that
are willing to love an idol. I support
them, but it's always the same, those
who throw themselves passionately into
these spasms, the punishment is death.

GURU SHAKSHAT PARABRAHMAN
We know the god of hate or love or

death, like a bow gone slack, silent
and beautiful, more than just the
move. One every threshing floor, hate
existed. I wish you had left me
unborn and now our days move
bitterly and are misery. The enemy
you have who loves them above
themselves, shall run before the fire
of the Lord on Good Friday. Young
jocks, whose birth is in sin, jerk, Adonis,
loiterer, stalker, hairier than before,
preening like teenagers, lost and
withered... Thou satan-sons are
eager, Their retribution, this crew of
energetic laborers, dusted and deadly,
is centuries silence.
Hadith

As brothers fight ye!

MUTILATIONS

PREFACE

"Existence is mutilation. To exist is to be subjected to a continuing procedure of degradation. This is my central theme, that we are the mutilated, that our generation has grown out of and grown up with a mutilating universe. Unlike those who came before, we were born into a world with no comprehensive view of itself. We were given nothing—adrift in contradictions, deserted. Our generation lacked even the hackneyed stalwarts of a generation before. The hippies had the advertised efficiency of the fifties. What do we really have? Woodstock II? Our generation, I would argue, is the first to completely lack any unifying 'hope' mechanism. We lack both reasons for our being and guarantees of our future. We were born into nothing but futility and fatality.

"From that point, the moment of our birth or even our conception, powers collide to destroy us—powers out of our past and from the edges of our present. It may also be that the generation before, having had their own hopes of a better world shattered, is primarily motivated by a culturally invasive sadism. To grow up in such a world is then a process of disassociated mutilations. Mutilations that at each moment fragment who we are and how we think of who we are. It then becomes the choice of the individual to fashion these moments into a rosary, that one may carry into a self-fabricated future, or be beaten completely, opening oneself to ever-increasing misery ending only in the rot of the grave.

"It is perhaps that the mutilations push us further. As Nietzsche argued, 'That which does not kill us, makes us stronger.' These moments, I propose, are something similar to

Foucault's 'limit-experiences'—moments that push at the envelope of transgressive possibility."

"How do these moments differ from the existentialist's 'extreme situations'?" Flux asked, lighting another Sobraine. She didn't want him to stall; it had been a long time since she had seen Cade this animated.

"I see them as a much stronger force than what Jaspers spoke of. The 'extreme situation' lifts one out of the everyday; it is a forced reprioritizing. It is something extraordinary. It's more than a momentary elevation above the forest to a vantage where one can see the entire valley. The 'limit-experience', the mutilating event or series, contorts the forest, changing its fundamental makeup before one's very eyes, thereby permanently transforming the perception of the trees."

"Is it in any way similar to the eastern methods of observing the course of life, but not judging its turnings?"

"The Eastern ways have always struck me as too passive. The whole notion of non-judging seems too positivist. You know that story of the guy who loses his horse? The old man of the village loses his horse; it runs away. All his neighbors say how unfortunate he is. The old man, however, refuses to look upon his situation either negatively or positively. The village suffers a tremendous thunderstorm and all the other horses run away. In the morning his horse returns. The villagers tell him how lucky he is, because his horse did not disappear with the rest of the village's herd. The old man again refrains from judging. His son falls off the horse and breaks his leg. The father again refuses to judge and subsequently his son's injury saves him from certain death in battle. There is something working under the surface in such a philosophy. It is the notion that somehow life will work itself out in the end. It implies that there is a method, or balance at least, to what is dealt out, by an otherwise randomly appearing universe. I'm sure we can both think of situations, where judging is completely appropriate. I cannot think that the universe is as fair or evenhanded as the dictum 'this too shall pass' implies. Are we to tell the poor person not to judge his poverty or his hunger; are we to admonish the raped woman not to judge her rape? What positive can come out of such situations?"

"What is the raped woman supposed to do then? How does she deal with her situation?"

"One survives them, that is all. It is of such situations that one makes them their own or runs in the face of them for the rest of their life.

"What stands us in the face of all this is our most primordial of drives, the will to live (evidenced in the act of breathing). The basic survival instinct forces one to confront the powers which seem allied against one. It is up to each person to face their mutilations and absorb them—reshape them and thereby reshape the possibilities open to the subjective 'I'. I don't mean a simple making sense of them. It is certainly possible that there is no sense to any of it. Such a concept would stink of metaphysics. I mean, rather, an approaching of the very experiences which have pushed one to the limits of endurance. I use experience here in the Heideggerian sense where 'experience' is an undergoing which both overwhelms and transforms. In such instances one has only a few choices. Initially one has the dual choice of succumbing—to die or to move through. In the face of these moments of personal darkness, contacts with the uncanny irrationality of existence, man either surges ahead, dies, goes mad or recedes into safety. Surging ahead is a picking oneself up moving forward transformed by the 'experience' of experiencing. Dying represents a complete overpowering which may result from either a complete satiation of ultimate pleasure or a general sacrifice of the fundamental will to live. Going mad, here, would also seem a perfectly viable option. Madness, in contrast to modern clinical foci, could easily represent a clarity of seeing the world for what it is—making life a continuing moment of 'limit-experience'. Is it that difficult to see the madness of Nietzsche or Artaud as the ultimate culmination of their pursuit of Being? The final option would be a recession into safety, the safety of the they. One of the principle mechanisms of a continuing society is the production of safety. Burroughs talks of this and the inherent danger of safety. Safety here would resemble an abdication of self, where one gives up any individualization in favor of a mode of non-experiential sleep. Safety then is a sacrifice of both pain and pleasure in favor of a life of external utilization and management."

"What of the New Age theory that we bring about our own situations and each event in our life is something that we, ourselves, have created to teach us some important lesson?"

"Bullshit. What could be a more disturbing theory? Where is the logic in such a proposition? If I am wounded in a hold-up, is it that I chose that particular store on that particular night because I subconsciously knew that I had to learn something? Who should go to jail in that case? It smacks too much of out dated notions of karma, or you 'reap what you sow' philosophies. It appears to work in some cases, where person X gets what we feel they deserve, but what of the man with cancer? Such a philosophy would make him search for the thing he did wrong, the reason for his punishment, or even more illogically in the case of terminal cancer, the life-lesson he is supposed to be learning from his experience.

"This is certainly not to say that there aren't mutilations, 'limit-experiences', which one undergoes freely and under their own volition. It may be that this is actually the preferred method—the image of one pushing themselves to their outermost limits. Pain, pleasure, it doesn't matter as long as it distorts and recreates the self-referential limits of personal being."

"This seems like a very depressing view of life. What about pleasure? Is this contained within the notion of seeking out mutilation? Can there be pleasure in abuse?"

"Certainly. A 'limit-experience' may actually be that point where concepts of pleasure and pain are completely confused, where the division between the rational and the irrational is surpassed. I don't think that it is at all surprising that Foucault, Mishima and Genet all found such experiences in sado-masochism, degradation and violence. What then of the abused? The modern concept of abuse, the criminalization of the abuser, contains the action into a juridical and/or medical zone of interpretation, which works to deny and alienate pleasure. What of those moments where the abused finds pleasure mixed with the pain? This would not be possible under either definition. The abused's only approach to any pleasurable moments in the experience would be through the lenses of shame and singular difference. The role of the victim does more than just depower, it also, simultaneously, destroys the capacity to integrate the experience of mutilation. A very gray area in terms of rape, I would agree, but doesn't that make it all the more damaging? The raped is trained away from seeing the actions of their attacker as anything other than a crime. They are trained in the new discourse of the 'survivor' which works to compound the contradictions in their experience through discursive denial.

"This whole process becomes even more damaging in the cases of child sexual abuse. This current hysteria over the sexuality of children—generally defined by law as anyone eighteen or younger—has completely occluded the notion of intra-generational sex. It's formed a medical movement blind in the face of its own historicity. We ascribe to post-pubescent children an illogical, fractured agency of consent. Age of consent laws focus primarily on *intra*-generational sexual relations as opposed to those that are *inter*-generational. Through our society's intentional ignorance of teen sex, we have given them license to have as much sex as they want within their own age group. On the other hand, we have, through our increasing concern over cross generational sexual relations, worked to criminalize the sexual impulse in such cases—a process which again functions alongside the simultaneous affect of alienating desire for the 'abused' 'victim'. A teenager can choose to have sex with one of his peers, but lacks the ability to make an equally informed decision when it pertains to a person on the other side of the arbitrary legal divide. What in different times was considered the highest of socially defined activities has now become the lowest of criminal, anti-social, behaviors. A couple of years ago I read a book out of Amsterdam which contained interviews with boys who had been involved with older men. In each case the youths spoke of themselves as the instigators. They described the pleasure and support that they found within their relationships. The researcher, for this was at least masking itself as a clinical study, found in these admissions the primary evidence demonstrating the extent of the young boys' abuse. In such instances, could it not just as easily be the case that it is the counselor who is training the boys' vision, warping their pleasure through a discourse of socially productive denial. It reminds me of an instance in Sartre's *Being and Nothingness*, where the jealous voyeur only notices himself through the intervention of another watching him. He sees himself not from within his own actions, but only at the moment that he feels shame. It's again the paltry assumptions of humanism.

"It's a disquieting, and often ignored, fact that humans can transform even the vilest of degradation into moments of pleasure. Perhaps you have to to survive."

"Yeah." Flux said still trying to piece something out of the onslaught.

"That's how it all came about. This piece, 'Mutilation,' is then an attempt to forge something out of my madness—a madness given to me which I eventually had to make mine in order to survive."

Cade drew in a deep breath and leaned back in his chair. Flux picked up the manuscript that he had laid before her at the outset of the conversation. Cade abruptly got up and walked to the kitchen to put on a supplementary pot of coffee. She looked down and began to read, "I am..."

"MUTILATIONS"

I am writing because I am years older. I'm sure you know very well that Saturday night when you last saw her, before you had said anything having to do with the arrangements, I remembered no one. You weren't asking for that this time. You did have pull with her that way. I have to deal with a few things but I still plan to come. I just have to work out the details. It doesn't mean that that's what she would have wanted above everything else. I can't get away for a few days. I'm crying—everything seemed so much later than now. Even here, far away, I share your pain. Like always we're taking turns staying hurt. But I guess we're through this week. Mom is a very special person; she will need you and me more than ever. That we didn't communicate more than anyone else in these last years means little. The important thing: "What now?" My answer among other things is that you always realize too late that we hurt each other—trying to get everything we want. Please try to understand, I can never take away your grief. It is hard to concentrate. I will call you tonight. I don't feel as acutely as you. My realization of what to say when you were here would not have been what you wanted. My own need is trite—but I wanted somehow to think that you would need me more. When you hurt both dad and mom, the other kids rallied around. I'm still not very good at expressing the meaning of those nights with her. That will happen person-to-person probably more profoundly when the immediacy wears off. I love you, Bran.

Camera moves through a hospital waiting room. A metal dulled white waiting room. The smell-feeling of pressure sterilization permeates the air. Pleather chairs and a couch ring the walls.

Dog-eared magazines fan on the center table and sit in racks hung on one of the walls. They're old, but the dates don't matter. They have never been read. Dog-eared, well handled, yes, but never read.

Cut to a room nearby. Connection shot of a magazine lying on a small equipment table. Hastily placed down on a syringe and some forceps. A woman, a mother, sits hanging on the edge of the examination table. A doctor in white lab coat and clumsy tie stands nearby. They both face a large vid screen that takes up the better part of the opposite wall. The doctor turns and flicks a switch on the wall behind the woman. The vid clicks on with a high pitched whine that continues for several seconds than disappears. The woman tenses. There it is the first image, a little boy lost on a field of video gray. He has a toy in front of him. He plays with it from time to time. This seems to disturb the mother. The boy continues to play with the toy—a yellow metal backhoe. The mother stares. The man in the white coat begins tapping his scuffed shoe but remains facing the screen. The mother stands. She moves closer, closer to the image till it breaks down into an ordered confusion of rectangular pixels.

The woman sees her son screaming on the screen but there is no sound. The mother pained watches his in silence. Doctor, can't you do anything? She turns around briefly. . . ? . . . The doctor looks at her, then the screen, then her. "Don't worry it is all in his mind." The doctor seems relaxed, a calm voice at her side. The muted screams and the smell of a mentholated breath mint, rising off the doctor, begin to make her reel. Isn't there any sound on this damn thing? Can't I at least hear what is doing this to my son?

"I don't know if you want to do that," the doctor places a reassuring hand on her shoulder. "It might be better this way. We are working on the audio connection, but. . ."

A third voice breaks into the room, crackling for a moment over the ceiling loudspeaker. ". .ther. I hate you. mother i hate you BRAN!"

Silence again.

Bran could feel, see taste the same memory played over and over again. Each time it meshed together with itself, compounded with variants and sped forth through a myriad of metamorphosis. Over and over again it played—changing, swirling, crackling. It was like someone was showing and reshowing the same scene from some movie, but the people watching it each time were different. They each watched with different eyes and divergent understandings. Occasionally Bran found his senses enough to wonder if it were the scene or the people's perceptions that were so chaotically disparate.

A fear shook Bran producing a sleeping hymn thrashing in closer. His friend now only the yellow whimper of cigarette smoke, he remembered their bodies moving against each other. His groin ached as he felt the night's tranquil fierceness. In the moonlight he noticed a hand dangling a hand. Bran reached up cautiously, remembering when he was a boy coming across his brother's lubricant in their basement. Now with the thought of his brother cornholing his best friend—their bodies drenched in sweat, their pants around their ankles, the Vaseline jar sitting beside them—he felt himself come down. That night his brother had eased himself into bed beside him, the contact of their naked skin as they felt each other through their underwear. Their lips had met, hands viciously massaging each other's bodies. Then their BVD's came off. Bran's brother bent his head, forcing his cock into his mouth. Understanding the challenge, he met the cock's plunging rhythm ruthlessly. His brother freed his hands and seized his hair, a burst of soft laughter, "Brothers always love each other." He held him down and lifted his legs over his shoulders. His brother pulled his hips into him. Bran felt the nudge of entry, sweaty legs, the cock growing again inside him. His resistance drained as he felt himself ripped open, "No. . ." Without slowing his thrusts, "I knew you were watching. Now I'm going to fuck you too." Their smashing bodies clamped together with arms and legs, all muscles alert, "That feels. . ." Bran stopped himself, the thought surprised him and filled him with renewed fear. It had never occurred to him that sex between two males could feel good for both. In the past this had always been for his brother's pleasure—returning from an unsuccessful date or a night out drinking with his jock friends.

Shaking himself conscious, almost petrified with fear, as his boyfriend thrashed in closer, his friend sleeping under him. Feeling their bodies against each other, a whimper of yellow smoke appeared at his groin. His chest ached as he felt the tranquil fierceness in him tonight. As he stirred, Bran noticed a dangling hand silhouetted by the moonlight. Cautiously he reached up to it. Bran reached across for the lubricant. He remembered when he was younger, he and his brother cornholing in their basement—an education with the Vaseline jar and drenching sweat. Once, when the pants came off and his brother eased himself beside him, they felt each other through their BVD's. The contact of their naked bodies, hands massaging lats and deltoids, their lips met again viciously. Then the cotton came off. He bent his head, his brother's cock in his face. There for a moment of challenge. He met it with understanding—an understanding that freed his hands to seize the cock ruthlessly. Brothers always love each other. Hair and a burst of soft laughter. Bran lifted his head. He pulled his brother into him. His brother felt for his shoulder. He pulled his hips, legs, his cock growing and the nudge of entry, as he felt himself beating into him. The strength drained as the rhythm grew, "I fuck you, just like we used to." A rip in the film, "No. . ." It continues without breaking. Smashing together bodies good and hard. "Is big cock, *maricone?*" Entwined, all muscles clamped with arms and legs . . . the distortion surprised him. He was alert and it felt good. It had never occurred to him that sex between two males could feel good for both.

Shaking himself, almost an understanding, as he thrashed in closer to his friend's cock ruthlessly. his brother, their bodies against each other, hair on end, a burst of soft laughter appeared at the groin. His other. . . . He held him by his shoulders in tranquil ferocity. He pulled his hips, as he cautiously reached up for the nudge of entry, sweaty. Bending across for the lubricant, his brother began to slide into him. The strength drained from him as his brother began to fuck him still wearing his ripped jeans around his calves, "No. . ." He continued without a break, reaching again for the Vaseline jar, "Good." Bran's head flopped back to some book somewhere, "Is big cock, *Maricone*. You like?" his brother came and then eased beside, clamped with arms and legs, feeling each other, again tangled in their BVD's— suddenly alert again. "That feels great." Bodies, hands caressing lats. It had never occurred to Bran that (his brother again entering his mouth viciously) two men could feel this good: his head and his brother's cock. With fear, Bran touched his brother now sleeping under him. New feeling freed his hands which suddenly seized onto a whimper of movie dust "Brothers always love." He ached as he felt at the air and lifted himself onto his brother. He stirred, as Bran guided his brother's cock into him. He looked down on his brother sleep-gauzed face illuminated by moonlight. Legs, the cock growing in his ass. Bran's brother reached as he seemed to feel himself remembered, younger, he began to direct the rhythm, "I'll fuck you." Their basement— induction smashing together bodies of sweat. Once when their pants intertwined, all their muscles side by side, they felt each other's surprise. It could be this contact of their naked sex—two males—fingers outlining pectorals,, lips meeting cotton. His brother bent into his face, "There."

Shaking himself awake trying for an understanding, his brother thrashing at his cock ruthlessly. His brother's body against him—his pubic hair a burst of fresh soft at his groin. His brother. . . he held him down forcibly, his fingers jabbing into his shoulders. As his brother pulled his hips hard into him, he thought he noticed a hand dangling from the cellar entry. Their mother's? Sweating, cautiously he reached up and it dissolved into him. Bran's strength drained as he perceived his friend reach across for the lubricant. . . His throat ripped, "NO...," deep from somewhere inside. Without a break, his brother began fucking him with a good big cock, "Sissy Sissy SISSY!" With the Vaseline jar discarded on the floor, arms and legs cramped, his brother continued to tease him. "That feels great, don't it?" He should never have felt his brother through his BVD's. He had never slept that hard. It had never occurred to Bran that touching a man's body was wrong. He had assumed that a vigorous massage always felt good for both. Then his brother's challenge, "What do you want to be treated like, a girl?" He met this and lowered his head to his brother's cock. With fear, he freed his hand and reached for the light. Feeling his brother's love, he whimpered, as his brother lifted his legs up, hands restraining ankles. Bran ached as he felt the push into him. The other felt nothing tonight. He stirred his legs, the cock growing with pain, their bodies illustrated by the gas lamp. As he felt himself becoming the phantom hand, he reached out to the rhythm. "I'll fuck you, you little shit. Remember when you were little, how you always ran to mother?" He smashed their bodies together—cold induction on wet basement floor—entwined, all muscles sweating to work. A thought surprised him. It put him outside himself. He felt that sex between two men could be more than the contact of their naked deltoids, their lips meeting, as they came in the white cotton. He bent forward and looked into his brother's face. There.

Shaking himself, preparing to face the challenge, he met the heat of flesh as it thrashed in closer. His friend freed his hands and seized their bodies against one another. He remembered that brothers always love each other; the first tickle of memory appeared at his groin. His friend held onto his ankles and lifted his legs up onto his shoulders. He perceived tranquil fierceness as he felt his friend's cockhead brought down into him. The other felt the depth-heat as he noticed a hand dangling, the cock growing cautiously. He reached up, as he felt himself being asked for the lubricant. He became the rhythm, "I want to fuck you..." brought back to images of he and his brother fucking, adolescent bodies smashing together with Vaseline jar and wet clothes tangled beside them. All muscles and dried come as his brother eased into him again. He remembered how the thought had initially surprised him, as they first felt each other through their BVD's. Suddenly sex between two men, boys, could open possibilities. Their bodies, hands massaging lats with not a little fear. Bran's brother again whispered viciously. Then back to this guy now sleeping under him. Feeling his head, his brother's cock now a whimper of yellow smoke on a far horizon, he began to form an understanding that ached as he felt for his friends sleeping cock ruthlessly. His brother, here, again, tonight. As his friend stirred, his hair became a burst of soft laughter illuminated by the moonlight. He held him in his hand, turned him over in his palm. Bran reached for his shoulder. He pulled his hips again to him, remembering when younger, the first searing nudge of entry, drenched, their basement initiation. The strength draining into sweat. Once when he was seven his pants ripped, "No..." Without break, he ran through the alleys home. His brother set himself beside him. He felt his brother's slightly older fingers on his neck. They felt welcome. Smashes again, another time, Mexico City family vacation, "Is big cock, *maricone?*" the contact of their naked clamped arms and legs deltoids all their lips meeting alert. "That feels great." Words emanating like rotten stenches coming off spent bodies.

Understanding the freedom implied, he met the challenge and relentlessly seized his cock in his teeth. His brother loved him, each hair a burst of soft light. He lifted one leg over the other...He held onto this part of him. The other felt the smooth shoulder. He pulled his hips separating his legs, the cock growing sweaty to his touch. As he felt himself being brought into him, the strength drained into the rhythm, "I'll fuck you better." "No..." Without a break, bodies together, limbs intertwined, all arms and legs clamped with tight young muscles. The memory surprised him. It alerted to the contact of men. It could have never occurred to him that...shaking himself to feeling. Both thrashed in closer, his friend suddenly tight with fear, as their bodies moved softly against each other. He feigned sleep beside him. An unwelcome feeling appeared at his groin, a whisper of tranquillity and fierceness. His cock ached as he felt his friend's breath. He noticed a hand moving toward him reflected in the low light. He stirred cautiously and reached up illuminated by the almost guttered votive. Bran reached for his brother's now fully grown lubricated hand. He remembered when they had both been younger, watching him alone with a Vaseline jar on the basement floor—magazines spread around him. He came with his brother as he eased closer to smell his brother's sweat. Once when they slept with each other, he felt him through his underwear, quieting himself beside him. He felt his body, his hand massaging the bulge, the contact of the naked flesh repeated now viciously. His lips met the head of his brother's cock.

Shaking, he met himself, challenging the freedom as his brother's hands met his throat. Brothers always love their bodies lifting against each other and their legs appearing and disappearing at the groin. The His in Him. The other felt the tranquil fierceness in his legs, the cock growing as he noticed an outstretched hand. He felt himself reaching up cautiously for the rhythm, "I'll fuck you." Using water from his cross as lubricant, he desperately smashed their bodies together. He and his brother entangled, cornholing, all muscles bathed in Vaseline and perspiration. The thought unnerved him. It asserted itself, but had no place. It didn't come off and his brother greased his sex. A rite between two males producing an admirable understanding of their bodies, hands massaging cocks ruthlessly. His brother grabbed his hair savagely, a burst of harsh laughter in his throat, his brother's cock holding him in fear. Another shudder. He pulled his hips under him, feeling the familiar nudge, missed initially but again entry, sweaty, a whimper of flesh sliding within. He ached as he felt himself being ripped, "No..." "Without break tonight." As he stirred, "Good, big cock, *MARICONE*." The moonlight illuminated a clamped hand and leg. Bran reached out, alert. "That feels great." He remembered when he was younger, that it had never occurred to him that their basement initiation could feel good for both the sweating participants. Once when he panted in beside him, he felt the contact of his naked chest, his lips meeting flesh. He bent his face and buried it there.

Shaking himself, he met the challenge. Freeing his hands, he seized his thrashing friend. Brothers always love their bodies against each other. He lifted his legs over and speared his groin into him. The other felt a tranquil tension in his legs, his cock growing as he noticed a dangling hand. He felt himself being cautiously reached up to. The rhythm of "i fuck you" reaching for the lubricant, smashing bodies together, his brother on him, fucking him, his older muscles hitting his body again and again. The feeling of the Vaseline smeared cock in his ass surprised him. It came to him, as his brother eased again inside him, sex between them could forge their love out of his fear. Bran's hands began massaging his brother's stomach and chest, hovering just above him dangerously. The yellow whimper of smoke in his head, his brother's cock burning inside him, he felt that there was an understanding tonight. As he stirred, his cock rigid again, his brother was illuminated by the moonlight, soft hair a burst of laughter in his hand. Bran reached tentatively for this other, but held himself suddenly back, remembering when he was younger, his broken shoulder. He pulled his hips on their basement floor—initiating the nudge of entry. Once when the pain drove into him, the strength seemed to drain from him and into his brother. He felt ripped in two, "No..." Without breaking the contact of their nakedness, he screamed, "Take my big cock, you little faggot. There is nothing else left in this life for a sicko like you. Everyone knows that disgusting cocksuckers aren't good for anything else." Their lips met, arms clamping his body to that of his brother, the cotton of his briefs mashing into Bran's face, the slight urine-sweat smell of his brother's day penetrating his nostrils. His brother, still inside him, bent forward and bit him harshly on the shoulder. "That feels great," Bran thought. In his face, invisible against the bed and cotton, occurred a smile.

Understanding the implied challenge, he met the freedom of his hands and grabbed the cock before him. His brother always said that he loved his hair. A tickle of soft laughter as he lifted his legs over his head. His brother held him, pinned against the basement mattress. He felt his brother shudder. He pulled at his legs, feeling his brother's cock growing toward the nudge of entry, sweating as he felt himself begin beating into him. The strength drained the rhythm, "I fuck you ripe..." "no..." Without breaking his movements, he smashed their bodies together. "Good? You like your brother's big cock in your tight pussy?" Faggots intertwined, all muscles clamped with arms and legs. The thought surprised him. It alerted him to something that felt good. The power of sex between two males had never occurred to him. With fear, he admitted to himself, that his brother felt good. Feeling shook him, almost a whimper, yellow smoke growing closer, his friend some great machine rolling on. He ached as he felt the movement of their bodies tonight. As he stirred, his erection appeared at his groin, illuminated by the moonlight's harsh edged, tranquil fierceness. Bran reached a hand across his brother's back and down over his ass. A dangling remembrance as he reached up in their basement. He thought across their bodies, across the lubricant, across to something new. He began to sweat, his joining the moisture already beginning to trickle rivulets off his brother's sides. He remembered back to when they shared a room, both thinking the other asleep they simultaneously reached out for the Vaseline jar and met. The contact of their nakedness came off and his brother had eased into bed beside him, his developing deltoids and abs rubbing his side. Their lips met each other and their hands searched beneath cotton. They bent bodies, hands massaging his face viciously, then his head and his brother's cock.

He tried to meet the challenge as Bran's brother freed his hand and seized his sleep from him. Feeling his brother's love, each a whimper of pale smoke, he lifted his legs aching as he felt his brother begin to probe into him. He felt like another tonight. As he stirred, his legs parted to receive a cock illuminated by moonlight. He perceived himself being felt for. He reached out to his brother, beginning to forget the reason he and his brother had both had to return home so quickly. "I fucked you; remember when we were younger, smashing our bodies together in the basement—initiation entwined with muscles and sweat?" When they were first naked together, Bran recalled, the thought had surprised him. It was himself beside him. When they felt sex between two boys, the contact of their naked shaking, their lips meeting, tongues thrashing, closer,

closer, his cotton shirt being ripped off. He bent their bodies against each other, face to face. There appeared the first movement in his groin. His was an understanding of the tranquil fierceness in his brother's cock, ruthlessly demanding. His brother as he reached up his hand dangling in his hair, a burst of soft laughter cautiously building, as he reached up. His brother held him as he reached out for the lubricant. He bit his lips his brother's cock nudging for entry, slick with Vaseline and wet with mixing sweat. His strength drained off and his brother ripped into him. "No." Without breaking his forward movement, "It's not such a big cock. I'm sure you can take it." Bodies, hands massaging lats, clamped viciously with arms and legs. Then the alert: "That feels great." His head, his brother's cock. The opening for this feeling had never occurred to him.

The challenge met with fear, as Bran freed his hands and touched the sleeping friend under him. Feeling brothers always love each other, sometimes in nothing larger than a whimper of yellow smoke that lifted his legs over his arched back as he melted into him. The other felt the slipping of night. As he stirred his legs, the cock gored, illuminated by the moonlight. As he felt himself becoming the hand of his brother's touch, Bran reached for the rhythm. "I fucked you when we were younger, remember?" He recalled how they used to smash their bodies together in the basement—becoming nothing more than a tangle of muscles and sweat. Once when they had stood pants off the thought had surprised him. His brother had become an extension of himself beside him, they felt their sex mutual between them, an understanding of their naked skin forging contact between them. Their lips met each other's cocks ruthlessly and unflinchingly. His brother came first. He bent over, his hair a burst of soft laughter in his brother's face. There, it was always the other... he held him by his shoulder shaking himself. They pulled their hips closer, feeling the entry, sweating their bodies together. He moved further into him. A strength cry rose from his groin, "Yes." Without any sense of anything else he could feel his brother's sharp intensity inside him, clamping them tightly. His arms, his legs, everything alert. "That feels great." Cautiously he reached up and drew his fingers across the side of his brother's rigid jaw. He searched the images of both of them cornholing with Vaseline in their parents' basement. Sensations wet with come and his brother's caressing hands massaging his body and then again entering him viciously. Never asking, just forcing his head down onto his cock.

Shaking himself, almost free of the deluge, he met the stranger's gaze, brought him into a closer focus. He fought to free his hands in order to seize the projector controls... Their bodies against his brother's. A contact love for each other rested in his groin. The man lifted his legs over his shoulders with a fierceness that sent terror into him. The other felt this as he noticed a severed hand dangling on a cord between his legs. Despite himself, his sex grew and reached up. As he felt his heart beating, the man looked for the lubricant. He could become the rhythm nothing more. "I fucked your brother." The words became a drumming. A man and his brother fucking, like they had used to in their basement, smashing bodies coated with Vaseline and phosphorescent sweat, all muscles pearly white. He often came first, but his brother never eased off. The recollection repulsed him, thinking of this man fucking him mixed with him and his brother. The two of them groping for each other through their jeans. Sex between two bodies could encode meaning with such fear. The man pounded him again viciously. Then sleep overcame him. Bran could almost feel his head resting against his brothers cock, brushed by blond pubic hair. An understanding ached as he felt the foreign cock, this was his brother here tonight. As he stirred, patting down his own hair, a burst of cruel laughter illuminated the dark. "I fucked your brother, you know." Other? He held him in his hand. He felt his brother reach for his shoulder to comfort. He pulled his hips in tight and remembered when they were much younger, sweaty from their game, his basement introduction to sex. His strength drained with the sweat that poured off him. This man ripping off his pants, "No..." Without breaking down completely, he remained himself, kneading his hands. They would have felt good around his brother's big cock. "I'm going to get married and make lots of money. You're never going to be anything but a fag and everyone knows that fags will always be miserable." His teeth clenched with the memory of their contact, of their naked alertness, of their bodies and lips melting wax. It had never occurred to him that he was one of them—those men that the other boys talked of trying to kiss them. He felt the prickling beginnings of his beard, now nothing more than raw cotton. He bent his other hand to his face; it felt good.

The doctor's gaze quickly went to the vid screen as he heard the distinctive noise of white light projected. He saw a hurried flash of simultaneous images forming a collage that moved outward from the haze. They appeared to be scraps of paper, laid out across a desk. The doctor looked closer, scraps of paper... telegrams, wrinkled telegrams carefully smoothed again and again, spread meticulously across what seemed to be the blotter of a desk.

TAD STOP.
I

TAD STOP
JUST WANTED TO SAY IM STILL HERE STOP
LOVE BRAN STOP

TAD STOP
IN KINGSTON STOP
KIKI TAKEN SICK STOP
NOT ABLE TO MAKE NEW YORK STOP
MAYBE NEXT MONTH STOP
LOVE BRAN STOP

KNOW I LOVE YOU STOP
BRAN STOP

The images went back to the playing of cinematic movements, regaining itself after its momentary freeze. The doctor now saw a priest standing just at the edge of an old, weathered porch out of some far Midwest town. White paint pealing off to reveal long ago grayed wood. The doctor noted all the accouterments of such a scene, the porch, the overgrown lawn, the rocking chair, the matron leaning from a window across the street. Even the priest struck the doctor as appropriate.

With a clean left hook, he ambiguously shouted, "Kill him!" He reached the end of the porch and jumped, the preacher staggering to stay on his feet. "Well, preacher man, you've got to decide. 'Oh, honey, give him a chance.'" The preacher shot back a confused but murderous gaze: "You can make it through this." Mrs. Sawyer screamed from her window, "Get him preacher." He hit him again and the preacher staggered barely remaining upright this time. "Got to decide." "Oh God, they're killing each other," screamed Mrs. Sawyer from her perch. Another clean left and the preacher fell into her nasturtiums. The boy stood at the edge of the porch. The preacher didn't stand a chance once he had got a look into his eyes. The preacher rubbed at his face, ignoring the second story window, above, Mrs. Sawyer leaning out fatly cheerful screaming like an eagle: "Kill Him!" The boy stared at the preacher splayed in the flowerbed gasping like a cold wet dog. "You've got nothing to do with us boys." The preacher lifted himself off the Sawyer nasturtiums, but billy boy continued his level stare direct into his eyes. During all this the form in the upper window rose and fell, hooking and cackling joyously. He knocked him back into the bed of flowers. His sister came out onto the porch, the matronly din still chiming above, "Kill him! Kill him!" The preacher again struggled to get to his feet. He wheezed, "You..." Little sister said calmly, "You've got to kill him." "KILL HIM!" reiterated the voice above. The boy walked over to the gasping priest, "You didn't have to do that to us boys. You decide."

With a clean, pure look he jumped after him. Once preacher got a hold of his chance, even Mrs. Sawyer leaning out of her window screaming like an old bird couldn't rub him out.

The doctor rose and flicked the wall switch. The vid screen went blank.

excerpt from the Journal of Dr. Benjamin Weg, final entry dated 27 March 1997:

This will be my final entry in the log of this particular case, Bran Hartman. I am tired and think that I can bear no more. I feel for his mother, one son dead and the other suspended in this state indefinitely. The woman is completely distraught and no longer comes to the hospital. Her calls are becoming increasingly infrequent as well. It is as if she no longer wishes for his recovery. But then, can I blame her? Can anyone with a humanist conscience blame her? How she has stood it for this long, I cannot fathom. To see the life of one's last son reduced to nothing—nothing but this incessant replay of pornographic fantasy.

I will myself unhook the machines tomorrow. It is simply unfortunate that he may be able to breath on his own without the assistance of the life support systems. How can any of us be comfortable gazing upon him, even in a completely vegetative state, after getting such a glimpse into his mind? I will destroy the tapes we have obtained as quickly as possible. I can see them being of no productive value to anyone, besides those philosophers bent on denying the value of human existence.

It will be with a degree of heaviness that I will begin caring for my regular patients again tomorrow. I will however, phase out my counseling based practice. I will instead begin to concentrate primarily on chemical avenues of diagnosis and treatment. I do all this with trepidation, for I know that I may well spend the rest of my life avoiding the questions raised by this abortive experiment. I will not ponder upon them here, nor indeed, I believe, anywhere. It may be the case into which man was not supposed to journey far. But it continues to nag me, gnaw at me from the inside out:

Is this it?

Is the self nothing more than a repetitive falsification of memory?

AFTERWARD

Flux ground out the stub of her gold butt in the now overflowing ashtray in front of her. She flipped the last page over and laid it atop the pile to her left. She leaned back against the wall and withdrew a cigarette from the open pack beside her. She clicked her Zippo and lit the fresh black and gold roll. "Well... What do I say now?"

"What did you think?" Cade asked hesitantly.

"It's a little depressing. I feel this overwhelming need to ask if you are all right." Her Sobraine held tightly pinched in her lips, she shuffled the papers before her, turning them over and straightening the edges against the hard floor. "Where is this coming from? I got some of what you were saying before about mutilation, but where is the redemption? Where is the growth?"

"Apart from, or aligned with, what I outlined earlier, I guess that my premise is that memory is a constant and ongoing process of fictionalization. It represents a cut-up formed of selective recollection colluding with those specters which lie both above and below the demarcation line of conscious recall.

"The story is concerned with those points, instances, which leave their hieroglyphic mark indelibly engraved on the self. They may be large or small, but they are those that remain, like the smell of microwave popcorn invokes fathers and fall football. After the chaff has been separated, they are those symbolic moments which call one back. This may be a more poignant process for the modern gay soul, if one can be argued into existence."

Flux removed the cigarette from her lips, exhaled sharply. "And why is that, pray tell?"

"I tend to agree with an observation made by Michael Bersani. In 'The Rectum Is Not a Grave,' he observes that the gay ethos is more concerned with recollection, while the heterosexual is focused primarily on anticipation. While cruising is, or at least has been up until now, an undeniably important component of the gay encounter, the discursively definitive segment of the act seems to be in the time following. In an interview with *Salmagundi*, Foucault observed, 'For a homosexual, the best moment of love is likely to be when the lover leaves in the taxi.' It is the difference between *Wuthering Heights* and *My Secret Life*."

"What did you want to say in it then? Somehow I suspect it is not as simple as 'life is pure suffering.'"

"No, no. Its just a glimpse at an ongoing process. It is like placing a window in the side of a cow so that one can observe its stomachs in action."

Flux flinched slightly. "Nice analogy. Is the process going anywhere?"

"I certainly won't say that it isn't disturbing. It has got to be. Here is this guy, Bran, trapped in memory—permanently trapped in a subtly shifting loop of his own nexus points. Zenith and nadir continually impacting and traversing each other.

"Bran *is* limit experience, but unfortunately he is trapped with no means of jarring himself back to productivity. Externally he serves no good purpose; the observers stand to learn nothing. They will run in the face of themselves and declare another sick. And Bran? Bran is trapped by fate or his own inability to pull himself back form his head-on collision.

"Redemption? Who knows. Maybe that begs the overall question. After all, what form does redemption have to take?"

Spirit Guide

My spirit guide came to me in a dream.
Not as before, in the acid dripping night
Meditating at water's edge beneath stone bridge.
Not in the form of the cross-legged old monk,
Black silhouetted in the candlelight.
No, this time he came as a beautiful young man
Nervous college age queer
23, just a year out of school, he later said
pale slight dark brown hair sideburns
plaid cotton shirt t-shirt jeans
thick-soled black shoes.
he appeared in a bar
eyes meeting accidentally
breath catching in recognition

After several attempts,
I said hello—as he knew I would.
We went to a table
introduced ourselves
I finished my beer
He bought a second round,
Because he was nervous.
Another beer for me
A double vodka neat for himself.
We continued on
Through the awkward obligatory
praising of first meetings.
Strange light talk
Introducing the necessities

Like people who meet in a bar.
What is your Will, when all you want
is to fuck your Guardian Angel?

Et In Acadia Ego

His fingers drummed visible sound waves across the table. His trip-addled brain configured ripples of distortion across the shabby, hard luck, age-gone-by diner. Cade was nervous. He was always nervous before making a buy. Not drugs. A couple of doses of blotter was never an issue nor hassle. Meeting his other dealer, his real dealer, the one that counted, the vendor of need, made him nervous. Always had—always would, he supposed. A few seconds of stilted, unfriendly conversation and he would have his future, a new golden, barely conceivable future—or another expensive disappointment.

He looked at his watch. 2:58AM. Simon would be here. He was always on time. Or, at least, there about. Simon could be counted on for his punctuality, just as he could for the unpredictability of the initial call preceding their late night meetings. Cade's cell phone would ring. "Got it." No need for self-identification or reciprocating comment. Just two syllables and Cade knew the place and time.

Cade abruptly stopped the movement of his fingers and tried quickly to corral the acid waves into a quiet place. Simon slid into the booth across from him. Simon... He didn't even know if that was his first or last name. Simply Simon. He wore a dingy brown coat. He had a couple of days beard on his face— unkempt in a way that belied a careful attention lurking, hidden, just this side of not caring.

"Is it with you?" Fuck. Cade couldn't check his anticipation in time.

Simon didn't look at him. He signaled a waitress for a cup of coffee. Only then did he turn to Cade. "Yes," he said coolly. "Can you pay for it?"

For a second Cade thought he caught the hint of disapproval shifting at the edges of Simon's thin lips. Perhaps, but he knew that Simon had set a price that would absolve him of any guilt. Cade reached in his jacket and pulled out an envelope. He turned it over in his hand, steeling himself for the separation, before sliding it across the table. He kept a single finger in place, waiting for Simon to produce the merchandise.

A small square wrapped in burlap exposed, the envelope of money released and it was done. Simon finished the remainder of his coffee less than a minute later. His eyes said "Next time" and he was gone.

Cade squeezed the small rectangular parcel in his hand and slipped it inside his jacket. He left the money for the bill and tip on the table. He hurried back to his studio in a rough nominally converted warehouse, thankful he lived so close by. Exhilaration was already eating at him.

He locked the large sliding door into place and went immediately to his low meditation table, which he had moved into the center of the space before leaving to meet Simon. He took off his clothes, tossing them on his futon against a far wall, lit two candles and sat on the floor. Holding the parcel in his left hand, he slowly folded back the wrapping with his right to reveal a small leather-bound book. Cade turned it slowly looking for signs of forgery or deception. Nothing caught his experienced eye. Typical 17th century bookmaker's craft. Miraculous that you escaped the fire, Cade thought to himself.

He leafed through the first few pages until he came to the first conjuration. He began to read the Latin—fluent from years of living in his self-imposed hermitage of antiquarian books. He read aloud:

O dark Emporer, Master and Prince of all Rebellious Spirits, I adjure ye to leave thine abode, in whatsoever quadrant you may currently be quartered, and come hither to commune with me. I command, compel and conjure thee in the Name of the Great Triune Spirit to appear without noise and without any evil smell, to respond in a clear and intelligible manner... Venite! Venite! Submiritillor Lucifage, or eternal torment shall overwhelm thee, by the great power of this blasting rod.

Nothing appeared before him. No presence, fog or wisp of smoke. Just blank walls and sparse, uninspiring space. *I adjure thee!* The environment began to shift—a subtle fluid movement at the edges of his vision. Then, enfolding inwards from these edges upon him, the whole atmosphere began to collapse and then pull apart again. After his eyes adjusted and became aware of the stillness that as quickly reset, Cade saw he was in prison-like room, cement walls and floor, pealing cream-colored paint. Floor sloping slightly downwards toward a six-inch metal grate covering a small drain in one corner. No longer looking at the small leather block in his hand, he continued to read a conjuration he did not know, from long out of time, and no longer comprehending or mentally checking the words:

Not to Virility, thy spirit of the carnal cock, thou Ruler of Anguish, I see thee not. I chant the praises of your chaste balls that sing families of sperm, a draught to salve my parched flesh. Empty me as the mother dost offer alms to the poor. Set thou that want answers to the petitions of Hope that dance about thy avaricious loins. Lost in the long nights and days of the Lenten Womb, I assure the reason that mouths the spells that baffle even your own Master, the Lord of tortures and misdeeds, the meter of thy Justice. On your balls, unknown and unmoved and whose love gently implores your servants forward. I lower myself to your knees, savoring and supplicate, to receive your bootless praise. Poor carnal lost to the loins, down into the precum of your anguish. Virile Lord, take me empty, me that sings the supplications, the petitions—I implore thee, my Master, unknown getting delirious, unknown delectable spells, them that arise joy in those that forfeit thy justice. I get between the faithful supplicant with love, the origin of misdeeds, I whose mouth has been given over to satisfy thy servants, fucking thou not the Lenten asshole. Alone I receivest the carnal cause of reflex like avaricious empty praises. From thou I demand the mother petitions, the daughter of your loins...

Cade was no longer alone. He was not surprised to feel another presence in the room—though not an unearthly spirit. It had been years since he had seen him, almost twenty years since junior high, but his old friend was unmistakable. Age had moved itself along Ricky's body, lengthening and strengthening, but the image of Cade's memory was still written large upon his form as only possible in a dream. They stood only a few feet apart.

Ricky had his cock in one hand—emerging from the fly of his faded Levis. A pale white snake, laying a semi-hard 7 inches across a supporting palm. A solid stretch of flesh from base to head. Cade's first thought was that it was the head of a serpent. Long and uncut. He was surprised, though he didn't know why he should be. He'd never seen it before. The closest he'd ever come was midnight skinny-dipping—furtive glances of Ricky's milk-white ass reflecting moonlight. Surreptitious and dripping with paranoia and excitement.

Ricky began to urinate—a foot on either side of the drain. He seemed to pay little attention to Cade as he concentrated carefully on his aim. Cade mentally checked his hand. He could feel the tension in his arm muscles as he involuntarily began to reach around Ricky's side. He stalled himself, debating quickly in his head, weighing the odds, benefit and potential defeat. His desire took possession too quickly and proved uncheckable. As Ricky shook the last drops from its head, Cade took the flesh and began to kneel. He knew that he would be forced to stop. He felt tension quickly ripple surprise through Ricky's body— tightening his muscles to a single bowstring. Ten seconds and no recrimination. All tension releasing, Cade could feel the fiber of Ricky's body relax into his mouth. Now effortlessly willing himself on, Cade increased the intensity of his open-mouthed, cramped prayers.

Hope determined their petitions. Chastity demands long praises. He shifted slightly, satisfying the tension of his sweaty, unmoved knees. He moved along, the unknown opening around the baffles, his tongue deep in Ricky's ass. A groan swirled origin gently onto his lips. He sucked misdeeds, discomfort and anguish. Ricky groaned through this supplicating spirit of the avaricious fuck. Hope rose in Ricky's throat as his hole received

Cade's tongue. Precum sucked, hungry, between torture and spells coming slowly to rest as another groan slid from his perineum, through his chest and out his throat.

His cock, pushed by reflex, swelled painfully in carnality. A well of cum swirled slowly in his ballsack, fucking luscious balls searching out unknown justice. Throbbing wishing to empty deeply into this unknown servant, a massive battle of cock and will. His dick delirious sliding reason from head to mouth to firm ass and suddenly straight onto his lips. Hope, an empty reflex of discomfort, never anything but a dick-poor firm offering.

As Ricky's justice shot down his throat, Cade became aware of layers of men surrounding them obscured by sheets of fog or smoke. Each dressed in an identical black suit and dark glasses. All watching.

Cade's environment began its fold again. Ricky and he and these gray men in their black suits, stationary icons in a shifting meta-landscape. A thread-bare plantation house fifty years too late. Ricky's softening cock in his hand and the taste still on his lips. Pealing gilded wallpaper, chandeliers and the smell of shit and roses.

Seeing Red In Cattle Country
The Rise & Fall of Rajneeshpuram (1)

The Bhagwan Shree Rajneesh (later known simply as Osho) was born Chandra Mohan in the village of Kuchwada in the Indian state of Madhya Pradesh on 11 December 1931. Due to the grace with which the young boy carried himself, his family began calling him "raja" or "king." By his own account, he attained the state of enlightenment on 21 March 1953, though he kept it a secret for many years after. He taught briefly at a Sanskrit university and began traveling the country teaching. By the early 60's he was conducting large meditation camps at locations such as Mt. Abu in 1964. In 1970, Rajneesh settled in Bombay where he began to give regular discourses to a growing number. It was in Bombay that Rajneesh initiated his first disciples giving his twist on the ancient India tradition of *sannyas*.

In 1974, the movement, under the management of Ma Laxmi, bought land in the Indian town of Pune, north of Mumbai (Bombay). Laxmi was the first in a line of powerful female "personal secretaries" that would hold despotic control over the management of the business of running the religious movement. Rajneesh and his group of early disciples moved to Pune compound, located in the Koregon park neighborhood, and established the Acharya Rajneesh Ashram.

At the ashram, Rajneesh gave daily morning discourses (alternating Hindi and English) and held evening meetings, *darshans*, where he initiated new disciples and answered personal questions. Throughout the 70's, the ashram attracted increasing numbers of international visitors and became one of the focal points of the, then growing, phenomenon of spiritual tourism.

The topics of Rajneesh's talks ran the breadth of the religious spectrum—from Indian teachers through Jewish mystics to the wisdom of the Zen masters. He introduced several revolutionary "active" meditation techniques, designed specifically for the western mind combining exorcise and mindfulness. In addition to a wide and varied selection of meditations, a multitude of therapy techniques and workshops arose at the ashram. By the late 70's the "therapists" had become something akin to a priestly class within the movement.

In 1981, another female disciple, Ma Anand Sheela, displaced Laxmi as Bhagwan's secretary. Under Sheela's direction, the movement began searching for land large enough to establish a commune. Laxmi was effectively banished from the ashram, sent out to search for possible sites in India. Meanwhile, Sheela funneled several million dollars to a small New Jersey meditation center, Chidvilas. Later in that year, Rajneesh flew to the United States on a medical visa granted under the pretext that he was to receive treatment for his back. The group remained in New Jersey for a few months and then moved to Oregon where Sheela had purchased a defunct ranch known locally as "the Big Muddy." The ranch consisted of 64,000 acres (126 square miles) of Oregon desert land and very few buildings. Though Sheela presented herself a shrewd businessperson, she paid $5.75 million for land that was assessed for the previous year's taxes at only $198,000.

Over the course of the next three years, Rajneesh sannyasins would transform this unpromising parcel into a city that supported at its height 7,000 regular residents with 15,000 annual visitors (mostly concentrated into annual July-August "World Celebrations"). The city, incorporated briefly as Rajneeshpuram, Oregon, had its own post office, school, fire and police departments, downtown malls and restaurants. Its state-of-the-art reservoir even won an award for its innovative ecological design.

Change of this scale, of course, put stresses on the local community. The commune residents, especially the management, were very quickly at odds with the near-by town of Antelope. The Attorney General of Oregon, David Frohnmeyer maintained throughout that the incorporation of Rajneeshpuram violated the constitutional separation of church and state. His action against Rajneeshpuram was still working its way toward the Oregon Supreme Court in 1985. An environmental action group 1,000 Friends of Oregon also fought the incorporation of Rajneeshpuram from the first public hearing onwards. Due to the questionable standing of Rajneeshpuram and the objections of 1,000 Friends to commercial use of the Ranch, the Oregon Land Use Commission suggested that the sannyasins locate their publishing and distribution business in the closest town, Antelope. The commune began to purchase real estate in the town and sannyasins registered to vote. Before sannyasins relocated there, the population of Antelope, OR was 40 mostly elderly and retired. Due to the influx of new residents, 3 sannyasins were elected to the 6-person town council. The 3 older councilors refused to sit in the same room with the newly elected sannyasins and effectively resigned their seats. Through default the Rajneesh followers took over the city government. Around this time the 40 original Antelope residents attempted unsuccessfully to disincorporate the town.

A similar chain of events occurred with the town school board. At the resident's request, the sannyasins had agreed to educate their children at Rajneeshpuram and not Antelope schools. The school tax the residents of Rajneeshpuram paid, however, continued to support the Antelope school. Sannyasins were then elected to the Antelope school board. The previous board had gerrymandered the school district in an attempt to keep Rajneeshpuram outside of its boundaries. The county invalidated the election of the non-sannyasin board members, because in the redrawing of the district they had mistakenly drawn their own homes outside the new district. Not residing in the school district they were no longer eligible to be on the board. Again, the sannyasins "took over" by default.

Both of these occurrences and the sannyasin purchase of real estate in Antelope—the mayor herself working as real estate agent for most of the transactions—were used against the Rajneesh sannyasins. Attorney General Frohnmeyer, state congressmen, state senators Hatfield and Packwood as well as the "concerned citizens" of Oregon viewed these actions as a take-over and argued that the aggressive sannyasins would not stop short of attempting to take over the county and then the state. The sannyasin presence was quickly characterized as a threat to the very way of life of eastern Oregon. Sannyasin control of Antelope was seen as a coup de tat and not the democratic process at work. By many of the government players, the taking over of the school board was the moment that the tide turned completely against the commune and its residents.

Throughout this period, Rajneesh himself was entirely silent. When he came to America, he had entered a silent period—never speaking publicly, instead, he said, teaching through his presence. As the Oregon battle began to hit the national media, first appearing on an episode of ABC's Nightline in 1983, the U.S. immigration service began arguing the invalidity of Rajneesh's visa. His medical visa had been renewed as a teaching visa and, the authorities argued, one could not be a teacher if one did not teach, i.e. talk publicly. Ironically at the same time Oregon's Attorney General was arguing that Rajneesh and his followers were a religion and as such were violating the constitutional separation of church and state.

Rajneeshpuram exemplifies both the best and the worst of modern cult phenomenon. The collective activity of the commune residents gave rise to the greatest intentional community experiment the modern age has seen. In an article in The New Yorker, journalist Frances Fitzgerald detailed some of the accomplishments the commune had managed by 1983: cleared and planted 3,000 acres of land, built a 350-million-gallon reservoir and 14 irrigation systems, created a truck farm that provided 90% of the vegetables needed to feed that Ranch, a poultry and dairy farm to provide milk and eggs, a 10 megawatt power substation, an 85-bus public transportation system, an urban-use sewer system, a state-of-the-art telephone and computer communications center and 250,000 sq. feet of residential space.

On the other side, the commune was a complex business structure built to centralize absolute power in one person, Ma Anand Sheela. She and her band of loyal supporters ran the commune with an extremely heavy hand and provided a combative public face that was readily and appreciatively displayed by the media. By 1985 there was increased hardship and unrest within the commune itself. Sheela and her coterie of female managers, known collectively as the "Mas," created what Rajneesh himself would later refer to as "a fascist concentration camp." Upon entering the U.S., Sheela had established the religion of Rajneeshism, created a bible in the three volume *Book of Rajneeshism* and began to style herself a high priestess. By 1984 she had begun wearing papal style robes. Bhagwan's own silence lent de facto support to Sheela's transformation of the movement.

It is without question, that power corrupted Sheela. She described herself as Queen (and Rajneesh, presumably, was her king) and started to speak of sannyasins as "her people." She relished confrontation and pursued rather than backed down from a fight—whether with the media, local officials, INS inspectors or a fellow sannyasins. When she spoke, it was taken as if Rajneesh spoke. She was the metatron speaking for the silent, remote godhead.

During the later period of Rajneeshpuram, a tension arose between Jesus Grove, Sheela's compound, and Lao Tzu House, Rajneesh's residence. In late 1984 Rajneesh began speaking again to small groups of sannyasins invited into his house. When Rajneesh informed Sheela he would begin speaking, witnesses report, she begged him not to. When he finally did begin talking publicly again, Sheela spent days in her room crying. Rajneesh's talks were video-taped and later played to the full commune. During the summer of 1984, Sheela attempted to cancel the public display of the talks, claiming that they were interfering with the work of building the commune. A minor rebellion erupted and she relented, allowing the videos to be shown late at night when few of the exhausted sannyasins could manage to stay awake to view them.

Satya Bharti in her book *Promises of Paradise*, describes one night where the video was not shown. Sheela announced that the tape had been accidentally destroyed. In this talk called simply "number 20," Bhagwan spoke out against Sheela and her management of the commune, saying that she had transformed paradise into a "fascist concentration camp." He also outlined his concept of a world filled with autonomous communes where no person would have absolute power.

Ma Nirgun (Rosemary Hamilton), Rajneesh's cook during the later commune period, relates her experiences of living in Lao Tzu House in *Hellbent for Enlightenment*. Under the pretext of security, Sheela ordered the construction of a large fence, complete with guard towers, around Rajneesh's residence. Guards armed with Uzi's followed Rajneesh and his entourage everywhere. No one entered or left Lao Tzu without Sheela knowing about it. Nirgun tells of one day walking outside the house and realizing that the fence was not to keep attackers out, but to keep the residents in. "When I got back to Lao Tzu, I suddenly saw it with new eyes: a prison. The high link fence, the gates that delivered a powerful shock; the guardhouse towering over us, manned round the clock by two still figures holding guns—until this moment I had seen them as a deterrent to hostile outsiders. Now they seemed to be directed against us." She also relates a conversation she had with one of the sentries, a sannyasin who had previously been a friend. She asked why the sannyasin's attitude toward her had grown cold and distant. He replied, "Sheela's orders." Nirgun asked if Sheela had explained her order. "She says it isn't good to get friendly with people you might have to shoot."

During this time Rajneesh issued lists of "enlightened" sannyasins. These lists were interesting more for the people that they excluded rather than those they included. Sheela and her group were conspicuously absent. It's my feeling, that Rajneesh was using these lists as a means of destabilizing Sheela's power, which rested ultimately on her connection to the guru. Simultaneous with this, Rajneesh orchestrated a relationship between his personal physician Amrito and Ma Prem Hasya. The latter was a member of a wealthy clique of Hollywood-connected sannyasins. In this way, Rajneesh established a connection with an alternative to Sheela's management team.

In September 1985, Sheela and a small group of core supporters abruptly left the commune for Europe. The day of her departure, Rajneesh held a press conference where he accused Sheela of stealing millions of dollars and attempting to murder him, several sannyasins and local politicians. He publicly repudiated Rajneeshism and his role as guru. "I don't give them any commandments," Rajneesh in a 17 July 1985 interview with Good Morning America. "I insistently emphasize that they are not my followers, but only fellow travelers." He also called on the FBI to conduct an independent investigation. The FBI quickly found an extensive eavesdropping system that was wired throughout the commune residences, public buildings, offices and even Rajneesh's own bedroom. Authorities also uncovered a secret lab where, according to later court testimony, Ma Puja, the commune nurse referred to by some as "nurse Mengale," had run a poison lab experimenting with biotoxins—including HIV and salmonella.

It was later revealed in court testimony that Sheela's group had attempted to poison two local communities by dumping salmonella into salad bars of several local restaurants. According to a report published in the Journal of the American Medical Association, the true cause of the mysterious outbreaks would never have been discovered if it were not for the testimony of conspirators. Salmonella sample disks discovered at Rajneeshpuram were subsequently matched to the strain of bacteria isolated from the salad bars. This episode has the unfortunate distinction of being the first instance of modern bioterrorism in the U.S. Sheela's group also allegedly fire-bombed a county records office in The Dalles. One of the charges most heavily investigated was the poisoning of Swami Deveraj (later Amrito), Bhagwan's personal physician. After the July 6 discourse, Ma Shanti Bhadra hugged Deveraj and jabbed him with a needle. The syringe contained a still unidentified poison concocted by Rajneeshpuram nurse Ma Puja. Deveraj became gravely ill and almost died at the Madras hospital.

In October 1985, Rajneesh himself was on a private plane headed secretly out of the country accompanied by Amrito and new secretary Hasya. The plane was seized in Charlottesville, North Carolina, and all on board were arrested. This began a long process of returning him to Oregon to face immigration charges for allegedly arranging sham marriages. Rather than flying him to Oregon, federal authorities opted for driving him across country. For several days during the journey, even Rajneesh's attorneys did not know where he was.

Within a month, Rajneesh was again on a plane headed out of the country having entered an Alford plea to two counts of immigration fraud. He briefly returned to India and then onto Kathmandu. This began what his followers term his "world tour" which included refusals from more than 17 countries and forcible deportation from two, Greece and Uruguay. He and his followers maintained that the resistance of countries to allow his entrance was due to secret behind-the-scenes pressure from the Reagan administration—a charge not entirely lacking in credibility.

By the end of the Oregon experiment, 25 sannyasins were charged with electronic eavesdropping conspiracy, 13 immigration conspiracy, 8 lying to federal officials, 3 harboring a fugitive, 3 criminal conspiracy, 1 burglary, 1 racketeering (RICO), 1 first degree arson, 2 second degree assault, 3 first degree assault and 3 attempted murder. A complex series of plea bargains followed. Sheela  was fined $400,000 and ordered to pay $69,353 in restitution. She was sentenced to concurrent prison terms of 20 years for the attempted murder of Sw. Deveraj, 20 years for first-degree assault in the poisoning of county commissioner William Hulse, 10 years for second-degree assault in the poisoning of commissioner Raymond Matthew, 4 years for the salmonella poisoning, 4 for wiretapping and 5 years probation for immigration fraud. She served only 2.5 years in a federal medium security prison and was released for good behavior in December 1988. Ma Puja also received concurrent sentences: 15 years for the Deveraj murder attempt, 15 for the Hulse poisoning, 7.5 for the Matthew poisoning, 4.5 for her role in salmonella poisonings and 3 years probation for wiretapping conspiracy. Puja also served only 2.5 years of her sentence. Like Sheela, she served her sentence at the federal prison in Pleasanton, CA and was released in December of 1988. Rajneesh was charged with one count of criminal conspiracy (RICO) and 34 counts of making false statements to federal officials (INS officers). He entered his plea on two counts of immigration fraud and agreed to pay $400,000 fine. He was given a 10 year suspended sentence and ordered to leave the country and not return for a minimum of 5 years. Rajneesh corporations agreed to drop all appeals to the ruling that Rajneeshpuram's incorporation was unconstitutional, abandon all claims to the money and jewels impounded in North Carolina, to pay $400,000 to the State of Oregon in compensation for investigative costs, $500,000 to settle the claims of four restaurants who suffered losses due to the poisonings, an additional $400,000 to the restaurant owners, $5 million to the Oregon state victim's fund and to sell the ranch. In exchange David Frohnmeyer agreed to drop all RICO charges against the corporations.

Sannyasins in India finally reached a settlement with the Indian government concerning back taxes on the Pune ashram and Rajneesh returned to his homeland. Through the second half of the 1980's, Rajneesh fell off the spiritual radar. He dropped the title Bhagwan and, later, even the name Rajneesh. His followers began calling him simply Osho, a Japanese honorific used when referring to a Zen master.

In 1989 Bhagwan again stopped talking publicly due to his failing health. His final discourse ended with the last word of the

Buddha, *samasati*, "...remember that you are all Buddhas." In that year he instructed his followers to build him a new marble bedroom following his detailed design. He spent only a short time in this new space, before saying he preferred his old bedroom. In January 1990, Osho passed from his body instructing his physician to place his favorite socks and hat on him. When asked what they should do with him after he died, he said simply, "Stick me under the bed and forget about me." The marble bedroom he had designed was in fact his mausoleum.

Through the course of the 1990's, Rajneesh, now packaged as Osho, again became an important figure in the spiritual and New Age landscapes. His ashram in Pune transformed into a meditation resort (complete with an air-conditioned modern hotel and "zennis" courts) is now, once again, a popular destination for Western seekers. His books are again available in U.S. bookstores. The Indian government, once his adversary, now respects the potential tourist dollars represented by Osho and his resort. The library of the Indian congress has established a separate Osho collection, an honor only held by one other individual—Mahatma Ghandi. *The Times of India* named Osho one of its 10 most influential Indians of the 20th century.

The events that comprise the rise and fall of Rajneeshpuram raise many more questions than can be answered in a single introductory article such as this. Rajneesh stated that he wanted everything that happens after a religious teacher dies to happen while he was still alive. He often spoke of the mechanism that led from a Buddha to the creation of a Religion and how that process destroyed the religiousness of the teacher's message. I think that the Oregon experiment was an attempt by Rajneesh to facilitate this process through the simulated death of his silence and ceding control to Sheela. In this way he could himself short-circuit the development of a religious orthodoxy and protect his sannyasins, later termed "fellow travelers," from the deadening of meditative/devotional religiousness.

This obviously leaves many larger questions unaddressed. Most notably among these is the question of the responsibility of a master for his disciples. Rajneesh himself asked pointedly after the departure of Sheela, why the sannyasin residents of Rajneeshpuram had not done anything to stop her.

Perhaps the facts, lies and enigma surrounding Rajneeshpuram will permanently occlude the full appreciation of what attracted thousands of people to him. All else aside, Rajneesh's teachings represent a post-modern synthesis neither equaled nor paralleled in the 20th century. The breadth of his knowledge and his deft interpretation of ancient masters is unique. His influence, mostly unacknowledged, has been widespread throughout both modern devotional spirituality and the New Age movement. Many a Rajneesh therapist, dehypnotherapist, has become a popular guru or teacher. When one reads in a biographical sketch that the teacher spent years in India studying under an unnamed guru, it is, more often than not, Rajneesh to whom they refer.

The Pune resort is now run by a group called the Inner Circle, a body designed by Osho prior to his death. A second group of sannyasins has coalesced around the Delhi meditation center, led by Indian disciples Swami Chaitanya Keerti and Ma Yoga Neelam (Hasya's successor as personal secretary and former Inner Council member). A multitude of issues mark the divide between these two groups over the role of the guru, devotion vs. meditation (described by Rajneesh as the "path of love" and "path of meditation"), the copyright of his books and art, access to his teachings, the management of the commune/resort, etc.

Better Dead Than Red
The Rise & Fall of Rajneeshpuram (2)

In the course of four years, the followers of the Bhagwan Shree Rajneesh did what no one thought they could. They raised a city from the desert of Oregon. They established an almost completely self-sustaining community of several thousand on land that was thought capable of supporting only nine head of cattle. Now almost 20 years later, it is evident that the episode of  Rajneeshpuram stands for other things as well. The events of 1981-1985 expose the pervasiveness of American xenophobia and the potential for the American legislative and judicial systems to be used by a few, with the backing of the masses, to destroy a foreign, unfamiliar, minority.

Even before coming to the United States, Rajneesh was on the radar screens of the U.S. State Department. After the murders and mass-suicide at Jones Town, the U.S. government began to monitor gurus and religious groups that attracted a large American following. In the late 70's, CIA agents were often rumored to be among the visitors at the Rajneesh ashram. At the very least, the American consulate in Bombay sent reports to Washington regarding the activities of Rajneesh and his Pune ashram. Those reports contained specific references to State

Department concerns that Rajneesh would try to relocate to the United States.

In 1981 Rajneesh and a small selection of sannyasins rented the entire first class section of a commercial airliner and flew to New Jersey. Notable for her absence was Ma Laxmi who had been left behind in India with a directive to look for land suitable for building a large commune. At the time that Rajneesh traveled to the U.S., everything points to his visit being temporary and actually related to the medical concerns which had provided the reason for his visa. Ma Anand Sheela appeared to be the only person then working toward making Rajneesh's stay permanent. Soon after the group arrived at the New Jersey meditation center, the recently purchased "castle," Sheela set off to find land for a commune in North America.

From the moment that Rajneesh first stepped foot on American soil, he was a matter of "concern" for the U.S. government. By 1984, 17 different local, state and federal agencies were actively investigating the activities at Rajneeshpuram. White House documents show that Edwin Meese III, the "shadow president" of the Reagan administration, noticed the Rajneesh "situation" as early as 1982. The presence of the Rajneesh commune almost immediately created fear among the local Oregonians—especially the few remaining residents of Antelope. Destruction of the commune became a crusade for Oregon Attorney General David Frohnmeyer. In a 1984 interview in *The Oregonian*, congressman Bob Smith stated he had begun "pounding" the INS to resolve the Oregon-Rajneesh "issue" in April 1982.

As the old saying goes: Just because you are paranoid, does not mean they aren't out to get you.

From very early on, the town of Rajneeshpuram was tied up in a constant barrage of litigation. Numerous lawsuits were filed by 1,000 Friends, the Attorney General's office and private citizens. In April 1983, a horse owned by Harry Hawkins, a former Jefferson county sheriff who had been hired as Rajneeshpuram's first police officer, was killed by buckshot. On 29 July 1983, three bombs exploded at a Rajneesh owned hotel in Portland. Oregonians began wearing T-shirts that had a picture of the Bhagwan driving a Rolls Royce caught in the cross-hairs of a riflescope while another shirt read "Not Wanted Dead Or Alive." The bumper sticker "Better Dead than Red" became a common sight throughout eastern Oregon. In 1985 several attempts were made to enact legislation that specifically attacked the legitimacy of Rajneeshpuram and sannyasin activity. The Oregon Secretary of State authored a ballot question, wording approved by Attorney General Frohnmeyer, that read "Shall City of Rajneesh (Antelope) charter be repealed, city cease to exist, and Wasco County assume city's assets and liabilities?" (*The Bend Bulletin*, July 3, 1985)

One of the most persistent myths of Rajneeshpuram over the years following it's dissolution is the assumption that the commune blew apart from the inside. This notion, that the commune simply disintegrated due to internal fractures and tensions, fits snugly within the popular conception of cults, that they are inherently fleeting, frenetic, fluid and unstable. The truth is that the commune suffered an unremitting and coordinated harassment from the local, state and federal government. This coupled with the tide of resentment and distrust in the local communities created a situation of extreme pressure on Rajneeshpuram and its residents. Sheela's tactics and combativeness rose in direct proportion to the pressure exerted on the commune from outside. Her reactions, increasingly ludicrous, were generally the result of new attacks from authorities. Her strangle hold on control of the commune also increased in relation to these external forces. These threats also, ironically, became an element in her power providing the important element of us-against-them paranoia necessary for the success of an absolutist regime. This was only exacerbated when Rajneesh began speaking again in 1984—a fact which immediately began to work against Sheela's power base.

Rumors and myths about the strangers in red began immediately after their arrival at the Big Muddy. The commune was spending tremendous sums of money on development and the creation of city infrastructure. This seemingly limitless supply of ready-cash convinced federal law enforcement officials, that the money stemmed from illegal activity such as drug smuggling, gun running or both. In fact the cash was coming from a series of lucrative and highly successful business ventures abroad. Sannyasins operated almost half the vegetarian restaurants in Germany and Rajneesh discotheques were springing up all across Europe. These businesses coupled with the growing number of meditation centers and local communes were sending millions of dollars to support Rajneeshpuram.

Another persistent rumors of illegal activity at Rajneeshpuram remains that the sannyasins were stockpiling weapons. Media reports of the day often focused on images of Uzi toting sannyasins. By 1985 Sheela was always shown wearing a gun on her hip. The reports all failed to mention that the photographed sannyasins were members of the Rajneeshpuram police force—a state recognized law enforcement agency whose members had been trained at the State Police Academy. Sheela and other sannyasin spokespeople, such as mayor Krishna Devi, did nothing to dispel these rumors. Instead through 1984 and into 1985, they stepped up the rhetoric and counter-threats. Newspapers quoted Devi as warning that they would take 15 Oregonian heads for every sannyasin killed. Sheela repeatedly asserted that the residents of Rajneeshpuram were ready to defend themselves—use of the words "war" and "blood" were common. When federal agents searched Rajneeshpuram after the Bhagwan's departure, no stockpile of weapons was discovered. Divers from the Navy Seals were brought in to search the two lakes at Rajneeshpuram. Media reports of the searches failed to mention that no cache of weapons was present. According to subsequent reports, the Rajneesh sannyasins did not possess any weapons inconsistent with a municipal police force.

In his book *Passage to America*, Max Brecher interviews two soldiers-for-hire who allege that they were offered money to kill Rajneesh. In both instances, the individuals were sure that the CIA was ultimately behind the payment offers. John Wayne Hearn, now serving three life sentences for three gruesome murders for hire, admits to working for the CIA on several covert operations, including running guns to Nicaragua and assisting in a plot to overthrow the government of French Guyana. Hearn claims to have been offered a significant amount of money to blow-up several trailers at Rajneehpuram in an attempt to scare the sannyasins. The second man Don Stewart recorded his conversations with his contact who went by the name Wolfgang. In these conversations, Wolfgang specifically mentions government agencies targeting Rajneesh. Wolfgang's plan was to assassinate the Bhagwan during one of his daily drives. Once a day Rajneesh would drive his car along a commune road and sannyasins would line up to watch their guru drive by. For Wolfgang, and presumably his backers, the killing of a couple of hundred devotees was more than acceptable if Rajneesh was taken out. It is ironic that in both these instances, the soldiers turned down the offer due to the rumors they had heard about the commune being an armed camp. The prospect of being trapped by a couple of thousand armed zealots proved an unacceptable risk.

Under the guise of fighting terrorism, the President authorized the CIA to investigate foreign entities on U.S. soil, thus sidestepping the congressional mandate against domestic CIA operations. In December 1981, President Reagan signed Executive Order 12333 which authorized federal law enforcement agencies to hire outside people to conduct illegal break-ins for the purposes of obtaining evidence. The executive order specifically allowed that evidence thus collected could be used, in turn, to obtain a legitimate search warrant.

Beginning in 1983 and increasing through to the dissolution of the commune in 1985, military jets from Whidbey Island Naval Base conducted regular flyovers of Rajneeshpuram. In violation of FAA regulations, the plains routinely flew extremely low over the commune disrupting daily life and, in several instances, jeopardizing civilian air traffic at the Rajneesh airport. These flights were ostensibly routine training missions—at times even using the commune buildings as fake targets for bombing runs. The flights also included reconnaissance and surveillance. Twin-engine Mohawk surveillance plains from the reconnaissance unit in Boise, Idaho also conducted recons over the commune. In the taped conversations with Wolfgang, he also mentions participating in aerial surveillance. Both the INS and U.S. attorney's office conducted aerial recons over Rajneeshpuram in 1985 as part of their preparation for arresting Rajneesh.

On 13 May 1985, the police of Philadelphia, PA dropped a C-4 bomb onto the headquarters of M.O.V.E., a back-to-Africa movement. The police had attempted to serve warrants on members of the movement and they were allegedly fired upon during the attempt. After a brief siege, Philadelphia Police Commissioner Gregore Sambor ordered the dropping of a bomb onto the headquarters building—one of several row houses in the Philadelphia residential neighborhood. (*The New York Times*, 14 May 1985) The ensuing fire destroyed 61 row houses and left 251 people without a home. (CNN, 24 June 1996) Following the bombing, Commissioner Sambor was reelected and U.S. Attorney General Edwin Meese III applauded the operation as a superb success for American law enforcement. By 1996 the city of Philadelphia had paid out almost $30 million in lawsuits resulting directly from the M.O.V.E. operation.

In the summer of 1985, Sheela retained a top immigration lawyer, Peter Schey, to represent Rajneesh in his ongoing battle with INS. Schey immediately began negotiating with U.S. District Attorney Robert Turner, who had already secretly convened a grand jury to investigate alleged immigration fraud at Rajneeshpuram. Schey wanted to insure that if indictments were handed down that the indictees would be allowed to surrender themselves to authorities at a location outside of Rajneeshpuram. Schey was confident that he had an agreement to this affect with Turner and that he, Rajneesh and any others indicted would be notified 24 hours in advance and be allowed to turn themselves in to the court house in Portland. Despite this, according to INS deputy counsel Mike Inman, Turner had no intention of allowing Rajneesh or anyone else to surrender peacefully. Instead, in Inman's words, Turner was set on "storming the Bastille." According to Inman, Turner wanted "to utilize the Oregon National Guard, the FBI and the Immigration Services Border Patrol, and storm the compound with force, and go through the barricades and fences." (Brecher, p. 275) Turner had developed a plan, according to Inman and others involved, of serving the warrants unannounced. INS agent Joe Greene testified under oath that Turner had no intention of allowing the Bhagwan to surrender at a neutral location. According to the plan, state and federal law enforcement, including the Bureau of Alcohol, Tobacco and Firearms, would show up unannounced at Rajneeshpuram and on a bull-horn inform the residents that they were surrounded and that the indictees had 1 minute to surrender. National Guard troops would be concealed in the nearby hills to provide back up if necessary. Given the then generally accepted rumors that the commune was a "militarized camp," this plan would seem to have been intended to provoke an armed confrontation.

The government's plan for Rajneeshpuram eerily foreshadows the later federal assaults on the Branch Davidian compound at Waco, Texas and Randy Weaver's cabin at Ruby Ridge, Idaho. In these two instances, similar tactics, to those proposed by Turner, were employed with very tragic results. In these cases, the fear that stockpiles of weapons were present was used to justify the excessive force employed. Through the period leading up to the arrest of Rajneesh and again during the siege at the Branch Davidian compound, media pundits repeatedly raised the specter of Jonestown. The deaths of the Davidians is still often represented as mass suicide, rather than the consequence of the government's assault. It is not difficult to imagine what would have happened, if Robert Turner had been able to proceed with his surprise entrance into Rajneeshpuram. One can also assume who would have been accused of "firing first." Turner's plan was unexpectedly thwarted before it could be implemented, when on the afternoon of Sunday 27 October 1985, two privately chartered planes departed Rajneeshpuram Airport and began to make their way across the continent. Rumors were flying that arrests were imminent. In actuality sealed indictments had been handed to Turner the previous week. Rajneesh's non-sannyasin attorney Peter Schey twice flew from Los Angeles to Oregon to discuss the rumored warrants and to arrange for the peaceful surrender of Rajneesh. On both occasions Turner denied the existence of warrants for Rajneesh or any other sannyasin. Turner, later, claimed that he believed that a peaceful surrender was impossible and that by telling Schey he would be tipping Rajneesh off and allow him time to flee. Sheela had departed the commune the month before under a cloud of accusation and suspicion—the Bhagwan, himself, her principle accuser.

Despite the fact that no indictments had been announced nor warrants served, frantic calls went out to law enforcement agencies across the country to apprehend the "fugitives." The planes landed at a small airport outside of Charlotte, North Carolina for refueling. Agents were waiting and the Bhagwan and his entourage were arrested without incident. Though they had been warned that the passengers would be heavily armed with automatic weapons and armor-piercing bullets, the agents found only one small handgun on the planes. At Rajneesh's bail hearing the next day, prosecutors were unable to present an arrest warrant from Oregon. Despite this discrepancy, the judge denied Rajneesh's bail. An unsigned, incomplete Oregonian warrant was later presented to the Charlotte court. Court records in Oregon hold a different arrest warrant, however, one that appears to have been forged after the fact and pre-dated.

In a jailhouse TV interview conducted by Ted Koppel and aired live on ABC's Nightline, Rajneesh asserted that he was not leaving the country or fleeing impending arrest. When asked by an incredulous Ted Koppel, if the Bahamas (their flight plans indicated North Carolina, but sannyasins were reported to have been inquiring about renting a plane capable of over-sea flight) was now part of the United States, Rajneesh claimed to not know where the planes were headed. He said, instead, that he trusted in his friends and all he knew was that they were taking him to some place safe, as detailed in Prem Shunyo's *Diamond Days With Osho*. Given Rajneesh's apparent lack of involvement in his travel decisions during his post U.S. "world tour," it is not out of the question that he did not know where the planes were headed. He would simply go where they were headed like a Zen sage, he was where ever he was.

One thing is certain; Rajneesh's departure from Rajneeshpuram stemmed off the government's plan for a major assault on the commune and, thus, likely spared several hundred lives. By late September 1985, 15 National Guard armored personnel carriers were positioned in the hills surrounding Rajneeshpuram. In addition to the many FBI agents investigating the allegations made by Rajneesh, the state was ready to commit 800 state troopers if conflict erupted and the National Guard had another 600 guardsmen on standby as backup. By September 30, the National Guard had three HUEY helicopters at Redmond airport ready to carry FBI agents and Oregon State Police SWAT teams into Rajneeshpuram. Turner also unsuccessfully requested U.S. Marshal's Service Fugitive Investigative Search Teams (FIST) and Border Patrol from the U.S.-Mexico border to assist with "mass arrests."

Even if one rejects his claim that he was not fleeing the country, one question does remain about Rajneesh's mysterious flight: why did they turn east rather than west? If they had chosen to fly out over the Pacific Ocean they would have very quickly been over international waters outside of U.S. jurisdiction. *A Passage to America* author Max Brecher asked this question directly to Rajneesh in 1989, "I left for Charlotte," Rajneesh answered, "because for six weeks previously the National Guard was on standby around the commune, ready to enter the commune. Obviously, if they had arrested me there, the 5,000 sannyasins would not have tolerated it. There would have been bloodshed. To avoid this, I went to Charlotte. It was just to avoid bloodshed of the sannyasins. There was no sannyasins in Charlotte to be involved if I was arrested there. And there was a beautiful house in the mountains there for me to stay." (Brecher, p. 289) When Weaver was asked about the government's concern about a bloodbath of innocent sannyasins at Rajneeshpuram, if the commune was stormed by force, he simply stated, "It's not the government's job to make those guy's jobs easier."

In retrospect, Rajneesh's cross-country flight did not meet the legal definition of fleeing prosecution and he and the other passengers could not rightly be considered fugitives. U.S. District Attorney conceded in the Charlotte court that he lacked the evidence to support his claim that Rajneesh and co. were attempting to evade arrest. Despite Turner's contention to the contrary in court, the pilots filed flight plans that listed Charlotte as their final destination. According to the account of the air traffic controller on duty that night, the pilots did not behave in a fashion consistent with someone who was either nervous or paranoid. Above all else, they could not be called fugitives since at the time of their arrests no warrant existed for any of them. The following morning, the federal indictment was unsealed but there is still no evidence that an arrest warrant was issued for Rajneesh or anyone else on the plane. The warrant that is currently on file in Oregon, though dated Oct. 28, was not clerked into the courthouse until two weeks after the arrest. The warrant also lists the North Carolina arresting officer, a fact that could not have been known at the time the warrant was supposed to have been issued, since Rajneesh was still in Oregon at that time. Despite these facts, Rajneesh's attorney's conceded that a warrant existed, without having seen it, and the magistrate denied Rajneesh's bail on the grounds that he was a flight risk.

A theory proposed by Max Brecher, and supported by the account of deputy INS council Inman, is that the federal authorities—the INS and the State Deptartment—wanted Rajneesh to flee the country. Then they could use the existence of indefinitely active warrants to keep him from ever returning. This plan would have effectively prevented Rajneesh from ever entering the United States again without having to go through the process of lengthy deportation proceedings and the possibility a court could rule in his favor. This would help explain why the INS pulled their support for the U.S. District Attorney's investigation and ordered their field operatives not to assist in the arrest of Rajneesh, despite the fact that all the charges against him were for immigration violations. Turner takes full credit for the arrest. He and a Charlotte INS agent, working against the directives of his superiors, coordinated the bringing in of the U.S. Marshals and the subsequent arrests. It appears that Turner in his zeal to prosecute Rajneesh may have thwarted the governments quiet solution to the Rajneesh problem.

In 13 July 1986 a monument was dedicated outside the Wasco County Court House. Beneath the statue of a stately Antelope read the inscription "Dedicated to all who steadfastly and unwaveringly opposed the attempts of the Rajneesh followers to take political control of Wasco County: 1981-1985." Below this, the plaque carries a quote from Irish politician Edmund Burke "The only thing necessary for the triumph of evil is for good men to do nothing." Above the statue flew a flag that had once flown above the U.S. Capital Building—a gift from Congressman Bob Smith. Were the residents of Rajneeshpuram really "evil" and were the Oregonians really "good"? What is true of erecting monuments is also true of history, they are constructed by the victors. The defeated almost without exception go down as villains within the orthodox historical record. Only two members of the commune could rightfully be described as "evil"—Ma Anand Sheela and Ma Puja. A few others committed evil acts.

Studies like the Zimbardo experiment have shown that even red-blooded, all American college students can commit the most atrocious acts if given absolute power over another. In the experiment designed by Philip Zimbardo, a group of male college student volunteers were randomly separated into two groups—

prisoners and guards. The guards were given uniforms and dark glasses and no one was permitted to address another by name. A long list of petty prisoner regulations was provided to the guards. The experiment originally designed to last a fortnight had to be ended after only one week, due to an unexpected level of violence and humiliation inflicted on the prisoners by the guards. In his analysis of the experiment, Zygmunt Bauman observes in his book *Modernity and the Holocaust*, "clearly and unambiguously, the orgy of cruelty that took Zimbardo and his colleagues by surprise, stemmed from a vicious social arrangement, and not from the viciousness of the participants." (Bauman, p. 167) In a separate study conducted by Stanley Milgram at Yale University, Milgram demonstrated that most humans possess the capacity of harming another if the instruction to do so comes from one that the subject holds as an authority figure.

Were all sannyasins indeed "evil"? This is certainly the explicit message of the Antelope monument. When the sannyasins first moved to Eastern Oregon, buying land that no one else wanted, they made serious efforts towards creating a positive impression on their neighbors. Sheela regularly held information meetings in 1981, where she presented a pleasant face and attempted to charm the wary Oregonians. The sannyasins went above and beyond in complying with local laws and state land use regulations throughout the creation of their city—a fact that infuriated their opponents in the 1,000 Friends of Oregon and the Oregon Attorney General's office. Their comprehensive plan was even held up as an example for other municipalities to follow. At its outset the commune developers tried to get along with their neighbors and comply with all U.S. laws. They only moved into the neighboring town of Antelope when pushed by 1,000 Friends lawsuits and at the suggestion of the state Land Use Commission. At the time that the sannyasins began buying property in Antelope, the town was listed prominently on the list of Oregon ghost towns.

Throughout the creation of Rajneeshpuram, Sheela's arguments and public appearances became increasingly vitriolic and provocative. Also through this time, the commune and its residents were the victims of an escalating bombardment of harassment and threats of harm. The intimidation came from multiple directions and was fully supported by several arms of the federal government. Against this opposition and with the backdrop of the unwelcoming sagebrush desert, it is amazing that the Rajneesh sannyasins accomplished what they did—creating a sustainable, ecologically friendly city capable of supporting thousands of residents.

The history of the United States began with religious dissent—the puritans forging a life in the wilderness of New England to escape persecution. It is also a history of repressing religious difference. The same puritan pilgrims established a cluster of communities ruthlessly intolerant of religious difference—Cotton Mather and the Salem witch trials being but one example, extreme among many. Attorney General Frohnmeyer asserted that a city founded by adherents of one particular religion was unconstitutional. If American history is to suggest anything, the opposite would certainly seem to be the case. Many U.S. cities were established by religious followers in an attempt to establish their own area where they could freely practice their faith. The settling of Utah and the incorporation of Salt Lake City is an obvious example.

The anti-cult movement has been an equal and counter-running force within the history of religion in the United States. Just as so-called "new religious movements" have been common since before the revolution, anti-cult movements have been equally ubiquitous. It was this strain of intolerance that necessitated the migrations that led to the establishment of new cities based on religious communities. Philip Jenkins argues in his book *Mystics & Messiahs* that anti-cult paranoia has frequently taken hold of the American mass psyche. Phillips notes that the arguments of this reactionary movement were solidly in place by the late 19th century—lurid stereotypes, xenophobia, accusations of mind-control and stories of sexual scandal. We can see all these elements displayed in the concerned voices speaking out against Rajneeshpuram. "When a modern critic attacks a deviant religious group as a cult," Jenkins writes, "the images evoked are ultimately a mélange of rumors and allegations variously made against Catholics, Masons, Mormons, Shakers, radical evangelicals, and others." He further argues that the concern over cults does not necessarily correlate to actual threats posed by the cult's activities. Jenkins observes that "the level of public concern about cults at any given time is not necessarily based on a rational or objective assessment of the threat posed by these groups, but rather reflects a diverse range of tensions, prejudices, and fears."

So, again, one has to ask, were the Rajneesh sannyasins "evil" for attempting to build their City on a Hill? Or were they simply victims of a cyclic resurgence of the pernicious hatred of difference that has run through the darkness of America since it's earliest days?

References:

Bauman, Zygmunt. *Modernity and the Holocaust.* Cornell University: Ithaca, NY, 1989.

Brecher, Max. *A Passage to America.* Book Quest, Bombay, 1993.

Carter, Lewis F. *Charisma and Control in Rajneeshpuram: The Role of Shared Values In the Creation of a Community.* Cambridge University: Cambridge, 1990.

Fitzgerald, Frances. *Cities On a Hill.* Simon & Schuster: New York, 1987.

Franklin, Satya Bharti. *The Promise of Paradise.* Station Hill: New York, 1992.

Hamilton, Rosemary. *Hellbent For Enlightenment: Unmasking Sex, Power, and Death with a Notorious Master.* White Cloud Press: Ashland, OR, 1998.

Haney, Craig, Curtis Banks & Philip Zimbardo. "Interpersonal Dynamics in a Simulated Prison," *International Journal of Criminology and Penology* vol. VI. (1968), pp. 69-97. Cited in Bauman.

Jenkins, Philip. *Mystics & Messiahs: Cults and New Religions in American History.* Oxford University: Oxford, 2001.

Joshi, Vasant. *The Awakened One: The Life and Work of Bhagwan Shree Rajneesh.* Harper & Row: New York, 1982.

Milgram, Stanley. *Obedience to Authority: An Experimental View.* Tavistock: London, 1974.

Rajneesh, Bhagwan Shree (Osho). *The Last Testament: Interviews with the World Press,* volume I. Rajneesh Publications, Inc.: Boulder, CO, 1986.

_____. *The Perfect Way.* Motilal Babarsidass: Delhi, 1993.

Shunyo, Prem. *Diamond Days With Osho.* Motilal Banarsidass: Delhi, 1993.

The Plastic Ideal
The Androgyne In *fin de Siecle* Occulture

INTRODUCTION:
THE SYMBOLISTS

As the second half of the 19th century got under way, naturalism predominated French art and literature. Figures such as Emile Zola and Edouard Manet exemplify the philosophical impulse upon which naturalism was founded. Referring to Manet's work, Zola wrote, "Our art's essential aim is to objectify the subjective (the exteriorization of the idea); instead of subjectifying the objective (nature seen through a temperament)." With its roots in the century's earlier Romanticism and influenced by the sensibilities of the midcentury Pre-Raphaelites, the Symbolists arose in direct opposition to the concrete objectification underlying naturalism.

The Symbolists diverged from their contemporary Impressionists such as Monet, Cezanne and Seurat. As the two movements moved away from naturalism, the latter was influenced by the awakening of scientific discovery, while the former embraced the religiously motivated resurgence of hermeticism, myth and allegory. The Symbolists had a mutually influential relationship with the Pont-Aven School. Gauguin gave the Symbolists color and an expanded capacity for expression, while the Symbolists influenced Gauguin by elevating the importance of signifiers within his work.

The official beginning of the Symbolist movement is marked by the publication of the Symbolist manifesto by Jean Moréas in the Literary Supplement to *Le Figaro* on September 18, 1886. "Romanticism," wrote Moréas, "after having sounded every tumultuous alarm of revolt, after having had its days of glory and battle, lost its strength and its grace, abdicated its

heroic audacities, made itself orderly, skeptical and full of good sense." His manifesto heralded the establishment of a new poetry that saught "to clothe the Idea in sensual form which, nevertheless, would not be its goal in itself, but which, while serving to express the Idea, would remain exposed."[1]

"The Idea," Moréas continued, "in its turn, must not be deprived of the sumptuous simars of external analogies; because the essential character of the Symbolic art consists of ever going until the concentration of the Idea in itself." For Moréas "concrete phenomena"

Poster, Carlos Schwabe, 1892, Lithograph, Picadelly Gallery, London

did not arise of their own accord, but were, rather, "the sensual appearances intended to represent their esoteric affinities with primordial Ideas."

Important Symbolist poets included Charles Baudelaire, whose *Les Fleurs du Mal* is considered the first literary expression of the movement, Paul Verlaine and Stéphane Mallarmé. Symbolism was most influential in the visual arts, however, and included painters such as Gustave Moreau, Fernand Knopff, Odion Redon, Edvard Munch and Pierre Puvis de Chavannes.

---

[1] Translation by Eamon Graham, *Bohème Magazine*, 2004, II(6).

It took only a few years before the movement founded on Moréas's manifesto merged with the growing interest in hermeticism, Gnostic Christianity and the occult that arose as the fin de siecle approached. Sâr Péladan and others founded a Rosicrucian-styled order whose public face was the Salon de la Rose+Croix. Their first exhibit opened in March of 1892 and included more than seventy-five exhibitors. The Salon began with an overture especially composed by Eric Satie and followed a mass at St. Germain l'Auxérrois that

Sâr Péladan

included excerpts from Parsifal. Carlos Schwabe designed the poster for the inaugural salon. The first Salon included the notable Symbolist artists Jean Delville, Knopff, Alexandre Séon and Alphonse Osbert.

In his accompanying book, Péladan declared his goal to be nothing less than "to restore the cult of the IDEAL in all its splendour, with TRADITION as its base and BEAUTY as its means [and] to ruin realism, reform latin taste and create a school of idealist art."[2]

---

[2] Quoted by Robert Goldwater, *Symbolism*. (New York: Harper & Row, 1979), pp. 186-7.

The Plastic Ideal

A preoccupation with fundamental duality is deeply rooted in the philosophical history of Western civilization. This notion of dual existence, or binary opposition, most commonly manifests as a tension between male and female, masculine and feminine, but extends to a greater force-relation of humans and the external world. In one-way or another, metaphysicians have long sought a means of reconciling or escaping this dualism. Often, historically, the solution has been resulted in a configuration of the androgyne as a spiritual ideal—an ideal being that exists outside of the split domain of the male and the female.

Most of the Western mystical tradition rests on myths that humanity developed out of a primal void. The Bible begins, "In the beginning of creation, when God made Heaven and earth, the earth was without form and void." (Genesis I:1-2) Medieval alchemists portrayed this void as the *prima material* given form by Mercurius, who was often depicted as a hermaphrodite. (Singer, 131) Qabalistic cosmology rests on the concept of Ain Soph, the veils of chaos (nothingness) that exist before the first emanation of the Divine (Kether on the tree of life). Within these three creation myths, division is a necessary precondition of creation. Organizing the chaos of the void depends upon the development of a binary system. Nothing coalesces into the point, creating tension between the form and the formless, which, in turn, splits the point into two forming a dynamism. The search for an escape from this dualistic state has formed one of the great pursuits of philosophers, mystics and occultists alike. This current manifested strongly in the fin de siecle occulture, with the Symbolist artists of the Salon de las Rose+Croix, and in the 20th century with the notorious occultist Aleister Crowley and the futuristic philosopher William S. Burroughs.

In his analysis of early man, Arthur Evans sees the sexes as living very separate lives. Stone age people lived apart from each other in sexually segregated houses and, at times, even villages. (Evans, 15) According to Evans research, the sexes only came together for procreative purposes, while recreational sex was primarily same-sex. Although several religious artifacts from this period depict hermaphrodites, within the practical levels of religious ceremony, there generally appeared to be room for only one mystery and that female. There is evidence from numerous cultures that the first male shamans were transgendered, being initiated as female. In some cases, male shamans even underwent ritual castration in order to receive the mysteries of the cult.(Evans, 17)

Medieval Qabalists were among the early proponents of androgyny as a solution to the problem of an existence based on duality. The Qabalists describe three levels of 'negative existence' preceding the first emanation of the Divine. Crowley poetically described these three states as "The Ante-Primal Triad That Is Not-God: Nothing is. Nothing Becomes. Nothing is not."(Crowley, 10) Out of this chaos God created pre-Edenic man, Adam Kadman, the archetypal androgyne. Rabbi Simeon writes in *The Zohar* that "the man of emanation [Adam Kadman] was both male and female from the side both father and mother for he was all light."(Singer, 87) The human became complete, with the second creation of man in the Garden and his split into male and female. *The Zohar* explains that a person in this nonwhole form is not capable of receiving diving blessing:

> Therefore we know: what is only masculine or only feminine is called only part of the body. But no blessing rules over a faulty or incomplete thing, but only over a complete

place, not one that is divided, for divided things
cannot long endure or be blessed. (Singer, 161)

The Kabalists' solution to this "faulty" state is the
androgyne, a careful combining of the male and female natures
within each person. This action thus creates a unified being
worthy of the blessings given over a complete place." The
apocryphal gospel according to Thomas, utilized by many
contemporary Gnostics, exemplifies this requisite for
benediction:

> When you make the two one, and when you
> make the inside like the outside and the outside
> like the inside, and the above like the below,
> and when you make the male and the female
> one and the same, so that the male not be male
> nor the female female; and when you fashion
> eyes in place of an eye, and a hand in place of a
> hand, and a foot in place of a foot, and a
> likeness in place of a likeness; then will you
> enter [the Kingdom]. (Lambdin, 129)

In the latter half of the nineteenth century, the artists of the
Symbolist movement exalted the androgyne image as the human
ideal. The Symbolist artists attempted to break from the cult of
realism, which they felt incapable of finding meaning, due to
intentional limitation. Des Hermies, in J.K. Huysmans' *La Bas*,
outlines the faults the Symbolists found in Emile Zola and his
associates:

> The fault I find with realism is not the dull
> monotone of its ponderous style, it is the
> uncleanliness of its compositions; the fault I
> find is its having embodied materialism in

Literature, and having glorified the democracy of Art! . . . What a low-minded theory, what a petty, narrow system! Voluntarily to limit oneself to the off-scourings of the flesh, to reject the suprasensible, to deny the visionary not even to realize how the mysticism of Art begins at the point where the senses cease to help us! (Huysmans, 1)

The movement away from realism toward a new religious art manifested clearly within the artists of the Salon de la Rose+Croix. For the Salon's founder, Sar Joséphin Péladan, and artists such as Jean Delville, Georges Minne, Armand Point, Fernand Khnopff, and Jean Dampt the androgyne played a fundamental role in their idealized mythic configuration. The androgyme, as differentiated from the hermaphrodite employed by others of the period, represents no less than the absolute goal of human spiritual evolution. By depicting the androgyne, the artists of the Salon de la Rose+Croix were creating/recreating a form of mystical art that served, at least in the mind of Peledan, to reestablish the role of religious art in intellectual society. Sar Péladan proclaimed categorically, "the androgyne, is the plastic ideal!" (Pincus-Witten, 44)

In 1884 with the collaboration of several prominent occultists including Stanislas de Guaita and Papus (Gerard Encausse), Péladan formed the Rosicrucian order le Ordre de la Rose+Croix+Kabalistique. The intent of this organization was to strip the system of Kabalistic magic of the frivolous accumulations of centuries and revitalize the Western mystical tradition. Péladan soon became uncomfortable with the Eastern influences within the ideology of the order, and in his Salon of 1890, announced his departure from the order. On 23 August 1891, article 9256 in *Les Petite Affiches* made the schism legal, with the formation of the Association de l'Ordre de la Rose+Croix du Temple et du Graal—otherwise known as the Rose+Croix+Catholique. With the financial backing of Count Antoine de la Rochfoucauld, Paladan wished to move away from the former order's Orientalism and return to the Papist church. (Pincus-Witten, 77) On a more practical level, the break with Guaita allowed Péladan to embody explicitly his religious ideals in the order structure and gather together a collection of artists with similar views toward the primacy of the androgyne archetype.

Throughout his involvement with the Rose+Croix+Kabalistique and the Rose+Croix+Catholique, Sar Péladan experimented with the theme of androgyny in his literary works. The androgyne plays an important role as the ideal within his 1884 novel *Le Vice Supreme* as shown in Leonora's dialogue with Antar. She advises the artist to "make an angel, without sex, the synthesis of a young man and a young woman." (Olander, 118) In 1888 Péladan's *Istar* was published, with a frontispiece by Khnopff, depicting a woman, head thrown back in ecstasy and completely devoid of surrounding except for an extremely phallic flower that grows toward her groin. Péladan described Khnopff's frontispiece as "the emotional nude, that is to say, the expression of the model apart from its surrounding." (Pincus-Witten, 68) The hint of muscles and wide jaw that Khnopff gave the model evoke a haunting, androgynous tone. They strengthen her without reinforcing her feminity. While the frontispiece of *Istar* is an example of the way in which Khnopff's women differ from the traditional androgyne, the angle of the head and the inclusion of the florabunda suggest a subtle cross between the androgyne and the femme fatale, containing glimpses of other thematic depictions prevalent in the Symbolist movement.

Jean Delville, also an exhibitor at the Salon de la Rose+Croix, noted in his comment on Khnopff's work:

> Khnopff has created a type of ideal woman. Are they really women? Are they not rather imaginary feminites? They partake at the same time of the Idol, of the Chimera, of the Sphinx and of the Saint. They are rather plastic androgynes, subtle symbols, conceived according to an abstract idea and rendered visible. (Howe, 48)

This passage shows that Delville saw in Khnopff's work a combination of several precursors of the androgynous form: the Greek hermaphrodite, the Babylonian Tiamat, and da Vinci's saints.

Eighteen-ninety saw the publication of Péladan's *L'Androgyne*, the plot of which centered around the androgyne Samas. Alexandre Seon drew the frontispiece for this work. It depicts, in the words of Péladan: "Above the strange rocks of the Brehat, licked at by the waves, there rolls in the sky in piece of the moon, the head of the androgyne Samas, stupefied by the sexual enigma." (Pincus-Witten, 71)

Since *L'Androgyne* is an autobiographical depiction of Péladan's childhood in a Jesuit school, Péladan is equating himself with the androgyne. By presenting Samas' head in the place of a celestial body, Seon's drawing exalts Samas, and through him Péladan to the role of divine being. This representation also strengthens Péladan's view of himself as magus, since the moon symbolizes, in its relationship to the tides, the power over the flow of nature.

Following the legal establishment of the Rose+Croix+Catholique, Péladan began preparations for the first exhibition of the Salon de la Rose+Croix scheduled for the following year. Fernand Khnopff was among those exhibiting in the first Salon and continued to exhibit in the Salons of 1893 and 1894. His work embodies two of the major themes within the Rose+Croix movement, the androgyne and the mage. Péladan felt that Khnopff's philosophy was closely aligned to his own, which led him to proclaim in *Salon de Champ de Mars* of 1893 that Khnopff was an "Admirable and Immortal Master." (Pincus-Witten, 153) In the Salon of 1893, Khnopff exhibited "L'Offrande" and "I Lock My Door Upon Myself," both of which contain references to the androgynous nature of their subjects. Khnopff created this androgynous feeling by giving his women a massive jaw, "a jaw so massive," in the words of art historian Micheal Gibson, "that Mussolini himself, with his ham-sized jowl might have envied them." (Gibson, 109) The over emphasizing of the model's jaw gives her an atypical female face.

I Lock My Door Upon Myself, 1891, Oil on canvas; 72 x 140 cm,
Neue Pinakothek, Munich, Germany

In "I Lock My Door Upon Myself" Khnopff used the model's clothing to create her sexual ambiguities through de-sexing her body. Her long hair and a subtle softness of the features are the only elements that outwardly denote her sex. The female in "L'Offrande" possesses even fewer clues that allude to her gender since unlike the model in "I Lock My Door Upon Myself," the model has her hair back, forcing her face to stand alone and appear all the more ambiguous.

The inclusion of the arum lily in "I Lock My Door Upon Myself" serves to reinforce the androgynous interpretation of the painting. Khnopff employed this particular lily throughout his work to allude to androgyny, it reappears in "Arum Lily," "The Secret Reflection," and "Le Reflet Bleu." The arum lily belongs to the class Gynandric, which is distinguished by having both male and female characteristics, and is thus the floral embodiment of Khnopff and Péladan's ideal. These women also embody the chaste ideal of Péladan's androgyne. It is impossible for these women to satisfy sexually, since both are removed from sexual physicality into a moment of isolation and introspection. This looking inwards displays the role of the magus, since magic is a search for internal union, especially when coupled with the depiction of the androgyne. The model in "I Lock My Door upon Myself" rests her arms on a table which has a coffin like appearance. This particular use of death imagery is more than a reference to suicidal contemplation; it represents the power that the magus has gained over the mysteries of life and death. The lilies in the painting's foreground can be viewed as a further reification of the magus's harmonious understanding of life's progression. They move from birth to death reflecting the magician's acceptance of natural laws.

Through the iconography of his work, Khnopff linked the androgyne and the magus with the internal search of the artist. He drew the comparison between himself and the magus most strongly in his depiction of Oedipus in "Des Caresses" (1896). Like Gustave Moreau in "Oedipus and the Sphinx," Khnopff depicted the victorious Oedipus as an androgyne. In both paintings, Oedpus carries a staff symbolizing his newly gained dominance over the physical world. In Khnopff's depiction, he wears a wreath of flowers in his hair drawing on the image of the laurel wreath, serving to establish further that the Oedipus of

Des Caresses, 1896, Oil on canvas; 50 x 150 cm, Musees Royaux des
Beaux-Arts de Belgique, Brussels, Belgium

"Des Caresses" is indeed Oedipus the victor. He has answered the Sphinx's riddle and gained the wisdom of the magus. This knowledge has taken him outside the world of opposites and recreated him as the androgyne. For the Symbolists, Oedipus is both prototype and allegory. He exists simultaneously as the mage and the archetypal androgyne. For Khnopff he represented even more than the androgyne and the mage. He equated these two with the artist. Péladan echoed Khnopff's visual idealism in his religious/artistic rhetoric, when he exclaimed, "Artist thou art priest."(Howe, 53)

Khnopff's painting and Péladan's writing attempted to explore other levels of reality perceived by the initiate. As Charles Morice points out, "Art is not only revelator of the infinite, it is also the very means to penetrate into it."(Howe, 53) Since Khnopff considered all nature but reflections of higher realities, it was through this search, both internal and external, that he derived the androgyne as ideal. Art became the means of attaining the desired state of androgyny.

For Péladan art's most important role was that of transcendence. In *L'Art Idealiste et Mystique* he wrote, "I believe I have seen in the aesthetic emotion a luminous and heightened equivalent of the emotions of passion; and at a certain attitude of impression, art averts sin."(Howe, 49) In Péladan's conception sexual desire formed the greatest enemy to spiritual growth. Article VII of the Rose+Croix+Catholique's constitution reads "The order has one single motivating goal: to ruin sexual love, passion and to substitute the abstract and aesthetic rites,"(Howe, 141) This "motivating goal" stemmed from the androgyne's perceived dependence on initial realization of sex or sexual potential would destroy the androgyne by bringing it down to the material realm of physical desire. Péladan explained, "the androgyne exists only in the virgin state; at first affirmation of sex, it resolves to the male and the female."(Olander, 120) This split caused by sexual awakening draws greatly on Péladan's background. In *The Symposium* Plato points to the sin of the Hermaphrodites as the trigger to their split "for our sins, God has scattered us abroad." (Hamilton & Cairsis) Within the Kabalistic structure, the fall of Adam Kadman is precipitated by his corruption into physicality.

References:

Crowley, Aleister. *The Book of Lies*. York Beach, ME: Samuel Weiser, 1984.

Evans,.Arthur. *Witchcraft and the Gay Counterculture*. Boston: Fag Rag Books, 1978.

Gibson, Michael. *The Symbolists*. New York: Harry N. Abrams, 1984.

Hamilton, Edith and Huntington Cairsis. *The Collected Dialogues of Plato*. New York: Viking, 1961.

Howe, Jeffrey W. *The Symbolist Art of Fernand Khnopff*. Ann Arbor: UMI Research Press, 1982.

Huysmans, J.K. *La Bas*. Paris: Collection "Le Ballet des Muses", n.d.

Lambdin, Thomas O. "The Gospel of Thomas," in *The Nag Hammadi Library*, James M. Robinson, general editor. San Francisco: Harper & Rowe, 1978, pp. 124-138.

Pincus-Witten, Robert. *Occult Symbolism in France: Joséphin Péladan and the Salon de la Rose+Croix*. New York: Garland, 1976.

Singer, June. *Androgyny*. New York: Viking, 1976.

One Made for Exceptions Not for Laws:
Wildean antinomianism in *de Profundis*

Antinomianism has diverse historical precedents and, one may suspect, reaches back to the very beginning of moral codes and religious strictures. Structured taboos and religious edicts have often give rise to counter-doctrines of transgression. This can be seen in certain Gnostic sects as well as the Tantrik practitioners of the *vama-marga*, or "Lefthand Path." Shri Mahendranath, last  guru of the Nath line of Tantrism, describes the role of the seeker as based on amorality, "a path, way, or outlook which is neither moral nor immoral." (cited by Belarion, 19)   The leader of a twentieth century Ophite-Cainite Gnostic church speaks of Carpocrates' theory of "salvation by reincarnatory fulfillment" as a notion "that if one does not commit some immoral act in *this* lifetime, he or she will likely commit it in the *next*." (Belarion, 19) In these doctrines it is the goal of the adept to reach a point that is beyond good and evil, free of social conditioning. For the adept to attain this higher vantage point, he or she must experience the evil as well as the good, for one cannot leave behind what one does not know. One cannot truthfully reject what one has not experienced; rejection without experience is based on conditioning, not personal knowledge, and therefore can never be complete.

In *De Profundis* Wilde rejects morality, saying, "I am a born antinomian." (Wilde, 583). In light of the spiritual nature underlying much of his work, it is certainly arguable that Wilde means here more than just simple moral transgression. He appears to acknowledge a purpose within his antinomian stance. In "The Soul of Man Under Socialism," Wilde writes, "Disobedience... is man's original virtue." In this 1891 piece, Wilde links disobedience with rebellion, but by the writing of *De Profundis*, he had given up rebellion as being too debilitating. In 1897, Wilde states, "He who is in a state of rebellion cannot receive grace," for "rebellion closes up the channels of the soul, and shuts out the airs of heaven." (Wilde, 595) He sees antinomianism, then, as more than just rebelling against social norms; he is attempting to utilize his suffering and degradation for spiritual purpose.

Early in *De Profundis*, Wilde states "that the fool in the eyes of the gods and the fool in the eyes of man are very different." He continues, "The real fool, such as the gods mock and mar, is he who does not know himself." (Wilde, 511) Since the fool to the gods is one who lacks self-knowledge, it seems that Wilde is implying that the one who seeks to know himself is likely to be a fool to man. Wilde is very careful to avoid entangling self-realization with a moral requirement for goodness. At the root of his literary device, the transgressive paradox, resides a theory that one must know all sides of life to pass beyond their social definitions. He stresses the soul's ability to transform all that one does and experiences, even evil and suffering, into something right. "The supreme vice is shallowness. Everything that is realized is right." (Wilde, 511)

Wilde describes his friendship with Lord Alfred Douglas, "an unintellectual friendship, a friendship whose primary aim was not the creation and contemplation of beautiful things," for his fall from Art. (Wilde, 511) He blames his fall from the graces of proper society on his turning to that society to protect him— "The one disgraceful, unpardonable, and to all time contemptible action of my life was my allowing myself to be forced into appealing to Society for help and protection against [the Marquess of Queensberry]." (Wilde, 624) What most consider his true fall, making his name, as he says, "a low byword among low people," Wilde construes differently. (Wilde, 566) Wilde had used those acts hidden in the dark parts of London, as a means of stimulating his art and as a vantage point to look upon the Beautiful. He explains, "Tired of being on the heights I deliberately went to the depths in the search for new sensations. What the paradox was to me in the sphere of thought, perversity became to me in the sphere of passion."

Later in the work, he writes:

*People thought it dreadful of me to have entertained at dinner the evil things of life, and to have found pleasure in their company. But they, from the point of view through which I, as an artist in life, approached them, were delightfully suggestive and stimulating. It was like feasting with panthers. The danger was half the charm... They were to me the brightest of gilded snakes. Their poison was part of their perfection. (Wilde, 626)

The darker side of life, constructed by society as sinful, seems to have formed the grounding for Wilde's exalted privileging of Art and Beauty. He states this explicitly in this description of Dorian Gray, "There were moments when he looked on evil simply as a mode through which he could realize his conception of the beautiful." (Wilde, 305) These three examples appear to hark toward a higher, more spiritual, definition of antinomianism.

What distinguishes Wilde's theory, of experiencing beauty through evil, from Lord Alfred's appetite-driven search for pleasure and Dorian's fall toward degradation is that Wilde sees in it a path toward realization. Wilde places his faith not in a higher power, but rather in the ability of the soul to transform actions. For Wilde the Soul is the ultimate spiritual alembic. In Wilde's opposition to denial he argues that the Soul "can transform into noble moods of thought, and passions of high import, what in itself is base, cruel, and degrading. (Wilde, 586) This reflects itself in the refrain of De Profundis, "The supreme vice is shallowness. Everything that is realized is right." (Wilde, 511) In Wildean morality there exists no pure evil; nothing one does or undergoes can be inherently bad. One always stands in relation to one's actions and possesses the ability to shape and reshape their reflexive meaning. Like his near contemporary, Nietszche, Wilde levels out the constructed difference between good and evil and envisions a metaphysical space beyond their duality. In Wilde's cosmology the transformative capacity of the Soul is dependent on one's self-defined relation to one's actions. In De Profundis's refrain "realized" is the key word—"Everything realized is right." (emphasis added)

Wilde places no emphasis on what is traditionally considered good or what is oppositionally conceived as evil. In his eyes, he sees that God, or the gods, do not distinguish between the two. "The gods are strange," Wilde writes. "It is not of our vices only they make instruments to scourge us. They bring us to ruin through what in us is good, gentle, humane, loving." (Wilde, 537) This sentiment is echoed later in the same text, and with more certitude, "I must accept the fact that one is punished for the good as well as for the evil that one does." (Wilde, 587) Wilde's acknowledgement that one is punished equally for all actions, regardless of their conventional definitions, does not lead him to a conclusion of nihilism. Surprisingly, it brings him instead toward a heightened, spiritually centered transcendence of the good/evil binary paradigm. For Wilde the gods indiscriminate punishment is not so strange after all. He actually possessed "no doubt that it is quite right one should be [for] it helps one, or should help one, to realize both, and not to be too conceited about either." (Wilde, 587) Here again Wilde places his importance on the act of "realizing." It is through the act of realization that the Soul becomes capable of transforming actions into deeper significances—a level where all conditioning, such as social constructions of good and evil, are removed or transfigured. For Wilde, "one only realizes one's soul by getting rid of all alien passions, all acquired culture, and all external possessions be they good or evil." (Wilde, 602) Wilde places this power of realization and the Soul in a concept of subjectivity and the seemingly paradoxical requirement of repentance.

When describing his philosophical outlook, Wilde adopts a skeptic's philosophical stance toward the notion of subjectivity: "I said in *Dorian Gray* that the great sins of the world take place in the brain, but it is in the brain that everything takes place." (Wilde, 609) As Wilde continues he could easily be paraphrasing from the dialogues of Sextus Empiricus or one of his successors. He bases his subjectivity on Sextus' argument of the senses, as he continues:

> We know not that we do not see with the eye or hear with the ear. They are merely channels for the transmission, adequate or inadequate, of sense-impressions. It is in the brain that the poppy is red, that the apple is odorous, that the skylark sings. (Wilde, 609)

From his theory of subjectivity, he posits his quest after "realization" internally. He writes, "If I may not find its secret within myself, I shall never find it." (Wilde, 584) The relation between Wilde's subjective self and the Soul's transformative capabilities is self-definitional. For Wilde, the act of repenting, or "realizing," one's actions is essential.

Though Wilde does not place a judgment on particular actions, he does make an important differentiation between various modes of relating to one's own actions. He argues "that there is nothing wrong in what one does," but "there is something wrong in what one becomes." (Wilde, 584) Wilde centers spiritual importance on a differentiation between one who remains in a singular realm of degradation, a slave to his appetites and drives (such as Lord Alfred), and the person who repents, thereby recognizing or "realizing" his actions. This separation is the crux of Wildean morality. "Of course the sinner must repent," Wilde states in *De Profundis*, "simply because otherwise he would be unable to realize what he had done. The moment of repentance is the moment of initiation." (Wilde, 616) Wilde's trial taught him, in retrospect, that it is not important to have one's actions recounted to one, or to be forced to confess them. In Wilde's conception, these are all spiritually meaningless. It is not what is said that is important, but that one says it oneself. Wilde defines "man's highest moment" as "when he kneels in the dust, and beats his breast, and tells all the sins of his life." (Wilde, 641) This marries nicely to *De Profundis*'s signature couplet; shallow people are the fools of the gods and it is the process of realization that distinguishes right from wrong.

When one looks at Wilde's own analysis of his scandalous fall, during and after his trials, one finds a developed cosmology based on antinomianism, transcendence, repentance and realization. Wilde's antinomianism is constituted in a knowledge of "evil" and "sin" based on a sense of active exploration, rather than passive acceptance of one's actions. He feels that "there is not a single degradation of the body which I must not try and make into a spiritualizing of the soul." (Wilde,

585)   For Wilde amorality is both artistically and spiritually stimulating. Wilde relies on a subjective stance relative to good and evil, where antinomianism allows one to remove oneself from a position of moral conceit. Repentance is the fulcrum of Wilde's relativist morality. It is through the act of repentance that one realizes one's actions and can learn from them. Ultimately Wilde's philosophy is one of action—"people whose desire is solely for self-realization never know where they are going." (Wilde, 617) Wilde's understanding of antinomianism is based on a requirement to experience all sides of life, just as Wilde accepts the importance of suffering as well as pleasure, one must learn equality from good as well as evil.

References:

Belarion [James M. Martin]. (1988) "Liber LXIX: On Sexual Antinomianism." Abrasax 1(1): 17-25.
Wilde, Oscar. *The Portable Oscar Wilde*. Richard Addington and Stanley Weintraub, editors. New York: Penguin, 1981.

Over the Hills and Far Away
The One God Universe and Dreams of Space

A critical analysis of control and control structures rests at the core of William S. Burroughs writing from *Naked Lunch* to the channeled voice of the cut-up experiments to the wondering thoughts captured in his final journals. Burroughs associates Control,(the capital his) with a process of imprinting objectives onto an unsuspecting general population. Burroughs artfully illustrated the ways in which culture and the media are utilized to produce a crisis of contradiction in the viewer that acts to reinforce a position of safety.

Within his work, Burroughs outlines the objectives he perceived underlying Control's plan and exposes the ways in which Control reinforces the concept of the One God Universe (OGU) as a reality of contradiction that negates the dreaming subject. Burroughs argues that under the guise of the OGU, secular Control attempts to eradicate free thought by producing a world that is nonmagical, lacking both dreams and multiple gods. Burroughs theorizes that a universe predicated on a myth of multiple gods is necessary for one to dream. What is at stake in Control's attempts at maintaining a static OGU is a monopoly on Space, or immortality. Burroughs asserts that humanity is moving toward its own annihilation—both due to the implementation of the OGU and problems inherent in humanity itself as a species. Since Burroughs views the human condition as biologic dead end, the only choice humans have is to mutate or become extinct.

Burroughs argues Control masks itself behind the façade of the OGU, since, as he says, "all control systems claim to reflect the immutable laws of the universe."(Burroughs 1974, 43) The universe of the One God is a world of absolute control and "rationality." The OGU is created in opposition to what Burroughs views as a magical universe consisting of many gods and a privileging of the dream space. Burroughs proposes that the objectives of the OGU are the destruction of the magical universe through the destruction of humans as a dreaming subject. Burroughs writes that the OGU "is controlled predictable, dead."(Burroughs 1987, 59) For Burroughs, the OGU is a world of absolutes, where no one is allowed to be free to think for him/herself. Such a universe ensures its power through the destruction of critical communities, achieved by the processes of constructed contradiction and determined "safety." In a system such as this, free or critical thoughts pose a substantial threat to the stability of the Control systems. Burroughs writes in *The Western Lands*:

> So the One God, backed by secular power, is forced on the masses in the name of Islam, Christianity, the state, for all secular leaders want to be the One. To be intelligent or observant under such a blanket of oppression is to be 'subversive.'(Burroughs 1987, 111)

The motivation behind the OGU, then, must be the eradication of intelligence and free thought. The immediate objectives of Control, as manifested under the guise of the OGU, are, for Burroughs, the destruction of magic, as characterized in a mythic component to human existence, and the cutting off of dream space. Through these secondary objectives, Control seeks to ensure its primary goal of maintaining a monopoly over Space, variously characterized in Burroughs' work as immortality and evolution.

The world Burroughs presents in his writing is one filled with myth, magic and dream experience. The mythic components of Burroughs' writing can be read as an expansion of his personal cosmology of a subversive magical universe within a world under the control of the One God. He states, "The most basic concept of my writing is a belief in the magical universe, a universe of many gods, often in conflict. The paradox of an all-powerful, all-seeing God who nonetheless allows suffering, evil and death, does not arise."(Burroughs 1991, 266) Burroughs here is not merely resurrecting archaic forms of human religion—myths such as utopian matriarchies or primal androgyny. He is, instead, positing a cosmology, where mutation is a necessary corollary to existence that is in direct opposition to the OGU and the objectives of Control. If Control's manipulative power rests on a world of contradiction, then the OGU is the only acceptable cosmology. A magical universe, as Burroughs discusses, is a world without contradictions, since all seemingly inherent contradictions can be ascribed to the contendings of diverse gods, each with their own objectives and agendas. Burroughs perceives safety as an artificial construction on Control that cannot exist in a universe without a Supreme Being.

Burroughs, like his character Joe the Dead in *The Western Lands*, is engaged in a "desperate struggle" to alter the outcome of Control's deployments. His fiction is an attempt to track down "the Venusian agents of a conspiracy with very definite M.O. and objectives," i.e. Control. Joe understands these objectives to be the propagation of an "antimagical, authoritarian, dogmatic" universe. Control, therefore, is the "deadly enemy of those who are committed to the magical universe, spontaneous, unpredictable, alive." (Burroughs 1987, 53)

Burroughs views dreams as one of the most important components of human existence. Free thought cannot exist without them and, therefore, Control attempts to destroy the dreaming self through the imposition of the OGU. Burroughs describes dreams as a "biologic necessity."(Burroughs 1987, 181) Dreams are the only things that humans possess which are outside of the sphere of Control's influence. Being spontaneous and unpredictable, they are contrary to its dogmatic objectives. When one is free to dream, Control's power cannot be absolute:

> These magical visions are totally devoid of ordinary human emotion and experience. There is no friendship, love, hostility, fear or hate. There are no rules, no series of steps by which one can see. Consequently such visions are the enemy of any dogmatic system.(Burroughs 1987, 241)

Dreams remove one from the conscious assumption of the forces that seek to define and confine one. Existing outside of Control's direct conditioning, dreams can produce random constructions that have the potential to work to undermine Control's influence over the reactive mind. Dogmatic paradigms must, therefore, alienate people's connection to their dreams since as Burroughs argues:

> Any dogma must postulate the way, certain steps that will lead to the salvation, which the dogma promises. The Christian Heaven or pearly gates and singing angels, the Moslem paradise of eternal whores and plenty of water, the Communists' heaven of the worker state. Otherwise there is no place for the hierarchical structure that mediates between dogma and

man, that dictates *the* way.(Burroughs 1987, 242)

Dreams provide a space where random options and alternatives can arise, and this possibility represents a threatening field of uncertainty for Control. In Burroughs' fiction, Control's very survival is based on its ability to establish and re-present *the way*. Thus a world with multiple ways of seeing is one where Control cannot long retain power.

The importance of the mythic, magical universe, as manifested in dreams and multiple deities, is central to Burroughs' work. As cited above, Burroughs regularly casts this as a basic premise underlying his theories. For Burroughs, humanity, dreams and the magical (multi-god) universe are fundamentally connected. In *The Western Lands*, he writes, "You need your dreams, they are a biologic necessity and your lifeline to space, that is, to the state of God. To be one of the Shining Ones. The inference is that Gods are a biologic necessity. They are an integral part of Man."(Burroughs 1987, 181) Control prevails when dreams are policed, since dreams allow one to project a future which is intrinsically different from one's present condition. Burroughs argues that the lack of dreams, or the alienation of the dreaming subject, works to contain one in a mode of stasis where future projection and creative thought are impossible. Control's ultimate objective, produced through the elimination of dreams, is the continuation of its monopoly on space.

Space is a central metaphor within Burroughs' work, which he uses as a signifier of all that is at stake in the resistance struggle against Control. Burroughs argues that in order to progress, humans must make the jump into space—a jump he sees as characterized by a movement outside of the confines of the body. Space for Burroughs, is a goal that requires a basic mutation of human life. He sees dreams as representing our connection to a fantasy of space. Control in its attempts to destroy human's capacity to dream through the construction of the OGU, is, then for Burroughs, manifesting Control's need to keep all thoughts of space, and thereby evolution, out of the minds of the populace.

Dreams on their deepest levels are projections of a future. Burroughs argues that "the function of dreams is to train the being for future conditions." Burroughs sees this "future condition" as space, or a future in space. "The human artifact is biologically designed for space travel," he writes.(Burroughs 1985, 136) Throughout Burroughs' work, he quotes his friend Brions Gysin's mantra, "We are here to go" along with his corollary phrase "Over the hills and far away." These maxims establish their opinion that a movement into space is necessary for human survival. Burroughs writes in the introduction to *The Place of Dead Roads*:

> The only thing that could unite the planet is a unified space program [...] the earth becomes a space station and war is simply *out*, irrelevant, flatly insane in context of research centers, spaceports, and the exhilaration of working with people you like and respect toward an agreed-upon objective, an objective from which all workers will gain. Happiness is a byproduct of function. The planetary space station will give all participants an opportunity to function. (Burroughs 1983, iv)

Burroughs thus hypothesizes space, both the physical movement into space and the mutational step away from the body that he argues this implies, as the answer to human problems of happiness and survival. Indeed, he argues, it may well be the *only* answer possible.

For Burroughs, space provides a motivating force, a unifying goal, which is contradictory to the divisive objectives of Control. In his essay "Immortality," he writes, "Space exploration is the only goal worth striving for."(Burroughs 1985, 134) The exploration of space represents, in Burroughs' opinion, a goal that has the potential of unifying people in a way that excludes the current divides that characterize society. In his last interview, Gysin suggested that "the future is fairly predictable from a historical point of view, and it all points toward ecological, military, political, psychic ruin." Like Burroughs, he suggested that "from this planet, somebody, some people are going to try to escape."(Gysin 1982, 115)

Burroughs sees that the fundamental human drive is for immortality and he proposes that space is the means of obtaining immortality. Burroughs began the writing he termed his mythology of the Space Age with the material that became *The Wild Boys* and *The Port of Saints*. In a 1972 interview with Robert Palmer in *Rolling Stone*, Burroughs stated, "The future of writing is to see how close you can come to making it happen." (Palmer 1972, 53) Like his namesake William Seward Hall in *The Western Lands*, Burroughs is attempting in his fiction "to write his way out of death." (Burroughs 1987, 3) This process is the attempt at creating a modern mythology suited for humanity at the brink of the mutational breaking point. Burroughs holds the theory that the process of writing actually creates something real. This is expressed in his use of the Arabic work "mektoub," meaning "it is written," a word traditionally used to seal magical spells to insure their success. This word embodies Burroughs' belief that writing has the power to create, alter or transform actual events.

Burroughs texts then work at two levels. As signified by the word "mektoub" as a magical seal, his work reflects his understanding of the process of writing where the act is itself an evocation of future events. On another level, his texts work themselves as frontal assault on present conditions. His words are as potent a weapon as those wielded by the wild boy tribes in the book of the same name. The work of creating a mythology for the space age, represents, for Burroughs, the actual attempt at creating a new reality. In this manner Burroughs sets himself in opposition to the forces of Control, that seek to keep careful check on any possible movement into space. Burroughs argues that Control does this through its program of dream destruction as presented in the OGU film. Control is therefore an absolute enemy, which stands in the way of the realization of free people. Burroughs writes, "You will know your enemies by those who attempt to block you path. Vampiric monopolists would keep you in time like their cattle." (Burroughs 1985, 134) Control is a force that acts contrary to human evolution, blocking the means of moving beyond present human conditions.

Burroughs cites studies that have shown that a person deprived of REM, dream sleep, will eventually die as a result of the deprivation. (Burroughs 1985, 135) It follows then that the policies of Control, the destruction of dreams and magic, can be seen as nothing other than genocidal. The current situation which Burroughs terms "control madness" is the implementation of a policy of human extinction. In *The Western Lands* Burroughs compares his theory of Control to George Orwell's image of Big Brother:

> The program of the ruling elite in Orwell's *1984* was: 'A foot stamping on a human face forever!' This is naïve and optimistic. No species could survive for even a generation

under such a program. This is not a program of eternal, or even long-range dominance. It is clearly an *extermination program*. (Burroughs 1987, 59)

Burroughs is not optimistic about the outcome for humanity if we remain at our present stage of development. He views the world as a prison, one created by Control, for the purposes of its own preservation. Its means of survival, however, is like a cancer cell whose will to live ultimately results in the death of the host, humanity. Later in *The Western Lands*, Burroughs writes, "The door closes behind you, and you begin to know where you are. This planet is a Death Camp. . . the Second and Final Death." (Burroughs 1987, 254) This second death is "soul death," which begins with the destruction of humanity's capacity to dream.

For Burroughs, however, this movement toward extinction is not simply a product of Control. It is also a situation that has been the logical outcome of factors endemic to the human condition since its inception. "Thoughtful citizens are asking themselves if the whole human race wasn't a mistake from the starting gate," Burroughs wonders. (Burroughs 1985, 124) Burroughs' texts have often been attacked for being misogynistic. He himself stated in *The Job* that he felt that women "were a basic error, and the whole dualistic universe evolved from this error." (Burroughs 1974, 116) In the decade following this problematic statement, Burroughs' position on women softened—or, more appropriately, his position on humanity in general hardened. In "Women: A Biological Mistake?" Burroughs writes, "Women may well be a biological mistake; I said so in *The Job*. But so is almost everything else I see around here." (Burroughs 1985 p.124)

Burroughs asserts that the causes of our extinction as a race have been with us since the beginning. He argues that the virus of our destruction has always been an endemic element of being human—"we are all tainted with viral origins." In *Cities of the Red Night*, the virologist Dr. Peterson maintains that "the whole quality of human consciousness, as expressed in male and female, is basically a viral mechanism."(Burroughs 1981, 25) Burroughs often writes that we carry our own death with us; Dr. Peterson further suggests that humans, as a species, carry their own extinction with them. This extinction is based on a world of humans trapped in a state of binary existence. Burroughs wonders if "the separation of the sexes" isn't "an arbitrary device to perpetuate an unworkable arrangement."(Burroughs 1985, 126) Burroughs theorist Robin Lydenberg writes that Burroughs sees "the only possible relationship between two sexes defined in binary opposition to each other is one of conflict."(Lydenberg 1987, 162) For Burroughs this arena of perpetual conflict, enacted through and on the zone of the body, is one of the largest elements that stands between humanity and the potential to mutate into something with even half a chance of survival.

Burroughs suggests that these divisions have trapped humans in a state of neotany, arrested evolutionary development. He states that "I am advancing the theory that we were not designed to remain in our present state, any more than a tadpole is designed to remain a tadpole forever." (Burroughs 1985, 125) Elsewhere he writes that "it is inconceivable that Homo sapiens could last another thousand years in present form." (Burroughs 1987, 223) What he suggests is an evolutionary step away from binarism, which entails a movement out of the body itself. Dreams are the connection between humans and this mutational step, since they are, in Burroughs words, the "lifeline to space." Burroughs views this movement to space a requiring a leap in evolution, since the body cannot exist in space.

In *The Place of Dead Roads*, Burroughs' spokesman Kim
Carsons points out that the body's weight is inappropriate for
space travel. (Burroughs 1983, 41) In his interview with Jorgen
Ploog, Burroughs refers to studies that have shown that a body in
weightless environment quickly loses its skeletal structure. He
faults both modern immortality experiments and space
exploration procedures for attempting to continue the body
beyond its usefulness. Modern research meant to prolong life is
centered on the replacement of body parts, which Burroughs sees
as creating a world of tenuous immortality for the rich and
rotting death for the poor. Those who can afford parts receive a
new heart in a week, while "the poor wait in part lines for
diseased genitals, cancerous lungs, a cirrhotic liver." (Burroughs
1985, 128) For Burroughs, immortality experiments along these
lines are guaranteed to fail, since they don't address the problem
of death itself. Instead they treat the symptoms of death as
expressed in atrophy, cell death and decay. Death is a condition
of having a body, as Gysin observes in *The Last Museum*, "When
we are born, we start to die." (Gysin 1986, 181)

On the other hand, Burroughs sees that the modern space
program is inherently flawed, since it is premised on the objective
of carrying present human bodies into space. "The space
program is simply an attempt to transport our insoluble
temporal impasses somewhere else." (Burroughs 1985, 126)
Burroughs likens modern space exploration to a fish attempting
to bring an aquarium with him in his adjustment to land. "You
need entirely too much," Kim argues. "To begin with there is the
question of weight. A raw H.A. [human artifact] weighs around
170 pounds. This breathing, eating, excreting, sleeping,
dreaming H.A. must have an entire environment essential to
accommodate its awkward life processes encapsulated and
transported with it." (Burroughs 1983) Burroughs believes that
all these methods are destined to fail, as the body itself is a viral

host and these solutions do not cure the human virus. He argues that ultimately "a problem cannot be solved in terms of itself. The human problem cannot be solved in human terms." (Burroughs 1987, 23)

Despite the pessimism above, Burroughs' position is not nihilistic. In *The Western Lands* he writes, "The human condition is hopeless once you submit to it by being born... *almost.* There is one chance in a million and that is still good biologic odds." (Burroughs 1987, 299) This "almost" is a very important almost for Burroughs, since it contains his hope that the present state of human affairs can be transcended or moved beyond. For Burroughs, the chance may be slim in human standards, but these standards, most importantly characterized by the relational construct of time, become entirely relative when one is discussing issues in biologic/evolutionary terms. Again in *The Western Lands*, he speaks of the Death Camp, that is Earth, as "the last game." (Burroughs 1987, 254) Burroughs thus argues that humanity may be in the last stages of its own annihilation, but he does not see this process as completely inevitable.

Burroughs' texts are his attempts to create a new mythology formulated to assist humanity in thinking in the terms that will be required for its continuation. His writing is in a sense both a glimpse of hope and an austere warning of impending annihilation. In *The Western Lands*, he discusses a picture "of a balloon suddenly and unexpectedly soaring and some people still holding the ropes." Most of these people, he writes, "didn't have the survival IQ to *let go in time.*" Seconds later it's too late—the distance to the ground having become too great. Burroughs points out that they did not heed the "basic survival lesson" of letting go "when your Guardian tells you to let go." He continues by posing a question to the reader:

> Suppose you were holding one of those ropes?
> Would you have let go in time, which is, of
> course, at the first upward yank? I'll tell you
> something interesting. You would have a much
> better chance to let go in time now that you
> have read his paragraph than if you hadn't read
> it. Writing, if it is anything, is a word of
> warning... LET GO! (Burroughs 1987, 213)

The above quote demonstrates that Burroughs does hold out
some hope for humanity. His fiction is an artful word of
warning. His message: "Let Go!" Throughout his work,
Burroughs tells his readers to let go of that which traps them,
outmoded forms of human existence, and move into the as yet
unknown.

The mutational escape Burroughs proposes is intrinsically
connected to sex. "This is the space age," he writes in *The Wild
Boys*, "And sex movies must express the longing to escape from
flesh through sex. The way out is the way through." (Burroughs
1992, 82) For Burroughs, sex, male homosexual sex in particular,
becomes the means of beginning the break with Control. While
engaged in sexual acts, one of the wild boys envisions himself as a
celestial body. "I see myself streaking across the sky line a star to
leave the earth forever. What holds me back? It is the bargain by
which I am here at all. The bargain is this body that holds me
here." (Burroughs 1992, 102) Space is again depicted as
requiring a move away from the body, a vision which begins in
sexual machinations.

For Burroughs the body itself forms the greatest obstacle to
human evolution. Burroughs' principle criticism of Egyptian
immortality experiments is that they included a reliance on the
corpse, the mummy, for one's survival in the afterlife. The
human flesh is regularly characterized as a prison within his

writing. When asked if a person could be truly free in the modern world, he answered "that free men don't exist on this planet at this time, because they don't exist in human bodies, by the mere fact of being in a human body you're controlled by all sorts of biologic and environmental necessities." (Burroughs 1974, 37)

In Burroughs' work, the moment of homosexual union represents the beginnings of a new imagining. In *The Place of Dead Roads*, he writes, "Sex forms the matrix of a dualistic and therefore solid and real universe. It is possible to resolve the dualistic conflict in a sex act, where dualism need not exist." (Burroughs 1983, 172) Thus, male same-sex desire represents the means of reaching a state beyond binary existence—a state where biologic mutation is conceivable. It stands in direct opposition to the sexual and cultural imperatives enforced by Control. Simply put, it is ill-defined territory.

The sex in Burroughs' fiction, especially as exhibited in *The Wild Boys* and *Port of Saints*, is the sex of young males—who are beginning the processes of sexual identity construction. When he speaks of the desire to "escape from flesh through sex" and the shift in "sex movies" that this entails, he follows with an example. Johnny and Mark are wild boy agents who "become astronauts playing the part of American married idiots," i.e. the traditional middle American, heterosexual, married couple. They remain thus until months after take-off, at which point they disconnect radio contact with Earth. At this point, Burroughs describes how "the sex scenes of their adolescence are seen as image dust in space through which they pass to other planets." (Burroughs 1992, 82-3) This routine, as Burroughs called his fictional sequences, then shatters with the images of their sexual memories lifted from their 1920's childhoods. "Lawn sprinklers," "classrooms," "frogs in 1920 roads" and "a naked boy hugging his knees sunlight in pubic hairs" are all resurrected in the explosion of space sexuality. Burroughs appears to view the personal sexual mememic landscape as a film written in early adolescence. This "sex film" then becomes in space, and his texts, a catalog of individual metaphor. Within his work, sex becomes the present-time invocation of these personal sexual encodings of history and memory.

This scene suddenly shifts from these loosely connected, isolated images to "a suburban room afternoon light bleakly clear." (Burroughs 1992, 83) Mark says he heard that Johnny "got laid" and Johnny replies that it was a prostitute "down on Westminster Place." He admits that since that encounter his crotch has itched. Mark orders Johnny to drop his pants and begins inspecting his genitals. During the process Johnny gets an erection: "Christ it is happening he can't stop it." The focus then shifts to fragments of solitary sexual conditions with "sad muscle magazines over the florist shop pants down green snakes under rusty iron in the vacant lot the old family soap opera look of yellow hair stirs in September." (Burroughs 1992, 84-5) The story continues to shift with brief glimpses of past sexual relations and fantasies. "The film stops..." and shifts again—moves to Mexico City, London and St. Louis—until "the film stops in his eyes" at the point of orgasm:

> A shooting star silence floats down on falling leaves and blood spit the smell of decay shredded to dust and memories pieces of legs and cocks and assholes drifting fragments in sunlight ass hairs spread on the bed dust of young hand fading flickering thighs and buttocks smell of young nights. (Burroughs 1992, 85)

Sex is a catharsis formed by "drifting fragments" of image and memory; each act is the product of all that has gone before. Burroughs presents homosexual intercourse as particulate matter in the light projection of Control's film, the OGU. In the case of Johnny and Mark, "the sex scenes of their adolescence are seen as image dust in space through which they pass." (Burroughs 1992, 83) As dust in the light, it both obscures and refuses the image on screen thus breaking down Control's monopoly on space.

In Burroughs' novels sex between boys begins the process of space exploration, but in his theories humans are actually incapable of envisioning the full scope of the movement into space. In his essay "Immortality" Burroughs suggests, "Mutation involves changes that are literally unimaginable from the perspective of the future mutant." (Burroughs 1985, 135) Elsewhere Burroughs compares the evolutionary step he projects for humans with the step made by fish onto land. As the great seas, which once covered much of the Earth, began to recede, certain fish developed rudimentary lungs. These they used to move over land from one body of water to another. At some point they lost the use of their gills and were forced to remain on land. In this way, in their search for water, they found land. Burroughs suggests that the human jump may be made in much the same way. "The astronaut is not looking for space; he is looking for more *time*—that is equating space with time... Like the walking fish, looking for more time we may find space instead, and then find there is no way back." (Burroughs 1985, 126)

The changes required in Burroughs' vision of an evolutionary shift are not conceivable to present humans. For Burroughs, space will involve taking "a step into the unknown, a step that no human being has ever taken before." (Burroughs 1985, 135) Just as the fish could not envision a world of gravity, Burroughs argues, humans are unable to conceive of a life in weightlessness. Also like the fish who can never return to water, humans once in space will never be able to reverse the evolutionary process. "Evolution," Burroughs points out, "would seem to be a one-way street." (Burroughs 1985, 125)

In one of his last interviews, mythologist Joseph Campbell was asked, "Why should we care about myths? What do they have to do with life?" His reply stressed the importance of myth as a constitutive component for understanding daily experience. Campbell blamed the nihilism and lack of direction evidenced within modern society on the loss of myth. He spoke of myths, "stories," as once providing ever-present interpretive paradigms with which to access experience. "When the story is in your mind," he said, "then you see its relevance to something happening in your life." (Campbell 1988, 4) For Campbell the lack of modern mythologies has created an environment where one has no choice but voice their lives as purposeless and random—a world without meaning or motivation. Burroughs continued importance is not as a erotic writer or literary experimenter, but as a creator of postmodern myths. Burroughs routines are most invigorating when they work as stories capable of providing paradigms that make lived experience accessible and intelligible. Burroughs often spoke of his work as being the creation of a mythology—"a mythology for the space age."

References:

Burroughs, William S. *Cities of the Red Night.* New York: Holt, Rinehart, Winston, 1981.

_____. "Immortality." In *The Adding Machine: Collected Essays.* London: John Calder Press, 1985.

_____. *The Job.* New York: Penguin, 1974.

_____. "My Purpose Is to Write for the Space Age." In *William S. Burroughs at the Front: Critical Reception, 1959-1989,* edited by Jennie Skerl and Robin Lydenberg. Carbondale, IL: Southern Illinois University Press, 1991.

_____. *The Place of Dead Roads.* New York: Holt, Winhart & Winston, 1983.

_____. *The Western Lands.* New York: Penguin, 1987.

_____. *The Wild Boys.* New York: Grove, 1992.

_____. "Women: A Biological Mistake?" In *The Adding Machine.* London: John Calder Press, 1985.

Campbell, Joseph. *The Power of Myth.* New York: Doubleday, 1988.

Gysin, Brion. *Here to Go: Planet R-101.* London: Quartet Books, 1982.

_____. *The Last Museum.* New York: Grove, 1986.

Lydenberg, Robin. *Word Cultures: Literary Form and Theory in the Radical Writings of William S. Burroughs.* Urbana, IL: University of Illinois, 1987.

Palmer, Robert. "William Burroughs." *Rolling Stone* 1972, 48-53.

Burroughs-ian Gnosticism
In His Own Words

Burroughs explicitly linked his philosophy to Manichaeism—a third century Persian religion. Manichaeism was founded by a young preacher, Mani in the early to mid third century of the Common Era. Mani was heavily influenced by Gnostic Christianity—calling himself a "disciple of Christ" and the "Paraclete," or biblical healer. The Manichaens incorporated many existing belief systems into their world-view. From Mandeanism and Gnosticism, they appropriated a strongly held belief in cosmic dualism. It is in this sense that Burroughs links his philosophy to that of the third century religion. Burroughs' fiction and nonfiction work (as the two are not readily separable) are best characterized as mythology. He himself described his effort as writing a mythology for the space age. His philosophy has many parallels to early Gnosticism that go beyond this simple invocation of Manichaeism dualism.

Burroughs first encountered the concept of the Johnson Family while still a boy reading the book *You Can't Win* by Jack Black. First published in the 1920's Black's autobiographical account of hobo life was immensely popular in its day. Burroughs describes the Johnsons in *The Place of Dead Roads*:

> 'The Johnson Family' was a turn-of-the-century expression to designate good bums and thieves. It was elaborated into a code of conduct. A Johnson honors his obligations. His word is good and he is a good man to do business with. A Johnson minds his own business. He is not a snoopy, self-righteous, trouble-making person.

A Johnson will give help when help is needed. He will not stand by while someone is drowning or trapped under a burning car.[1]

In his essay "The Johnson Family," Burroughs elaborates on the Johnsons' philosophical placement within his mythic system—explicitly linked them to Manichaeistic dualism:

> The Johnson family formulates a Manachean position where good and evil are in conflict and the outcome is at this point uncertain. It is *not* an eternal conflict since one or the other must win a final victory.[2]

In contrast to the honorable world of hobos and criminals, Burroughs describes a type of person known simply as a 'Shit.' Unlike the Johnsons, Shits are obsessed with minding other's business. They are the town busy body, the preacher, the lawman. Shits are incapable of taking the honorable road of each-to-his-own. Burroughs describes the situation in his essay "My Own Business" thus:

> This world would be a pretty easy and pleasant place to live in if everybody could just mind his own business and let others do the same. But a wise old black faggot said to me years ago: 'Some people are shits, darling.' I was never able to forget it.[3]

---

[1] *The Place of Dead Roads*, iv.
[2] "The Johnson Family," 75-76.
[3] "My Own Business," 15.

In Burroughs' mythology, the world is one of conflict between the Johnsons and the Shits. A Shit is one who is obsessively sure of his own position at the cost of all other vantages. Burroughs describes Shits as incapable of minding "their own business, because they have no business of their own to mind, any more than a small pox virus has."[4] This is more than an offhanded analogy. For Burroughs, Shits are, in actuality, virus occupied hosts—chronically infected by what he terms the Right virus. "The mark of a basic Shit," Burroughs reminds us, "is that he has to be *right*."[5]

The war between the Johnsons and the Shits is epic and runs throughout Burroughs' writing. Though of immense proportions, like the Gnostic battle between good and evil, the cosmic war is not figured across eternity. It has an end and, for Burroughs, that end is imaginable. It does not come without immense conflict, however. Burroughs tells his reader, "The people in power will not disappear voluntarily."[6] There is no turning back, once the battle is met. "Once you take up arms against a bunch of shits there is no way back. Lay down your arms and they will kill you."[7] "Hell hath no more vociferous fury than an endangered parasite."[8] But remember, also: "The wild boys take no prisoners."[9]

In discussing his mythology, Burroughs describes a classic Catch-22: "He who opposes force with counterforce alone forms that which he opposes and is formed by it... On the other hand he who does not resist force that enslaves and exterminates will

---

[4] Ibid, 16.
[5] Ibid, 16.
[6] *The Job*, 74.
[7] "The Johnson Family," 77.
[8] "My Own Business," 16.
[9] *The Wild Boys*, 148.

be enslaved and exterminated."[10] Burroughs' work begs the question, how does one resist the forces rallied against one without taking on the viral-taint of that opposing force. To imagine a permanent solution proves an all too easy flirtation. In his essay "My Own Business," Burroughs writes that "one is tempted to seek a total solution to the problem: Mass Assassination Day."[11]

In *The Place of Dead Roads* Burroughs imagines a scenario where the Johnson Family organizes into armed squads that fan out to hunt those infected with the right virus. Some Johnsons are assigned as "Shit Spotters" whose task it is to move out into cities and small towns across the country recording those who exhibit virus occupied behaviors. Acting upon the intelligence thus gathered, sharp shooters follow-up eliminating the detected Shits.[12] Ultimately Burroughs tempers his fantasy. He observes, "Probably the most effective tactic is to alter the conditions on which the virus subsists."[13]

In truth, indifference will prove the end of the Shit problem. "Conditions change, and the virus guise is ignored and forgotten."[14] Burroughs envisions the Shit position obsoleted by changes in normative culture:

> This trend toward sanity has brought the last-ditch dedicated shits out into the open, screaming with rage. Victimless crime, the assumption that what a citizen does in the privacy of his own dwelling is nonetheless

---

[10] *The Job*, 100.
[11] "My Own Business," 17.
[12] *The Place of Dead Roads*, 155-6.
[13] "My Own Business," 18.
[14] Ibid, 18.

someone else's business and therefore subject to denunciation and punishment is the very lifeline of the *right* virus. Cutting off this air line would have the same action as interferon, which blocks the oxygen from certain virus strains.[15]

And slowly the Shits are ignored into a dull, dated celluloid sunset.

Like many of the early Gnostics, Burroughs believed that humanity was tainted from birth by outside elements. Within his writing, all humanity is infected from the outset. "We are all tainted with viral origins."[16] "[T]he whole quality of human consciousness, as expressed in male and female, is basically a viral mechanism."[17] He posits a theory of 'inverse evolution.' Also like the early Gnostics, Burroughs cosmology contains a parallel to the Fall. He suggests that "Man did not rise out of the animal state, he was shoved down to be an animal to be animals to be a body to be bodies by the infamous Fifth Columnists."[18]

Due to this viral mechanism, the cosmic conflict is configured within the domain of our own bodies. Burroughs wonders if "the separation of the sexes" isn't "an arbitrary device to perpetuate an unworkable arrangement."[19] Theorist Robin Lydenberg writes that Burroughs sees "the only possible relationship between two sexes defined in binary opposition to each other is one of conflict."[20] For Burroughs this arena of

---

[15] Ibid, 16.
[16] *Cities of the Red Night*, 25.
[17] Ibid, 25.
[18] *Port of Saints*, 105.
[19] "Women: A Biological Mistake?" 126.
[20] Lydenberg, 162.

perpetual conflict, enacted through and on the zone of the body, is one of the largest elements standing between humanity and the potential to mutate into something with even the slightest chance of survival. In *The Wild Boys*, Burroughs writes, "What holds me back? It is the bargain by which I am here at all. The bargain is this body that holds me here."[21]

Lydenberg continues her analysis:

> Burroughs attributes the polarization of reproductive energy to structures of binary opposition which set two incompatible sexes in perpetual conflict, channeling the flow of creative energy into a parasitic economy based on power and property.[22]

Burroughs suggests that this division has trapped humans in a state of neotany, arrested evolution (A.E.). He writes, "I am advancing the theory that we were not designed to remain in our present state, any more than a tadpole is designed to remain a tadpole forever."[23] Within his mythology, there is very little hope that humanity will make it out. The necessary mutation that might spur us back onto the evolutionary path may prove unattainable. Bleakly, he writes in *The Western Lands*:

> Man is indeed the final product. Not because homo sap is the apogee of perfection, before which God himself gasps in awe—"I can do nothing more!"—but because Man is an unsuccessful experiment, caught in a biologic

---

21 *The Wild Boys*, 103.
22 Lydenberg, 156.
23 "Women: A Bioloogical Mistake?" 125.

dead   end   and   inexorably   headed   for
extinction.[24]

And...

It is inconceivable that Homo sapiens could last
another thousand years in present form.[25]

Burroughs did believe in reincarnation. In interviews, he described it as a 'given.' "I have written [in *The Place of Dead Roads*], Kim had never doubted the existence of gods or the possibility of an after-life and Kim is my alter ego and spokesman like Larry Speaks." Birth, however, "is something to be avoided... the worst thing that could happen."[26] For Burroughs, it seems, the real trick is not to be born in the first place. "The human condition is hopeless once you submit to it by being born...*almost*. There is one chance in a million and that is still good biologic odds."[27] *Almost*, and the slightest glimmer creeps in.

As Burroughs sees it, the only escape possible for humanity is biologic mutation. This is nothing less than an evolutionary jump into the unknown—a complete and total movement away from what one knows as human. Burroughs writes in *The Western Lands*: "A problem cannot be solved in terms of itself. The human problem cannot be solved in human terms."[28] And in his essay "Immortality" he warns us "Mutation involves changes that are literally unimaginable from the perspective of

---

[24] *The Western Lands*, 41.
[25] Ibid, 223.
[26] Maeck.
[27] *The Western Lands*, 199.
[28] *The Western Lands*, 27.

the future mutant."[29] The mutation he envisions represents "A step into the unknown, a step that no human being has ever taken before."[30] Once one takes the step there will be no turning back. "Evolution would seem to be a one-way street."[31]

The Gnostics believed that the world was created by an evil being, the Demiurge known as IALDABOATH. This being was an abortive creation of Sophia, the embodiment of cosmic wisdom, formed when she took creation unto herself without the knowledge of the non-dual prime-entity. The Demiurge is unaware of his own origin and thinks of himself as the one and only GOD of his creation. One finds strong parallels to this cosmology within Burroughs mythos. The world is actually at the mercy of an ephemeral, but all too real, force Burroughs calls simply 'Control.' In *The Western Lands* he writes, "We are controlled by the Powers. Not one, but many, and often in conflict. It is all part of some Power Plan."[32]

Burroughs views the modern period as characterized by an insidious display of Control's raw authority unprecedented in history. Within his fiction, he depicts a world of "control madness," which is predicated on the modern wholesale presentation of image and word, constructed through careful manipulation of the media, the state, religion and advertising. For Burroughs, the modern world is characterized by "random elements" that have come to power through accidental conditions. Modern leaders are the "unwitting" agents of control. Thus, "the iron-willed dictator is a thing of the past."[33]

---

[29] "Immortality," 135.
[30] Ibid, 135.
[31] "Women: A Biological Mistake?" 125.
[32] *The Western Lands*, 188.
[33] "No more Stalins, no more Hitlers."

In Burroughs' work the modern world is a horrific terrain of constructed knowledge—organically directed toward the eradication of all free thought. Contrasting this modern manifestation of Control with its historical antecedents, Burroughs writes, "To confuse this old-style power with the manifestation of control madness we see now on this planet is to confuse a disappearing wart with an exploding cancer."[34]

Just like humanity's precarious position in a state of neotany, Burroughs sees that the presence of Control is not perpetual. Again the cosmic conflict is not eternal. For Burroughs, humanity is in "the last game."[35] In *The Western Lands*, Burroughs writes of Control's ultimate plan:

> The program of the ruling elite in Orwell's *1984* was: 'A foot stamping on a human face forever!' This is naïve and optimistic. No species could survive for even a generation under such a program. This is not a program of eternal, or even long-range dominance. It is clearly an *extermination program*.[36]

Finally...

> The door closes behind you, and you begin to know where you are. This planet is a Death Camp... the Second and Final Death.[37]

Just like the evil God of the Gnostics, Burroughs' concept of Control masquerades as the axiomatic, natural laws of the

---

[34] *The Job*, 60.
[35] *The Western Lands*, 254.
[36] Ibid, 59.
[37] Ibid, 254.

Cosmos. In *The Job*, Burroughs notes, "All control systems claim to reflect the immutable laws of the universe."[38] Control wears the mask of religion, temporal law enforcement, the righteous politician. The greatest tactic of Control represented within Burroughs' work is that of the One God Universe (OGU):

> Consider the One God Universe: OGU. The spirit recoils in horror from such a deadly impasse. He is all-powerful and all-knowing. Because He can do everything, He can do nothing, since the act of doing demands opposition. He knows everything, so there is nothing for him to learn. He can't go anywhere, since He is already fucking everywhere, like cowshit in Calcutta.
>
> The OGU is a pre-recorded universe of which He is the recorder. It's a flat, thermodynamic universe, since it has no friction by definition. So He invents friction and conflict, pain, fear, sickness, famine, war, old age and Death.[39]

Compare this One God with the Gnostic conception of the Demiurge.

For Burroughs, the notion of One God is simply a method employed by Control. It is akin to the Mayan calendar system in which each moment was predictable as it was pre-recorded. No matter the holy book or the messenger, the notion of One God proves little more than a palliative film shown to prisoners on Death Row. In such a system, resistance is a dangerous move:

---

[38] *The Job*, 43.
[39] *The Western Lands*, 113.

> So the One God, backed by secular power, is
> forced on the masses in the name of Islam
> Christianity, the state, for all secular leaders
> want to be the One.   To be intelligent or
> observant under such a blanket of oppression is
> to be 'subversive.'[40]

While describing his concept of the One God Universe,
Burroughs outlines his contrasting view of a Magical Universe.
"The most basic concept of my writing," he writes, "is a belief in
the magical universe, a universe of many gods, often in conflict.
The paradox of an all-powerful, all-seeing God who nonetheless
allows suffering, evil, and death, does not arise."[41]   Like the
Gnostics, Burroughs held the belief that through contact with
this magical universe, one could break free of the confines of the
One God Universe, thus moving outside the grasp of Control.
Burroughs image of the Garden of Alamout is analogous to the
way the Gnostics employed the vision of the Kingdom.   A
glimpse of either is transformative—a Gnostic vision taking one
above the realm of the evil creator god, the Demiurge or Control.
For Burroughs, through dream visions, one becomes a god:

> You need your dreams, they are a biologic
> necessity and your lifeline to space, that is, to
> the state of God.   To be one of the Shining
> Ones. The inference is that Gods are a biologic
> necessity. They are an integral part of Man.[42]

Burroughs appropriates the Egyptian notion of an after life,
a paradise known as 'The Western Lands.' Unlike the Christian

---

[40] Ibid, 111.
[41] "My Purpose Is to Write for the Space Age," 268.
[42] *The Western Lands*, 181.

or Islamic heavens, entry to the Western Lands is by no means guaranteed through actions within one's life. It does, in fact, lie at the end of a dangerous journey—one in which portions of the soul struggle to reach immortality. Burroughs asks his readers to compare his mythological description of the Western Lands with the shoddy images of paradise promised by the proponents of the One God Universe:

> Look at their Western Lands. What do they look like? The houses and gardens of a rich man. Is this all the Gods can offer?[43]

> Well, I say then it is time for new Gods who do not offer such paltry bribes. It is dangerous to think such things. It is very dangerous to live, my friend, and few survive it. And one does not survive by shunning danger, when we have a universe to win and absolutely nothing to lose. It is already lost.[44]

In *The Place of Dead Roads*, he tells us unequivocally: "This is no vague eternal heaven for the righteous. This is an actual place at the end of a very dangerous road."[45]

Burroughs sees that historically "the Gods held all their keys and admitted only favored mortals."[46] This was the case in the Egyptian system, described in their *Book of the Dead*, where gods and demons had to be placated, propitiated and answered with their sacred names throughout the nearly impossible journey across the wasteland between earthly life and the Western Lands.

---

[43] Ibid, 184.
[44] Ibid, 184
[45] *The Place of Dead* Roads, 171.
[46] Ibid, 171.

Like the Gnostics, Burroughs' mythology proposes, no matter how remotely, the possibility that one may discover the hidden key (gnosis) that opens the secret wisdom represented by the Western Lands. Again like the Gnostics, Burroughs understood that this metaphorical key unlocked not just one revelation, but everything in an instant. This is the vision of the Kingdom conveyed by Jesus, or the Illuminator, in the Gnostic scriptures. Burroughs writes, "Once you find the key, there are not just one garden but many gardens, an infinite number."[47]

Throughout his own Book of the Dead, Burroughs frequently warns us of the treacherous nature of the journey:

> The road to the Western Lands is by definition the most dangerous road in the world, for it is a journey beyond Death, beyond the basic God standard of Fear and Danger. It is the most heavily guarded road in the world, for it gives access to the gift that supersedes all other gifts: Immortality.[48]

And...

> The Road to the Western Lands is devious, unpredictable. Today's easy passage may be tomorrow's death trap. The obvious road is almost always a fool's road, and beware the Middle Roads, the roads of moderation, common sense and careful planning. However,

---

[47] Ibid, 171.
[48] *The Western Lands*, 124.

there is a time for planning, moderation and common sense.[49]

Within his mythology, Burroughs appears to suggest that the end is all but a given. The final trains are moving inexorably toward the gates of the camp. There are many ways in, but no exit. For humanity, stuck for millennia just moments before mutation, there seems no escape for the soul. No windows give sight of the future, but the smell of the charnel fires are a dead give-away. Perhaps it is too late and we have already moved past the evolutionary point of no-return—already dinosaurs in dénouement. But, with Burroughs, there is always an *almost*.

Burroughs' close friend and collaborator Brion Gysin reminds us: "The outbreak of Armegeddon made things infinitely more complicated but all that much more urgent."[50]

---

[49] Ibid, 151.
[50] Gysin, 105.

References:

Burroughs, William S. *Cities of the Red Night.* New York: Holt, Rinehart and Winston, 1981.

_____. "Immortality," in *The Adding Machine: Collected Essays.* London: John Calder Publishers, 1985, 127-136.

_____. *The Job.* New York: Penguin, 1974.

_____. "The Johnson Family," in *The Adding Machine: Collected Essays.* London: John Calder Publishers, 1985, 74-7.

_____. "My Own Business," in *The Adding Machine: Collected Essays.* London: John Calder Publishers, 1985, 15-8.

_____. "My Purpose is to Write For the Space Age," in *William S. Burroughs at the Front: Critical Reception, 1959-1989*, Jennie Skerl and Robin Lydenberg, eds. Carbondale, IL: Southern Illinois University Press, 1991.

_____. "No more Stalins, no more Hitlers" on *Dead City Radio* (sound recording), New York: Island Records, 1990.

_____. *The Place of Dead Roads.* New York: Holt, Rinehart and Winston, 1983.

_____. *Port of Saints.* Berkeley, CA: Blue Wind Press, 1980.

_____. *The Western Lands.* New York: Penguin, 1987.

_____. *The Wild Boys: A Book of the Dead.* New York: Grove, 1978.

_____. "Women: A Biological Mistake?" in *The Adding Machine: Collected Essays.* London: John Calder Publishers, 1985, 124-6.

Gysin, Brion. *The Last Museum.* New York: Grove, 1986.

Lydenberg, Robin. Word Cultures: Literary Form and Theory in the Radical Writings of William S. Burroughs. New York: Routledge, 1988.

Maeck, Klaus. *William S. Burroughs: Commissioner of Sewers.* New York: Mytic Fire Video, 1986.

"I sent you a postcard today"

I sent you a postcard today
words quickly scribbled
on a post office desk
I've been working on your portrait
something to occupy the time
it made me think of you
haven't seen you in over a year
the summer before last
you stopped by twice

If not now, when?
If not here, where?

I have heard many Buddhist teachers remark that humans live as if they will live 500 years, while, in actuality, they could die tomorrow. You'll see this evidenced just by looking at those around you; you'll see this evidenced just by looking at yourself and the decisions that you make in each moment. We put off the big stuff to tomorrow, to get the little stuff done today. People all too often make choices sacrificing their needs in the now, for their projected future—trading youth, family, spiritual life for hours of overtime and the envisioned future retirement, the sandy beach and handsome cabana boy.

This is evidence of the dichotomy Buddhists refer to as the 'two truths' conventional reality and ultimate reality. The conventional is that we live today for a better tomorrow; the relative is that tomorrow is never guaranteed. With a recent death in my immediate family, this contrast has been brought painfully home. When brought into sharp contrast, the choices that most of us make day-to-day, moment-to-moment, look amazingly (and ironically) shortsighted. You could die tomorrow. Sometimes that can be a joyous and empowering revelation. Keep that in your mind for just twenty-four hours and see how it nuances your decisions throughout the day.

I can tell you from my recent experience, most people think you're nuts when you walk around with a shit-eating grin telling them that they could die tomorrow.

Another teaching that Buddhists like to use is the auspiciousness of one's current birth. In the simplest terms, if you are reading this (or any other spiritual material), or listening to a master, Vaishnava saint, spiritual friend, etc., than you are in the best place you can be for your spirituality Right Now.

As Buddhist teachers love to remind one, just think how unlikely your birth was. Think how vast the Universe is... how many galaxies there are... how many solar systems in each... how many planets in each solar system. And you were lucky enough to be born on a planet fortunate enough to have a Buddha incarnate. What's the Vegas odds on that?

Think how many beings there are on just this little planet Earth—not just human beings, but animals, bird, fish and insects, even protozoa and bacteria. Add to that the other realms (at least within the Buddhist worldview) of Gods, demi-gods, ghosts... Well, you get the point. There's a whole hell of a lot of beings you could have been born as and being born human makes you best positioned to get real spiritual work done.

While animal, demons, and ghosts are obviously not the best states to be in, gods and demi-gods, though seemingly better births, are also not considered helpful for spiritual progress. To Buddhists, the higher realms of gods and demi-gods, where all desires are satiated, provide no impetus for spiritual practice. A certain amount of resistance is necessary for one to look toward spiritual study and contemplative practice. Human birth represents the most auspicious balance of resistance and fulfillment—a potential for friction from gain and loss.

So consider how fortunate we are to have this improbable birth on such a planet affording such potential with spiritual teachers and scriptural wisdom. Of all human beings currently incarnated on this planet, think how few actually have the fine balance of friction, fulfillment and intellect to manifest an interest in spiritual life. Of these spiritually interested individuals, not all gather the means and motivation to actively pursue their course of interest. Of these few motivated individuals, only a small number have the fortunate convergence of circumstance to come into contact with a spiritual teacher, sacred scripture or divine friend. Of these few fortunate ones, even fewer have sufficient capacity of attention to listen and receive what is being offered. Of the few who do listen, only a very small percentage actually apply what they hear to their practice towards developing a spiritual life.

The Vegas odds are off the board at this point.

Just think for one moment on the nearly infinite improbability of you reading this—well, maybe not this, but the other material in this book—and having the interest to check it out.

I have heard Geshe Lobzang Tsetan comment that it is simply a matter of respect not to squander this amazing opportunity afforded one—whether we individually consider it a gift of the Supreme Personality of Godhead, the Universe or, simply, random circumstance.

It never hurts one's spiritual development to take a step back and look at the decisions we are making today not in terms of how they affect tomorrow, planning for our idyllic future, but rather how they affect, or what they cost, the present moment. We live our lives as if we will live forever, while the opposite is the only guarantee we have. The only thing one really can say for sure is that our decisions affect us now, allowing that they may, depending on course, nuance our future. There is a paradoxical Zen teaching that, like a John Lennon song, karma is instant. The decisions one makes now affect one right now.

Living in the moment does not mean living for the moment. "Be Here Now" only means that you're not there then.

"When you're so committed to the future, it's real easy to let your life right now to turn to shit" Brad Warner in *Hardcore Zen*

An Asceticism of Being:
Foucault & the Epistemology of Self, Post Modernity

I pay homage to the guru, the divine friend,
Mahatma Guru Shri Paramahansa Shivaji

The mental focus of the past several decades, in the West, has been marked by a heightened quest for essence, sometimes internal sometimes external—a quest always figured within the reputably "private" and, paradoxically, articulated in the unquestionably public. Identity politics, the contrasting concurrent philosophy of postmodernism, arose as a reaction to the egalitarian prerogatives of the post-60's humanist agenda and the latter's attempts to eradicate the social ills of racism, homophobia, heterosexism, anti-Semitism, etc. by erasing difference. This trend in the political has been mirrored by an even more pervasive, and persuasive, movement in the, at times, overlapping areas of religion and spirituality. This mirroring has proved all the more pronounced for its easy collusion with the "soul-searching" inherent in the polemic of historic religiosity. In general, spirituality in the West has been transfigured historically in terms of an heroic quest for the soul and through this knowledge obtaining a closeness to God. In the twentieth century this has been secularized into a search for the soul in order to gain a closeness to Self. The loosely connected grouping of overlapping mystical schemas and recycled pop self-improvements generally termed the New Age Movement typifies this essentialized spiritual quest.

To know 'who we are' has become increasingly synonymous with spirituality. Since the earliest roots of Christian mysticism knowing has been posited as *the* means for achieving a closeness to God. French post-structuralist philosopher Michel Foucault pointed out that the entire process was shaped around a search for increased "individualization." "We try to seize what's at the bottom of the soul of the individual," he said. "'Tell me who you are', there is the spirituality of Christianity." (Foucault, "Michel Foucault and Zen" 1999, 112) This internal, personal questing for the "secret" within is the philosopher's stone of the Western metaphysical alchemist. This quest relies on two presumptive assertions: it both reifies the soul and elevates it to the ultimate embodiment of truth. It remains almost unthinkable to question if there is a subjective self and that subjectivity should itself be the object of knowledge. Foucault artfully problematized both these, seemingly immutable, assertions. In his histories of the clinic, the criminal system, the epistemology of knowledge and sexuality, Foucault was examining the role of subjectivity and its relation to both knowledge and power. Foucault argued that modern man finds himself in an "ambiguous position as an object of knowledge and as a subject that knows." (Foucault 1970, 312) Outlining Foucault's position Daniel Palmer observes "for Foucault, such attempts to constitute individuals as objects of their own knowledge is both theoretically dubious and socially perilous." (Palmer, 1998 408)

The religious expression of Western Judeo-Christian culture has been marked by its imputation of and relation to the Soul. That each human being has a soul is the axiom at the central to its dogmas, while the redemption of the soul is the steel that forms the girders of its framework. The soul is something to be cared for—saved, purged, cleansed and protected in a circular movement of sin and confession. This is, of course, manifested with difference within the various prismatic subdivisions that have arisen since the Schism, but at the heart of it all remains the soul as essence. Over the course of 19th century, the previous century's imperative mechanism of the institutionalized religious confessional was secularized by transference to the analyst's couch.(Foucault 1980, 63, 65-7) Psychoanalysis, oxymoronic at its inception, proposed to assist one in (re)gaining agency over oneself by abdicating free will to a chaotic neurosis of bio-impulses and synaptic whim.

The soul figures no less prominently within Eastern philosophy. It is that which reincarnates and as such is an unquestioned facet in the cosmology of Hinduism and its proto-modernist child Buddhism. The soul moves as a static element within a dynamic structure of change and remanifestation across the boundaries of life, death and species. "A sober person is not bewildered by such a change." *Baghavad-gita* 2:13.(Prabhupada 1985, 93) Within the Brahman philosophical structure the soul is something that is at once distinct from the body while residing within the body. "The sky, due to its subtle nature, does not mix with anything although it is all-pervading. Similarly, the soul situated in Brahma vision does not mix with the body, though situated in that body." *Baghavad-gita* 13:33(Prabhupada 1985, 678) The soul is something other within—a particular of the infinite. In his comment on verse 13:34 Swami Prabhupada describes it as "a small particle of spirit soul ... situated in the heart."(Prabhupada 1985, 678-9) The soul provides the animus to the corporeal edifice of bone, sinew, muscle, and flesh. Verse 13:34 of the *Gita* likens the soul to the sun, illuminating the body with consciousness as the sun does the earth with light.

Buddhist philosophy, of course, extends the discussion to conventionally reify the soul in the relative while, simultaneously, arguing for the inherent emptiness of the same soul in an ultimate sense. Traditionally, Buddhists hold that beings do have a soul. It is the soul which is tied to the cycle of birth and re-birth—*samsara*—and it is the release of the soul which signifies the realization of *nirvana*. While accepting the Brahmic notion of *karma*, Buddhism rejects the essential nature of the soul or self. To the Buddhist, the soul is as empty (devoid of essence) as everything else in cyclic existence. Central to (Mahayana, Greater Vehicle) Buddhism is the teaching of the two truths, conventional and ultimate. The first, conventional truth, is the relative approach to the world which allows for the mundane perception and the utility of the phenomenal world. The second, ultimate truth, is the realization that all things are dependently arisen, mutable and lacking of inherent essence.

The religious modus historically has been marked by a search for absolute interiority—with the possible exception of certain Buddhist traditions (see postscript). (Palmer 1998, 408) Since the Delphic directive to "know thyself" the search has been on. This operative assumption has been that an essence of self exists within and that it is something to be discovered and revealed. This process is most marked in the doctrines of the Christian West, partaking as they do of the inheritance of their Greco-Roman forebears. The entire discursive and liturgical power of the church has been directed to this end. This is a phenomenology endemic to the past 2,000 years and initially articulated in the writings of Soranus, Rufus of Ephesus, Plutarch, Seneca and other physicians and philosophers of the first two centuries. The early Christians borrowed heavily from this "insistence on the attention that should be brought to bear on oneself."(Foucault, "About the Beginning of the Hermeneutics of the Self" 1999;Foucault 1988, 39-41) These early Christian philosophers and mystics differed from their Greco-Roman predecessors diverting "the practices of self towards the hermeneutics of self and the deciphering of oneself as a subject of desire." (Foucault and Kritzman 1988, 260) It should be pointed out that the shift from the ethos of antiquity to the compulsion to self-examination was not exclusively Christian. (McNeill 1998, 59-60) Throughout this period, the self-analytic imperative evolved through the Catholic confessional and protestant witnessing of the declaration of sinful acts to the modern focus on the secular confessions of psychiatry and self-referential identity discourse. The West has limited itself to the knowledge of the subjective "I." The dictum of Delphi to 'know thyself' has become both the spiritual and secular order of knowing. The Eastern conceptions of the soul developed along somewhat similar lines, though the fragmentary nature of Eastern practice (lacking Pope or Patriarch) allowed for marked divergence as well. Consequently the focus on interiority was not as markedly pronounced in the East as it was in the West. The Hindus posited a self as a fragment that resided in the body along side a Supersoul, which was nothing less than the face of the Godhead. This fragment, being part of the divine, was not changeable. The Buddhist sought through meditation to dissolve the self—more appropriately the reification of self—by the full and experiential realization of emptiness. In contrast to the Hindu belief, the Buddhists held that the soul, or self, is constantly undergoing change and is, therefore, ultimately empty of inherent existence.

Foucault argued that this interrogation of self was aligned with a compulsion to discourse first applied with the monastic confessional and then, later, moved outside of the monastery walls. Eventually, by the advent of the 19th century, the confession and its puritan counterpart, the public repentance of transgression, were a ubiquitous element of most social structures. The origin of this compulsion was the focus of Foucault's later work. His 1979-1980 course at Collége de France explored "how a type of government of men is formed in which what is required is not simply to obey but also to reveal, by saying it, what one is." (Eribon 1991, 317) In Foucault's analysis this compulsion was a productive rather than repressive force. In the groundbreaking first volume of *The History of Sexuality*, Foucault unilaterally rejected the "repressive hypothesis" favored by historians. He argued, rather, that the concern for self, as sexuality, was ubiquitous in the Victorian world. Rather than being repressed and unequivocally silenced, sex and transgression were routinely the subject of both academic concern and particular public dialogue. Even silence, he noted, was a particular type of discourse.

The repressive model rests on the notion that there are 'powers' that are doing this 'to us'—a model which is appealing by virtue of providing something to 'speak out' against. (Foucault 1980, 7, 27) The processes Foucault proposes differ greatly from this absolutist model. He observed power as multitudinous lines coming at one from all directions. 'Power from above' was far too simple, for Foucault. He replaced the theory of hegemonic power with a more subtle 'relations to power.' "Power is everywhere," he wrote, "not because it encloses everything, but because it comes from everywhere." He described this power as a "moving substrate of force relations." (Foucault 1980, 82)

In the 19th century the simple discourse of the Christian pastoral exploded into a diverse pleroma of scientific and pedagogic discourses. This process transformed what was once discreet acts into evidence of identity. Previous to this shift, acts were not constitutive of an identity. The Christian metaphysicians held that everyone was capable of sin, therefore a sinful, transgressive act, did not imbue an individual with any note of difference. Suddenly in the middle to late 19th century, a list of scientific, medical and psychological categories came into existence—the criminal, the insane, the invert, etc. The compulsion to discourse, once confined to confession and penitence, was easily transferred to this new arena. Over the course of just a few decades, science insisted on the labeling and placement of the individual. Even the concept of the 'normal' was codified later and only in relation to the polymorphous mass of categories.

Foucault argues that no essential element resides at the core of the subjective. Foucault stated in his critique of the essentialist position that the search for such an inner "self," the *raison d'être* of the modernist impulse defining identity politics, always proves fruitless at its ultimate extension.(Foucault, et al. 1984) This position can be easily extended to the larger view of self and soul: No essential nature (or identity) exists, thus the search for the root of subjectivity leads irrefutably to a dead end. No core exists at the heart of the onion, nor does a wagon remain once its constitutive parts are removed. In his critique of post-Hegelian identity, Chris Cutrone writes, "The idealist construction of the subject founders on its falsely taking subject to be objective in the sense of something existing in-itself, precisely what it is not: measured against the standard of entities, the subject is condemned to nothingness."(Cutrone 2000, 263)

Foucault's analysis asks the critical question why the relation one has to oneself has to be one of knowledge. Explicitly, this forced him "to reject a certain *a priori* theory of the subject." Foucault argued that such a rejection of the basis of Western ontology was necessary to achieve his examination of the "relationships which can exist between the constitution of the subject or the different forms of the subject and games of truth, practices of power, and so forth." (McNeill 1998, 59) Ultimately, Foucault fully rejects the assumption that knowledge equates to knowledge of self and that the only relation that we can have with ourselves is as a object of observation. (Palmer 1998, 408) Simply put, Foucault argues that there is nothing there to find. The Western mystics' Quest for total individualization is an ontologic dead end. Palmer states this position succinctly, "there is no deep truth about ourselves." (Palmer 1998, 408) In a 1982 interview Foucault articulated this position in a lighter tone, "I don't feel that it is necessary to know exactly what I am. The main interest in life and work is to

become something else that you were not in the beginning."
("Truth, Power, Self" 1988, 9) Palmer highlights two distinct
problems Foucault exposed with any attempt "to found a
systemic and positive knowledge about ourselves." The first
centers on the "plausibility" of successfully achieving such
knowledge; the second points to the "practical implications" of
positioning ourselves as subjects of our own knowledge. (Palmer
1998, 402)

Questions of subjectivity and the epistemic self have arisen
as the driving questions in the dialogue of modernism through to
postmodernism. Is everything relative to the subjectivity of the
perceiver? Does subjectivity exist? If so is it relative, empty or
absolute? What is the relation between self and other? Does
such a relation even exist and if so what are its constituent parts?
This philosophical (and political) dialogue has been paralleled by
the increasing personalization of the spiritual quest. As the
Golgotha of institutionalized religion has slowly eroded, the rise
of subjective relativist spiritual agendas have grown—either in
small to medium groups, the so-called "New Religious
Movements," or on a completely personal solitary level. More
often than not this has resembled the postmodernist artistic
aesthetic, creating a heterozygous amalgam of appropriated
imagery, icons and philosophical precepts. The trend has been to
center these historical and/or cultural fragments around a drive
for ferreting out the root of one's essence—whether termed
Being, self or inner child.

Foucault instead proposed a process involving a creative
approach to the self. For Foucault, the emptiness of self-essence
logically demanded a productive relation between one and one's
self. The self and its relationships (to others, to power and to
categorizations) is something that is mutable, dynamic, limited
only by the conceptual limitations of the self at any given socio-
historic nexus. Of this Palmer says, "Truth (for Foucault) is not

passively deciphered, but is dynamically created." (Palmer 1998, 409) Foucault termed this process '*askesis*,' 'ascetical practice' or creative expansion. In an interview he described *askesis* as "something else: it's the work that one performs on oneself in order to transform oneself or make the *self* appear that happily one never attains."(Foucault 1989, 206) *Askesis* is the Greek root of asceticism and Foucault intentionally uses this term to link back to a classical philosophical tradition he examined in depth in *The Care of Self*, volume three of his *History of Sexuality*. His taxonomic choice reflects Foucault's emphasis on a deliberate, hermeneutic approach. Through this he attempts to resurrect a notion that the self is something to be cultivated rather than explored. The soul is distinct for its potential not its inherency. Foucault, however, is not simply invoking antiquity, as some of his critics have charged, as a call to move back to some remote "golden age." He is using, instead, the oppositional model of Greek *ethos* to destabilize deeply ingrained, modern conceptions of self and identity.

In his discussion of Foucault's philosophy, Palmer describes Foucault's asceticism as a process "not to decipher what we 'really' are, but to strive to cultivate what me might become." (Palmer 1998, 408) Foucault himself argued that "the main interest in life and work is to become something else that you were not in the beginning." ("Truth, Power, Self: An Interview with Michel Foucault" 1988, 9) For Foucault the self is something to be "cultivated," tended, shaped through the application of a creative mechanism. Knowledge is the knowledge one presents to the world and discovers through the process of creation, not the knowledge that one finds hidden in one's self. The mind, body and spirit reach to grab at a great, limitless truth, rather than delving internally for an essential atom of meaning.

For Foucault who we are, our self if you will, is inextricably linked to where, when and how we are. No unified, pure, absolute self exists. Instead, the individual is a mosaic of fragmentary moments, memories, genetics and cultural genealogy. Here he is building directly off of Martin Heidegger's theories of Being. Palmer describes Heidegger's philosophy as "pointing our that we do not exist first as isolated Cartesian egos but are acculturated into a set of shared social practices that allow entities or beings to be disclosed to us in specific meaningful ways." (Palmer 1998, 403) It is impossible to separate who we are from where we have come from and where we have been. Our interpretations of the world (and, if directed inwards, ourselves) is shaped by our family, culture, past relationships; we are at each moment the totality of our conditioning. Again summarizes Heidegger, Palmer states "there can be no human nature as it were; there are only specific interpretations of what it means to be a human being in specific cultures." (Palmer 1998, 403) The entirety of Foucault's intellectual corpus is centered around the inseparability of self from conditioning. Despite later interpretations to the contrary, Foucault never argued for a totality of social-construction. Rather, like Heidegger before him, he endeavored to point out the social conditions in which being functions in an attempt to expose the unseen and, therefore, unexamined lines of power, which constrain the individual.

In this *askesis,* Foucault proposed a ongoing process in which boundaries are mapped so that they can be pushed at. His focus was the direct opposite of the internal quest. He argued for an expansion of self, pushing outwards towards a limit which is always just beyond reach. In an interview given just prior to his death, he outlined this view, "the relationships we have to have with ourselves are not ones of identity, rather they must be relationships of differentiation, of creation, of innovation."

(Foucault, et al. 1984) Foucault's *praxis* calls for the individual to stand in opposition to those forces which seek to hinder his knowledge. James Miller, in his *Passions of Michel Foucault*, summarizes this mode of being: "To be modern is not to accept oneself as one is in the flux of the passing moments" but, rather, as the result "of a complex and difficult elaboration."(Miller 1993, 333) In this way Foucault gives agency back to the individual. Our bodies and ourselves are not a territory to be mined but one to molded, shaped and re-shaped. "Where religions once demanded the sacrifice of human bodies, knowledge now calls for experimentation on ourselves."(Miller 1993, 346) Through this process one increasingly realizes the mutability of both identity and truth. As Palmer points out, one reaches the realization that "categories are precisely historical and contingent and not universal and necessary." (Palmer 1998, 407) Foucault's Genesis is a call for us to be something else—his Song of Solomon his own personal exploration of the sexual underground.

For Foucault the interrogation of self proved in fact to be a mechanism of oppression. Many of his works outline the process of knowing and the way in which the process constrains the individual. In his *History of Sexuality volume one*, Foucault methodically outlines the way in which the compulsion to discourse actually worked as a mechanism of power that effectively channeled sexuality rather than overtly oppressing it. The goal of his intellectual work, in his own words, was an attempt to explicate "the historical analysis of the limits that are imposed on us and an experiment with the possibility of going beyond them." (Palmer 1998, 406) Foucault brings into question the relation we have with knowledge and the relation one has with oneself. He proposes the application of a life-long process of personal unfolding, rather than private/public revelation. His theory, asks us to resist the impulse to analyze who we are and the corollary compulsion to confess incessantly. He calls on the individual to enlarge themselves through a process of perpetual redefinition—a process that culminates in the realization of the impermanent nature of the world and truth. Rather than seeking to reveal an internal hidden nature, he urges us to resist the categories that been placed within—a placement we have been blinded to by the inculcated focus on interiority. Foucault described his goal in very precise and eloquent terms: "That is *what* I tried to reconstitute: the formation and development of a practice of self whose aim was to constitute oneself as the worker of the beauty of one's own life." (Foucault and Kritzman 1988, 259)

POSTSCRIPT: FOUCAULT & ZEN

In the spring of 1978 Foucault traveled to Japan intending to be initiated into Zen Buddhism. At the suggestion of his master Omori Sogen, head of the Seionji temple in Uenohara, Foucault spent several days living the life of a monk. (Eribon 1991, 310) Foucault's discussion with the priests of the temple were published in the Japanese review *Shunjû* and, later, the French journal *Umi*. Foucault acknowledged his interest in Buddhism but admitted what interested him most "is life itself in a Zen temple, that is to say the practice of Zen, its exercises and its rules. For I believe that a totally different mentality to our own is formed through the practice and exercises of a Zen temple." (Foucault, "Michel Foucault and Zen" 1999, 110) During the course of these discussions, Foucault emphasized the principle difference he saw between Zen practice and the Christian practice of individualization:

> As for Zen, it seems that all the techniques linked to spirituality are, conversely, tending to attenuate the individual. Zen and Christian

mysticism are two things you can't compare, whereas the technique of Christian spirituality and that of Zen are comparable. And, here, there exists a great opposition. In Christian mysticism, even when it preaches the union of God and the individual, there is something that is individual. The one is he who loves and the other is he who is loved. (Foucault, "Michel Foucault and Zen" 1999, 112)

References:

Cutrone, Christopher. "The Child with a Lion: The Utopia of Interracial Intimacy." *GLQ* 6, no. 2 (2000): 249-85.

Eribon, Didier. *Michel Foucault.* Translated by Betsy Wing. Cambridge, MA: Harvard University Press, 1991.

Foucault, Michel. "About the Beginning of the Hermeneutics of the Self." In *Religion and Culture Michel Foucault,* edited by Jeremy R. Carrette, 158-81. New York: Rutledge, 1999.

_____. *The Care of Self.* Translated by Robert Hurley. Vol. 3, *History of Sexuality.* New York: Vintage, 1988.

_____. "Friendship as a Way of Life." In *Foucault Live,* edited by Sylvere Lotringer: Semiotexte, 1989.

_____. *An Introduction.* Translated by Robert Hurley. Vol. 1, *History of Sexuality.* New York: Vintage, 1980.

_____. "Michel Foucault and Zen." In *Religion and Culture Michel Foucault,* edited by Jeremy R. Carrette, 110-14. New York: Routledge, 1999.

_____. *The Order of Things.* New York: Vintage, 1970.

Foucault, Michel, Bob Gallagher, and Alexander Wilson. "Sex, Power and the Politics of Identity." *The Advocate,* 7 August 1984.

Foucault, Michel, and Lawrence D. Kritzman ed. *Politics, Philosophy, Culture: Interviews and Other Writings 1977-1984.* New York: Rutledge, 1988.

McNeill, Will. "Care for the Self: Originary Ethics in Heidegger and Foucault." *Philosophy Today* 1998, 53-64.

Miller, James. *The Passion of Michel Foucault.* New York: Simon & Schuster, 1993.

Palmer, Daniel E. "On Refusing Who We Are: Foucault's Critique of the Epistemic Subject." *Philosophy Today* 1998, 402-10.

Prabhupada, A.C. Bhaktivedanta Swami. *Bhagavad-Gita as It Is.* Los Angeles: Bhaktivedanta Book Trust, 1985.

"Truth, Power, Self: An Interview with Michel Foucault." In *Technologies of the Self: A Seminar with Michel Foucault,* edited by L Matin, H Gutman and P Hutton. Amherst: University of Massachusetts Press, 1988.

There Is No God Where I Am

Whether East or West, the religious modus of the Old Aeon has been marked by a search for absolute interiority. This operative assumption has been that an essence of self exists within and that it is something to be sought out and cared for. This process is most marked in the doctrines of the Christian West, partaking as they do of the inheritance of their Greco-Roman forebears. The entire discursive and liturgical power of the church has been directed to this end. This is a phenomenology born of the Aeon of Osiris (c. 1-1904c.e.) and initially articulated in the writings of Soranus, Rufus of Ephesus, Plutarch, Seneca and other physicians and philosophers of the first two centuries. The early Christians borrowed heavily from this "insistence on the attention that should be brought to bear on oneself."(Foucault 1988, pp. 39-41) Throughout the course of the Osirian Aeon, this self-analytic imperative evolved through the Catholic confessional and protestant witnessing of the declaration of sinful acts to the modern focus on the secular confessions of psychiatry and self-referential identity discourse. The West has limited itself to the knowledge of the subjective "I."

The Eastern conceptions of the soul developed along somewhat similar lines, though the fragmentary nature of Eastern practice (lacking Pope or Patriarch) allowed for marked divergence as well. The focus on absolute interiority was not as disproportionately pronounced as it was in the West. The Hindus posited a self as a fragment that resided in the body along side a Supersoul, which was nothing less than the face of the Godhead. This fragment, being part of the divine, was not changeable. The Buddhist sought through meditation to dissolve the self—more appropriately the reification of self—by the full and experiential realization of emptiness. In contrast to the Hindu belief, the Buddhists held that the soul, or self, is constantly undergoing change and is, therefore, ultimately empty of inherent existence.

The new modus of the Aeon of Horus and Set is developing along lines distinctly contrary to those of the previous aeon. In *Liber AL vel Legis: the Book of the Law* (AL), Lord Aiwass teaches that the seeker is no longer to be concerned with the soul as object. In the New Aeon, the Path moves in the opposite direction. Expansion versus contraction. The point moves outward reaching toward the circumference, instead of the worldly projection turning inwards seeking the essence of self. It is the core that manifests the world, rather than the world seeking the core. Lord Aiwass introduces a cosmology based on the counter relation of two principles, Nuit and Hadit. Nuit is the iconographic expression of infinite expansion. Hieroglyphically she is the lady of the stars whose arched body forms the night sky. Hadit, on the other hand, is the dimensionless point, unextended, the stars within her body. AL II:2 Nuit is the circumference while Hadit is the center of the circle. AL II:3

Questions of subjectivity and self have arisen as the driving questions in the dialogue of modernism and postmodernism. Is everything relative to the subjectivity of the perceiver? Does subjectivity exist? If so, is subjectivity relative, empty or absolute? What is the relation between self and other? Does such a relation even exist and if so what are its constituent parts? This philosophical (and political) dialogue has been paralleled by the increasing personalization of the spiritual quest. As the Golgotha of institutionalized religion has slowly eroded, the rise of subjective relativist spiritual agendas has grown—either in small to medium groups, the so-called "New Religious Movements," or on a completely personal individuated level.

More often than not this has resembled the postmodernist artistic aesthetic, creating a heterogenous amalgam of appropriated imagery, icons and philosophical precepts. The trend has been to center these historical and/or cultural fragments around a drive for rooting out the root of one's essence—whether termed Being, self or inner child.

In direct contrast to this flood of disparate self-searching philosophies are the words of Nuit, Hadit and Ra-Hoor-Khuit, spoken through their minister Lord Aiwass. In this tripartite image, reflected in the three chapter division of *Liber AL*, is encoded a model for the correct view of exteriority, interiority and subjectivity. Building from the analogy of the sphere utilized in *Liber AL* II:3, Nuit, as the circumference, is the limit of personal expansion; Hadit is the central, originating point; and Ra-Hoor-Khuit is the synergy arisen from the correct, direct experiential (as opposed to inferential) apprehension of these two. Hadit is "everywhere the centre" and Nuit "the circumference, is nowhere found." We are each the center of our own universe. (cf. the Khabs and the Khu of AL I:8) Ra-Hoor-Khuit is the projection of personality that the interrelation of Nuit and Hadit gives rise to. The ability to move forward, create and develop is the "reward of Ra-Hoor-Khuit." AL III:1 This process is *not* a unification of the one into the all but rather a dynamic play of expansion and contraction which results in the agency of the individual. "There is division hither homeward; there is a word not known." AL III:2 To functionally exist within the world means that the complete dissolution referred to in chapter one is not a place of permanent abiding—but may, rather, be more an attainment of an accessible realization or meditative nexus point.

In chapter two, Hadit states "I am alone and there is no god where I am." AL II:23 At the center is only Hadit, the dimensionless point. "Unextended," he is therefore empty of inherent existence as it would be defined by traditional phenomenology. Hadit describes himself as "alone" without reference to "god" or an essential element of self or spirit. If one were to say Hadit exists at all, it is not in a way that can be characterized as existing "as such" within the dimension that we are able to comprehend. Since Hadit is not perceivable and nothing else resides with him to be perceived, it follows that the quest for meaning at the core of self cannot result in realization. Hadit is the projective point from which we originate and not the end goal of our quest. Those who seek him, utilizing his image as focus, will discover nothing for he is, in actuality, "the worshipper." AL II:8 Hadit is the originating point, the impetus to begin the spiritual quest and the strength to carry on against the dark night. It is he that goes. AL II:7 The flaw of modernist subjectivity is that it mistakes the doer for the object of interrogation. Modern humanism is blind to the irony of the seeker seeking oneself. Or in the words of the enlightened master Osho, "The worshipper is the worshipped." (Rajneesh 1988, 23)

"You don't have to worship anyone else. Your innermost being is the highest and the most precious, the most existential and conscious point. There is nothing higher than it. You need no worship, you can only meditate." (Rajneesh 1988, 23)

It is not, necessarily, that the self does not exist. It is rather that one is incapable of perceiving the nature of the soul and it is thus an inappropriate focus of spiritual concern. The self cannot be known by the false ego or intellect. The intellect can only recognize the nature of the self, but this is still a veil. "The khabs is in the khu, not the khu in the khabs." AL I:8 Khu is the innermost veil that obscures the right perception of the khabs, inner light or flame. Of this Crowley writes, "It is the 'veils' that obstruct the relation between Nuit and Hadit." He further admonishes us "not to worship the khu, to fall in love with our magical image. To do this—and we have all done it—is to forget our truth."(Crowley 1986, 83) The self, khabs, is not the correct object of the path, since the seeker can never perceive it with any clarity. The khabs always remains obscured by the khu. The core, self, can only be correctly perceived in the "highest trances."(Crowley 1986, 156)

The relation of Hadit and Nuit is also figured in terms of the dualism of the knower and the known—the one who has the ability to realize and the object of that realization. Hadit, symbolic of the seeker on the path, is in the position of reaching toward Nuit, the "limit" to be strived for. In verse II:4 Hadit, speaking of Nuit, says "Yet she shall be known & I never." Hadit is the active principle, the "goer." Crowley writes of this relation, "Hadit possesses the power to know, Nuit that of being known."(Crowley 1986, 158) Exteriority (Nuit, the universe) and interiority (Hadit, the soul) is thus a mutually reciprocating relation where "the soul interprets the universe; and the universe veils the soul."(Crowley 1986, 155)

Crowley uses the philosophy of *Liber AL* to postulate that singular perfect emanations, "stars," self-limit in order to achieve Wisdom through lived experience. He uses the example of a carbon atom which goes through diverse connections, combining with oxygen to make CO_2 and then being subdivided back into pure carbon. In this analogy, the atomic element goes through processes but does not change in its ultimate constitution. The soul works in a similar fashion, undergoing change but carrying forward that change not in its ultimate constitutional make-up but in the form of memory and historicity. Crowley elaborates that Nuit is the "object of knowledge" while Hadit is "merely that part of Her which She formulates in order that she may be known."(Crowley 1986) The perfect creates the myth of duality in order to gain Wisdom. "For I am divided for love's sake, for the chance of union." AL I:29

To borrow from the post-structuralist philosopher Michel Foucault, *Liber AL* proposes the development of what he termed an *askesis*, a productive ascetic discipline of creative expansion—ultimately resulting in a dissolution in the body of Nuit. "The pain of division is as nothing, and the joy of dissolution all." AL I:30 Foucault describes *askesis* as "something else: it's the work that one performs on oneself in order to transform oneself or make the *self* appear that happily one never attains."(Foucault 1989, 206) This expansive notion of spirituality, the seeking to expand the very conception of self, as opposed to rooting out its 'source' echoes Crowley's theories. "The development of the Adept is by expansion—out of Nuit—in all directions equally."(Crowley 1986, 89) Hadit is a force which strives to be something greater, ever reaching toward a goal which appropriately remains just out of reach. Again the focus is external and not internal. The notion of the self is relational and not essential. "It is therefore wrong to worship Hadit; one is to be Hadit, and worship [Nuit]."(Crowley 1986, 166) The path is to seek toward the Orisha, to be enveloped in something greater than one's self. "Consciousness loses its sense of separateness by dissolution in [Nuit]"(Crowley 1986, 155)

It is up to us to create who we are—not to discover it. In an interview, Foucault stated it succinctly, "The relationships we have to have with ourselves are not ones of identity, rather they must be relationships of differentiation, of creation, of innovation."(Foucault, et al. 1984) He further proposed that "to be modern is not to accept oneself as one is in the flux of the passing moments" but, rather, as the result "of a complex and difficult elaboration."(Miller 1993, 333) In his construction of a positive, productive spiritual quest rooted in exteriority, Foucault gives agency back to the individual. "Where religions once demanded the sacrifice of human bodies, knowledge now calls for experimentation on ourselves."(Miller 1993, 346) Spirituality is now a choice, and not a de facto confluence of heredity, culture and (familial) heritage.

Crowley believed, "One should plunge passionately into every possible experience." (Crowley 1986, 166) His 12th and 21st theorems in *Magick In Theory and Practice* state that limits are self-imposed and merely represent the ability of the practitioner to measure and cognize the distance between self and a perceived boundary. For both Crowley and Foucault, the goal does not stop at the reaching of the boundary but actually moving past it through heightened experiences. Foucault terms these instances "limit experiences" a moment which pushes us beyond what we thought ourselves capable of perceiving, thus changing even the most basic conception of who we are. Experience keeps us fresh. The direct access that we have to the glories of the Orisha and Devas gives us an ongoing evolutionary play of expanding realities. We learn and grow though this contact and not, conversely, through internalized self-analysis. We meditate and rest in the quietude of emptiness; we experience the Divine and become more than what we thought we were.

"Nobody in the whole history of consciousness has been able to say why he is. All that one can do is shrug your shoulders: I am, there is no question of why." (Rajneesh 1988, 25) "If Will stops and cries Why, invoking Because, then Will stops & does naught." AL II:30 Shrug your shoulders and go on.

We do not pray. Our worship is contact with something greater than our selves and, through this contact, we are expanded. We can only ever begin to know ourselves by contact with the Divine—the Orishas, Devas and Divine Emanations.

The gods once again walk the earth as men—or the men once again walk the earth as gods. It is up to us to write our own mythology. Brion's clarion call echoes through Space: *We are Here To Go!*

References:

Crowley, Aleister. *The Law Is for All.* Phoenix, AZ: Falcon Publications, 1986.

Foucault, Michel. *The Care of Self.* Translated by Robert Hurley. Vol. 3, *History of Sexuality.* New York: Vintage, 1988.

_____. "Friendship as a Way of Life." In *Foucault Live*, edited by Sylvere Lotringer: Semiotexte, 1989.

Foucault, Michel, Bob Gallagher, and Alexander Wilson. "Sex, Power and the Politics of Identity." *The Advocate*, 7 August 1984.

Miller, James. *The Passion of Michel Foucault.* New York: Simon & Schuster, 1993.

Rajneesh, Bhagwan Shree. Zen: The Quantum Leap from Mind to No-Mind. *First ed. Cologne: Rebel Publishing House, 1988.*

Plain Brown Wrapper

This poem wrapped
in a plain brown wrapper.
This poem is gay,
but doesn't like to tell people.
This poem used to be Catholic
but now is lost.
This poem censored
by Meese porno commission.
This poem dreamed of
"No redeeming social value."
This poem put on the stand,
the religion of secular humanism.

This poem is of rape
but lies around alone in bed now.
This poem is a blowjob
sauced with blackmail
but never comes.
This poem has to fuck
to get to orgasm.
This poem doesn't speak
to others of like nature.
This poem is a preppy poem.
This poem is in a
plain brown wrapper.

Friendship & Forgery:
Michel Foucault and the Practice of Homosexuality

Michel Foucault perceived homosexuals as residing in a privileged space relative to the transformation of personal relationships. He viewed homosexuality as, in his words, "an occasion to re-open effective and relational virtualities," since it has the potential to "introduce love where there's supposed to be only law, rule or habit." (Foucault Live, 205) He characterized this redelineation of desire as a reconfiguration of "friendship." In an interview given just months prior to his death in 1984, he proposed that "the disappearance of friendship as a social relation and the declaration of homosexuality as a social/political/medical problem, are the same process." (The Advocate 7 August 1984)

In the modern world there exists very little to structure friendship. After the break down of the cult of friendship in the nineteenth century, as outlined in Caroll Smith-Rosenberg's "The Female World of Love and Ritual," friendship has become a very ambiguous and ill-defined area. It is under the rubric of "friendship" that Foucault begins positioning his notion of homosexual "askesis," or ascetic practice. Foucault means by "askesis" a process of creating or inventing what it means to be homosexual, rather than discovering an essentialized homosexual identity. He states:

> The world [regards] sexuality as the secret of the creative world; it is rather a process of our having to create a new cultural life underneath the ground of our sexual choices. (*The Advocate*)

For Foucault sexuality becomes meaningful through a dynamic process of creation, rather than a static realm of private revelation and confession. He asked gay men to begin to understand what can be established through the new ways of coming together which they are establishing. He said, "we have to understand that with our desires, through our desires, go new forms of relationships, new forms of love, new forms of creation." (The Advocate)

In the era after the sexual revolution, the gay liberation movement, gay assimilationism, and Queer politics, new possibilities for relationship exist. As homosexual relations begin entering a realm, relatively free from legal and social restraints, gay men need to refigure their relationships outside of the realms of "law, rule or habit." Through his discussion of homosexual askesis, Foucault argued that gay men should seek to establish an art of living, based on creating the domain of personal sexuality. "Sex," he wrote, "is not a fatality; it's a possibility for creative life."(The Advocate)

In many ways, homosexuality is still undefined territory. The definitions that the medical and scientific movements developed in the late nineteenth century never fully encompassed significant portions of the homosexual subcultures. One can not, also, live long under the assumption of sin; critical attitudes must develop in response to adverse conditions. The history of homosexuality in the modern West can, thus, be viewed as a search for meaning. The process can be observed strongly in the work of Walt Whitman with his attempts at creating a mythic system based around the Calamus symbol. It can also be seen in the work of early homosexual rights advocates, such as John Addington Symonds, Edward Carpenter, Karl Ulrichs and Aleister Crowley.

This formative process of homosexual definition is most poignantly manifested in the life and style of Oscar Wilde.

Indeed, to a large extent, Foucault's discourse can be seen as having been begun by Wilde. He always spoke of his life as a work of art—a work of creative presentation. He asserted, "I have put only my genius into my work; my art I have put into my life." Wilde seemed to feel that the act of living, especially as a homosexual, was a work of artifice. "The first duty in life is to be as artificial as possible," he wrote. Like Foucault, Wilde felt that, in a world lacking appropriate definitions of same-sex desire, the only choice a homosexual has is to begin a creative process of exploratory practice and presentation.

In the movement of definition that characterized same-sex desire in the nineteenth century, Wilde attempted to transpose his desire into a style of living. In many ways he seems to have recognized a certain element of social construction a century before Foucault's work. He argued that "most people are other people. Their thoughts are someone else's opinions, their life mimicry, their passions a quotation."(*De Profundis*) In the quips and maxims that characterize Wildean dialogues, he seems to evince his own methods for dealing with a desire that was at once dangerous and improbable. I must stop to say that I do not wish to be accused of hero-worship in relation to dear St. Oscar. He certainly problematized his social creativity, as can be easily observed in the arrogant banter that characterized his courtroom testimony during the three trials he endured. What I do want to point toward is the relatively long history of connection that has existed between modern homosexuality and the exploration of designing an art of living. What Foucault talks of in his later interviews on homosexual askesis does echo in several fundamental ways Wilde's cultural philosophy.

In his work on Wilde, *Who Was That Man*, gay novelist and theorist, Neil Bartlett argues that homosexual life has to be one of intentional forgery-self-creation. He writes:

There is no intrinsic value to homosexuality. There is no "real" us, we can only ever have an unnatural identity, which is why we are all forgers. We create life, not out of lies, but out of more or less conscious choices; adaptations, imitations and plain theft of styles, names, social and sexual roles, bodies.(Bartlett, 169)

As Foucault frequently argues, there is no "essential" homosexual nature, and any internal search for such a nature must result in a discursive dead end. This cul-de-sac of personal interrogation results, more often than not, in a reliance on the ideological assumptions which lie at the heart of the crisis of identity politics. The definitions that gay men have been given— by religion, medicine, and law-provide little basis for living a homosexual life. They do not speak, nor have they ever truly spoken to, the ways in which one has to see in order to survive. Culture provides few imperatives to which gay men can subscribe, they are therefore always posing as something. After one rejects the definitions of deviance and unnaturalness, what is left? Gay men have several choices in the modern cultural arena, but the central choice still lies in the division between attempting to shape one's life around the heterosexual imperatives that permeate every level of society or to remove oneself into a zone of identity presented by the gay subculture(s).

The history of homosexuality has been broken along these lines, since the word was first formed. Gay men have chosen between the marriage based family unit and the liberalizing agendas of gay politics (and some others remaining marginalized on the sidelines of both). As the existence of the support group Married Gay Men (MGM) attests, gay men have chosen, and continue to choose, to marry and stay married—often maintaining a cloak-and-dagger separation between married "heterosexual" life and furtive, clandestine hotel room "homosexuality." Gay men have also attempted, over the years, to find their own place of comfort within the marital ideal through an attempt at de-heterosexualizing the family. One recalls gay couples on Oprah, Donahue and Sally Jesse Raphael dressed up as young preppy boys/girls just out of college. Could anything be more natural than two young people attempting to find a life together after graduation? One of them always says, "We are not here to destroy the family; we just want the definition to include us." This choice implies a position of isolated homosexuality, where "the choice of love" is only a minor character difference from the American ideal.

On the other hand, gay men also choose to completely define themselves relative to their love of other men. They place themselves in one of several political/fetishistic camps that have shaped and re-shaped both before and after the mythic awakening of the Stonewall riots. For these men homosexuality is infused in an extensive portion of their lives. Both these positions are tenuous, however. A redefinition of the American family could only result in its destruction, since it has never been more than a myth existing only in the cultural eye. Homosexuality has always been one of the family's most potent defining others. Gay men are the antithesis of everything those few who still rely on the familial myth hold dear. Queers will never be welcome at their tables or reunions. Identity based on political positioning presents an alternative which isn't any more stable. Political ideologies and social pressures are continually shifting, aspects moving on and off of cultural center stage, while personal political stances remain all to often static. The political activist of today is all too quickly the dated stalwart of tomorrow.

In most countries where men engage in homosexual intercourse, such activity is criminal. We are indeed forgers, conscious or not, who routinely pose as law abiding citizens. Gay men have power when they refuse their criminality, as illustrated in the fiction of William S. Burroughs, Jean Genet and Dennis Cooper. More often than not, however, gay men ignore the implications of their criminality—carefully constructing a separation between the bar and the bank. Later in the same work quoted above, Bartlett discusses the ways in which criminality and personal homosexual interpretation play out their relation within gay male life. He writes of a weekend night at the bar:

> It is our commonest experience that after breaking the law we become law-abiding citizens. . . . We regularly watch ourselves turn into the most improbable creatures, transform back again, then set off to the office or the dole office just like anybody else. . . . Morning does not disrupt the night any more than the glamour, the ferocity and wickedness of the night challenges or abolishes the day. (Bartlett, 216)

He continues:

> After the moments of harsh intimacy with ourselves or with others we like the world to fall back into place again. We acknowledge, with extraordinary calmness, given how much this all costs us, that there is no radical impulse beneath our radical acts. (Bartlett, 216)

Bartlett argues that gay men's intimate actions move them momentarily "up or down" but never "forward."(Bartlett, 215) Gay men lack a unifying system, a mythic structure of interpretive stories, with which to critically engage with their "radical acts."

References:

Bartlett, Neil. *Who Was That Man?* London: Serpent's Tail, 1988.

Foucault, Michel. "Sex, Power and the Politics of Identity." *The Advocate, 7 August 1984.*

Wilde, Oscar. *The Portable Oscar Wilde.* Richard Addington and Stanley Weintraub, editors. New York: Penguin, 1981.

You Can Keep Your Rights,
I Already Gots Mine!

The licensing of marriage is the last uncomfortable intersection of law and religion left in our increasingly secular society. Marriage is, on the one hand, a religious ceremony—one of the three great rights common to all denominations of the priestly classes—and, on the other, a contractual union with an associated array of civil oversight and regulation.

Within the milieu of religion, marriage bestows a cultural recognition and support of the solemn promise of two people to live together in mutual love and respect. As an ideal, it is the moment when one's small community of faith, friends and family join together in celebration of a life shared.

As a civil contract, marriage is codified in over 1,000 federal 'automatic' benefits and countless more in the state and private sectors. With licensing certificate in hand, the couple becomes a unit, which is everywhere predefined in the laws that govern everything from inheritance to privacy protection and access.

This uncomfortable intersection, leads to an uncomfortable, and highly inappropriate, collusion between lawmakers and religious leaders. The religious estate of our republic, sees marriage as a purely religious issue—the civil license merely being a recognition of non-secular solemnization—ignoring the numbers of people who obtain a civil marriage, only, without interface with clergy. For their part, the secular leaders view marriage as much more than the act of licensing clerks, recognizing that it creates a legal class with more privileges and responsibilities than any other in our society.

When debating civil unions, the Vermont legislature admitted to being confused as on one day a religious leader would advise them against the proposed bill, while on the next another religious leader would speak in favor of the bill. It was obvious from the legislators' comments, that their collective confusion arose out of their inability to glean a consensus of religious understanding from the various positions articulated before them by the line of religious authorities. In a recent *Newsweek* editorial, Anna Quindlen posed the question, "In a secular nation, why should church leaders be required to acknowledge civil marriage—or, for that matter, be attended to when they pass judgment on what they will not acknowledge?"

The real crux of the 'gay marriage' question is not a religious debate. It is, rather, a wrestling for the retention of one of the last areas of religious control of secular life. Ultimately the question of marriage legislation is a secular one, positioned squarely in the domain of law and codified social custom. The spiritual solemnizing of unions is a religious question, while the licensing of a special coupled class of society is not.

Recently a colleague asked why gay men and lesbians would want to fight for marriage anyway. On the surface, it does seem a lot of energy to lay claim to the summit of an anachronism. It is, however, one of the last great vestiges of exclusion directed at a colonized people. One cannot help but feel something akin to the Berlin wall being torn down, as each new town is added to the list of gay marriage havens... On the other side the last stalwarts desperately trying to hold on to a history and golden age that never really existed.

The opponents of gay marriage argue that the concept erodes the foundations of the very concept of marriage itself. They paint an image of marriage that claims to look backward into time immemorial at a continuity of glorious union— pristine, perfect and biblically sanctioned.

The truth, of course, is that modern marriage has no historic antecedents. The history upon which they choose to premise their arguments never existed. In the 21st century, marriage is about love and commitment—a construction that would have been unthinkably scandalous in proper society just 100 years ago. For the centuries prior, marriage has been a contract of property and inheritance with little or no relation to the practice today.

Just a little over thirty years ago, interracial marriage was illegal in much of the United States. When it was legalized nationally, the country was less divided over the issue than it is today over the question of gay marriage. Unlike current polling, at that time an *overwhelming majority* of the country opposed interracial marriage. A Gallop poll conducted in 1968 showed that fully 72% of the country opposed interracial marriage with 48% openly expressing the opinion that it should be criminalized. It is no coincidence that Massachusetts governor Mitt Romney is using a 1913 anti-interracial marriage law to prevent non-residents from marrying in his state.

For me as an observer of this debate, the critical point in the current events and court rulings is a subtle, but vitally important, shift in the rubric of power in the debate of gay rights (so called). I have long been ambivalent about the notion of demanding rights, as I see a large, unintended, side-affect being the ironic, and often self-defeating, empowering of others to bestow rights. This has allowed the far-right to control the debate for the last 20 years, by casting the demand for equality under the law as a fight for 'special rights' and asking the loaded (rhetorical) question of how far should the 'expansion' of 'rights' go. In this environment, courts are deemed symptomatic of an 'activist judiciary' when they have the hubris to interpret the self-evident truths of our founding fathers as applying to *all* peoples.

Regardless of whether the members of the Enlightenment could foresee what they were setting in motion, courts are now beginning to correctly interpret the reach of those rights. The authors of the Declaration of Independence acknowledged that no mortal could ultimately bestow rights on another, leaving that to the avowed purview of a mightier universal power. It may seem like a subtle shift, but asking someone to give you what you already have, only gives them the power to withhold it.

When the Supreme Court overturned their own *Bowers v. Hardwick* (1984) ruling in *Lawrence & Garner v. Texas* (2003), the debate transformed overnight to a question of existing rights. This decision stands in sharp contrast to earlier legislative efforts easily cast as attempts at articulating new rights or extending novel protections. Justice Scalia, in his dissenting opinion, correctly observed that the court's overturning of *Bowers* called into question the "validation of laws based on moral choices" including, in his list of examples, same-sex marriage. For once, I actually agree with a Scalia opinion, though he and I are at complete odds as to whether this change bodes well or ill for society. Without question or exception, in a modern, secular country laws should *never* be based on "moral choices."

The Massachusetts Supreme Judicial Court was the first to correctly extend *Lawrence v. Texas*, ruling that exclusively inter-sexual marriage laws are unconstitutional (*Goodridge v. Department of Public Health*, 2003). In their decision, the court acknowledged that "many people hold deep-seated religious, moral, and ethical convictions that marriage should be limited to the union of one man and one woman, and that homosexual conduct is immoral. Many hold equally strong religious, moral, and ethical convictions that same-sex couples are entitled to be married, and that homosexual persons should be treated no differently than their heterosexual neighbors." The court ruled that "the State may not interfere with these convictions, or with the decision of any religion to refuse to perform religious marriages of same-sex couples." They held "these matters of belief and conviction" to be "properly outside the reach of judicial review or government interference."

The court's response to the Massachusetts Senate, went further, giving reality to Scalia's deepest fears, stating "neither may the government, under the guise of protecting 'traditional' values, even if they be the traditional values of the majority, enshrine in law an invidious discrimination that our Constitution [...] forbids." The court saw clearly that the existing state marriage law created a class relegated "to a different status." In rejecting the Senate's proposed compromise legislation outlawing same-sex marriage while, with the same stroke of the pen, creating 'civil unions'—same as marriage in everything but name—the Massachusetts SJC could deduce no rationality in creating a segregated group. In their response, they observed, "The history of our nation has demonstrated that separate is seldom, if ever, equal."

Apocalyptic queer American novelist William S. Burroughs observed prophetically in *The Western Lands*, "The more familiar something becomes, the less it will incite fear and hostility... But, and it's a big But, a certain percentage of individuals, varying with environment and context, act in the opposite direction: the more gays come out into the open, the more hysterical and frenzied and often violent they become." We are now living in both interesting and dangerous times—a time when a respected civil rights leader like Coretta Scott King can declare: "A constitutional amendment banning same-sex marriages is a form of gay bashing." The attacks from the Right certainly will become more violent as their position becomes more desperate and untenable. At the same time, a more insidious, and potentially more damaging, threat lurks beneath the surface of the cultural debate. In the long term, what price will we pay as a 'people' for assimilation and acceptance?

Gay culture is both myth and reality—but the same can be said of all cultures throughout time and place. A culture is little more (or less) than artifice developed from within (and all too often marketed from without) that assists in binding a group together whether by ethnicity, religious belief or clan heritage. This process is vital for the self-preservation of a colonized people, which, as Joan Nestle observed, gay people are. The inevitable homogenizing process of assimilating to a dominant culture may prove an even greater threat to Queer cultures—new and modern as they are, lacking the pull of centuries of contiguous heritage and the support of familial tradition. Couple this with the fact that we lost a generation before they had a chance to become our cultural elders and the situation becomes more precarious. It is my hope that we, as gay men and lesbians, will do as we have done before and take the mythic 'I Do' and make it our own in all of *our* irreverent, Queer culturally affirming, camp glory.

"I'm not sure..."

I'm not sure what you are to me
you couldn't replace
maybe make me forget
your looks your shoulders
the power felt within your arms
the restrained force of new york
gentle brown eyes brown hair
face fleshy ass and tanned cock
I'm reminded of your habit
of grabbing your balls
lifting them to hang higher
adjusting for comfort—while
making your package larger.

Looking into that third space
formed of the contact of two bodies
smooth chest against smooth chest,
silky semi-hard cock against semi-hard cock,
mouth against mouth.
Tongues, the source of the word,
tangle, intertwine, work against each other.
Breath transfers from body
to body and flows back again.
Spirit moves in a circle, melding
and seeding one into the other.

The angels of the night city
surround this talisman of flesh
and unapologetic desire.

Saints Sinners and all that lies between.
Dr. John, Marie LaVeau, Dantor,
St. Theresa "the Little Flower,"
Collected by the winds of Oya,
the flesh lifts them up
and bears them away on
secret verses toward hidden places.
Indistinguishable energies and shadows
fill the room, blanketing.

Outside in the air, an interlude,
walking the few blocks
through the night streets,
the spirits dance above—
reflecting light off a red cloud sky.
Afterwards two cling together, spent.
Holding to the night, tightly,
not wanting to cleave for the rising day.
Two enter in, a third is created
and none return unchanged.

Rant

Don't imagine that the ways you have sex make a fucking bit of difference. Your various positions, in all their apelike vicissitudes, predicate no politics and invoke no ideology.

As you penetrate yet another surplus cadaver or get impaled by one more in a string of hairless studs, don't delude yourself into thinking you're a revolutionary. Don't think that your "intimate" actions interest them; don't fabricate a polemic of the puerile.

The ways we fuck interest them about as much as dog shit on the pavement. It makes no change apart from fleeting disgust.

No matter to what height you take your sexual theatrics, no matter how elaborate your ecstasies, at the point of coming do you ever envision the destruction of tyranny or the dissolution of the unjust? Or are you dreaming of the man you would rather be with?

Neil Bartlett is right when he observed, in *Who Was That Man*, that our actions move us only up and down but never forward. How can we ever progress when you are too busy thinking with your dick and worrying about your hair?

Don't take me wrong: Have sex, a lot or a little. Fuck and enjoy it whether it be with your husband, a string of husbands or the dick of the moment. Just don't make of it something it isn't.

Titclamps and a ball gag are no basis for a revolution.

10:36PM Friday

He's gone now
only memories
nothing left
except one red
twisted pubic hair
tucked into
a Ginsberg anthology
and a stain
still wet on the sheet

REBEL SATORI PRESS
WWW.REBELSATORI.COM

Printed in the United States
85875LV00004B/136-156/A

9 780979 083808